HESTER W. CHAPMAN

LIMMERSTON HALL

JONATHAN CAPE
THIRTY BEDFORD SQUARE LONDON

FIRST PUBLISHED 1972
© 1972 BY HESTER W. CHAPMAN

JONATHAN CAPE LTD, 30 BEDFORD SQUARE, LONDON WCI

ISBN 0 224 00757 2

To
JOHN GIELGUD

PRINTED AND BOUND IN GREAT BRITAIN
BY RICHARD CLAY (THE CHAUCER PRESS) LTD, BUNGAY, SUFFOLK
PAPER MADE BY JOHN DICKINSON & CO. LTD

LIMMERSTON HALL

20l.

BOOK I

If thou dost play with him at any game
Thou art sure to lose, and, of that natural luck,
He beats thee 'gainst the odds; thy lustre thickens
When he shines by ...

Antony and Cleopatra

I cannot forgive myself. Why did I marry him? I was happy once: contented, at least. But one can never go back – and marriage seemed to be the only solution. So I shall set about remembering how it all happened: calmly, if possible. I must not despair. The rebuilding of a life – his and mine – might, somehow, be achieved. Yet have I the heart for it? With prayer, Help may come to me. I used to believe that that Help would not fail. Now – I am not so sure...

1

I had always considered myself reasonably scrupulous with
regard to the proprieties. It was therefore rather surprising
when Lucretia Mary said, 'I wish you may not get into a
scrape over this scheme. Your friends' doubts don't signify
– they will understand – but what will be thought by those
who hear that you are established, unchaperoned, in the
household of a single gentleman?'

'I thought I had made it clear. Miss Trevy is coming
with me. And besides, there is the children's governess.
She is a Frenchwoman – but even so – '

'You are uprooting that poor lady – in her fifties?'

'She would not hear of my going alone.'

'Dear Anne,' said Lucretia Mary gently, 'forgive me. I
know that your first concern is your duty.'

I would have liked to tell her how I had been led to this
decision; but neither she nor I cared to speak lightly of
such experiences.

As the maid withdrew, Lucretia Mary began her tea-
making. She put the hot cakes down to the fire, turned up
the spirit-lamp and said, 'You have met him – Mr
Quarrendon?'

'Never.'

'How long is it since you saw the children?'

'Some months. I have not seen Francis and Sybilla since
the death of Francis's twin – '

'You were the much-loved aunt, I know. Always ready
for play, or to tell stories.'

'I shall find it difficult not to spoil them. And now –
since my poor sister – ' Picturing that triple loss, I paused.
Sybilla was a baby still; but Francis, at eleven, had had too
much to bear. 'If I had been appointed as their guardian,'
I began, 'we should be together now. But Cecilia wished

me to help her with their education when my brother-in-law died – that was in 1864. So I am doubly bound.'

'And Mr Quarrendon?'

'He has written begging me to come to Gloucestershire. I should have offered, in any case.'

'What relation is he to the children?'

'He is their step-uncle. His elder half-brother, George, married Cecilia. It is perhaps fortunate that Francis saw so little of his father; he was away on business for weeks at a time.'

As she began to pour out, Lucretia went on, 'Do you know anything of Mr Quarrendon – as landlord, for instance?'

'He lives very quietly. He is comfortably placed, but not wealthy.'

She seemed to consider; I continued, 'He knows all about me – that I am no longer young – or irresponsible.'

'You never were, my dear. And at thirty-four – '

'You mean, I always was the staid, prim spinster.'

'And a very clever woman.'

'But not suited to this position?'

'Oh yes.'

'The only trouble is that I must arrive alone. Eliza Trevy follows in a few weeks. That may give rise to talk. But it will die down once she is installed,' I said, helping myself to bread and butter. I was hungry and tired after the journey: and unwilling to set off again. It would have been very pleasant to stay a little with this dearest of friends. As I put the thought aside, she said, 'I know something of this gentleman, although I have not met him.'

She got up; her shawl slipped from her shoulders. As if I had been stabbed, I recognized it: one of a pair that Herbert had brought us from Delhi. She continued, 'His *Tales of the Forest* was my children's favourite reading. I have it still – ' and went over to the bookcase.

I had thought, often, of giving my shawl away. As Lucretia came back, with a thick, blue-and-gold volume, I tried to interest myself in what she was saying. Opening the book at random, I saw Herbert's face, heard him speaking. But something must be said. I stared at a softly coloured picture of rabbits and birds, murmured 'Very pretty – ' and turned back to the beginning. Opposite the elaborately framed frontispiece of a forest glade I read the title, and beneath it, 'by Neville Quarrendon', in Gothic print.

'There is one in every nursery still,' Lucretia said.

The first picture I took in was that of a fox creeping down to a stream. The colours might have been evolved by, rather than for, a child. The effect was strange. If a fox did not look exactly like that – then it should do so. I turned over the page and read, 'There was once a lazy and mischievous family of foxes, who preferred to kill and eat helpless farmyard animals, when with a little more trouble, they could have fed on the wild creatures of the forest. They would tear the throats – '

'Let me show you another,' said Lucretia, holding out her hand.

'I did not know of this. He has been a widower for several years. And there are no children.'

'Look at that one.'

I nearly dropped the book – we were holding it between us – as I gazed down at a hunting-scene. 'But it's horrible! How could your boys like such a thing?' She said nothing. 'I declare, I shall dream of it,' I went on.

'That tale ends happily.'

' "The Fairy of the Forest rescues the Spirit of the Stag." Well! Is there more than one of these books?'

'Four, in all. Perhaps you should have refused that invitation,' said Lucretia, smiling.

I continued to turn over the pages. The meticulous delicacy of the pictures placed them in a category unknown to me. Every detail – a flower, a bird's claw, a ripple of water – had a translucent steadiness. Yet there was nothing static about this private world, in which the creator had portrayed the horrors, as well as the beauty, of wild life. The savage chase, the bloodshed, the killer and the slain – all were shown by an observer who had recorded them in a personal vision. 'He must be eccentric,' I said at last. 'Was this a hobby?'

'When he and Herbert were at Oxford, he used to hunt.'

I put the book aside. The connection had deprived it of all interest. As we had to go on talking, I asked after the boys, now, I was told, in their last term at school. Their father was not mentioned, and I concluded that he was still abroad. Lucretia bore her troubles as if to set me an example. I could not have borne them so. Presently it was time to rest, and then to change my travelling-dress for dinner.

Lucretia Mary had asked some friends to meet me: a married couple. I tried to like them. His conversation, unduly personal – Why was I burying myself in Gloucestershire? We were almost neighbours in Suffolk – verged on the indelicate. And she was plain and dull: a mere wifely echo.

Next morning, I so shrank from leaving that I would have sent away the brougham, given the courage. I thought of my home, abandoned for a principle. My parish work, the garden (I should miss all the spring flowers), my good Ellen and Lucy, the little Norman church I had helped to restore, those kind friends and neighbours – surely it was too much to sacrifice. Also I began to worry about dear old Trevy – what if her Pusey-ite tendencies irked Neville Quarrendon? And she was not strong. There was just time to attend morning service before taking the train; so help came. If I had been poor and dependent, this departure might have seemed adventurous. But I did look forward to being with the children once more.

The solitude of the journey brought back the hateful recollection of a cousin Lucretia and Herbert disliked – she had designs on him, it seemed – saying, 'So your engagement is broken off – on religious grounds?' I said nothing, and she went on to describe him as 'something of a philanderer', the implication being that he had deserted me. 'Let it wait till he comes back from Canada,' Lucretia suggested. I replied that all was at an end.

I was sure that we should both get over it. Hearts are made, not of glass, but of Indian rubber. Yet this new venture did not promise much happiness. And there had been something about those illustrations that made me feel I should not like the artist. Lucretia Mary, who still thought of me as marriageable, hoped, or so I guessed, for that particular solution. But I knew that Neville Quarrendon's appeal was the result of Cecilia's will which, leaving him a moderate fortune, yet made his guardianship a burden he intended me to share. Then I remembered his mention of his secretary, a young man just down from Cambridge, who was to tutor Francis. His employer might, nevertheless, let me help to train the children; I had a suspicion that their religious teaching had not been wholly connected with their everyday life.

It was impossible not to be overcome by doubt, dread even, as I prepared to descend from the train. And there they were, both of them, Francis holding his sister's hand! His mourning, not unduly crape-hung, well became him. Sybilla was in white dimity, with black ribbons.

When the greetings were concluded, Sybilla's nurse, who had been waiting with the groom, got into the luggage-cart; the children and I were ensconced in the victoria. I could then guess at Francis's frame of mind. I had to remind myself that less than three months had passed since his mother's death. He must have wondered why I had not come to them when his twin died; but that explanation could wait.

He had grown, of course; and he appeared serene. I noticed that he avoided looking at me. Sybilla, pulling at my sleeve, said, 'Mamma – dead – ' in a loud whisper – and he, turning scarlet, edged away.

Taking her hand, I said, 'I know, my darling – but we will not talk of that just now.'

She continued, 'Gone to Heaven – ' and with a flouncing movement, he muttered, 'Be quiet, can't you?' I spoke of the box of toys I had brought for them; as we went on talking, no mention was made of Pond House, nor of its owner.

Presently Sybilla, leaning against me, slept. I stared through my veil at the backs of the coachman and the groom, and then at the hedgerows, speckled with flowering parsley and whitened by dust. At last I resolved to speak of what most concerned me.

After a pause, Francis replied, 'Oh – yes – he's very nice,' in a tone that seemed to forbid further questioning. He went on, 'Are you coming only for a visit, Aunt Anne? Or to live?'

'I think we must call it a visit – as long a one as suits Mr Quarrendon,' I said, adding, 'Is Pond House a pretty place?'

'It's beautiful. There are two ponds, one in the wood, and the other near the house. I can sail my boats, there's one in the big pond now. Mr Lambton said he would keep an eye on it for me. But I don't think he will.'

'Why not?'

'He is – preoccupied.'

'With preparing your lessons?'

'Those don't trouble him. His Latin and Greek are as good as his French. I think he has had a blow. He wanders about the garden without seeing it – you know. He is distracted. But Aunt Anne – I thought Miss Trevy was coming?'

I explained about her sessions with the dentist, adding, 'It was very good of Mr Quarrendon to welcome her,' and hoping that Francis would say something more about his uncle. He went on, 'Is she bringing Whitefoot and Grimalkin?'

'We have left them with Ellen and Lucy. Cats do not like to be moved.'

'Perhaps that is just as well,' he said gravely. 'Because we have three, and they might not get on. Mademoiselle is supposed to look after them – but she has been crying too much. I don't know what for. She may be homesick.'

This budget of news silenced me. The picture of contented children and distressed grown persons was slightly alarming. Francis began, 'You know, I am not to go to school till next year – ' and was interrupted by Sybilla rousing herself to murmur, '*Awful* – ' with a smothered laugh.

As I put in, 'That is not a nice word – ' Francis said gruffly, 'She means orphan – ' adding, 'C'est de ces gens-là – ' nodding at the box – 'qu'elle l'a entendu,' with an accent that did credit to Mademoiselle. At this point the carriage turned into the drive of Pond House.

2

The drive was circular. Within it, lay the pond, backed by a shrubbery.

My first impression of the house, which provided, as it were, a clasp to the necklace of the drive, led me to believe that its owner was not as well off as I had supposed: for it was so unpretentious as to be almost humble. The date over the front door – 1825 – showed it to be no more than forty years old. I could not, then, appreciate its quality, and saw, merely, a two-storied, yellow-washed building with a slate roof and long windows beneath which were beds of tulips and daffodils.

At the front door stood a young man and a slightly older woman. Again, I was taken aback, for I had imagined Mr Quarrendon to be middle-aged. They now made way for an elderly manservant, who opened the carriage door. As I turned to lift out Sybilla, I was fore-stalled by the young man saying, 'Allow me – please.' He replied to my greeting with, 'My name is Lambton,' a hesitating smile and an inquiry about my journey.

Entering Pond House, I concluded that Neville Quar-rendon was waiting to receive us indoors. Mr Lambton then introduced me to Mademoiselle Hébert. As I stood in the hall, wondering how to put them at their ease (she seemed unable to speak), he suggested that tea should be sent up to my room. Francis said, 'But it's all laid for us here, sir, look.'

We sat down, Sybilla was placed in her high-chair, Mademoiselle began to pour out – and still there was no sign of the host. The general tension, slightly lessened by Francis's inquiries about his boats, was such that I found myself unable to ask when he was likely to appear.

We were sitting round a richly supplied table in a long,

stone-floored room, papered in dark red. On the walls were paintings of animals, interspersed with studies of wild flowers: all, obviously, the work of Neville Quarrendon. Later, looking at them more closely, I became convinced of a talent which, while pleasing (but I was never a judge of such things), yet verged on the bizarre. Nevertheless, this room had a happy atmosphere; it was as if the owner rejoiced in his gifts, and also in his possessions, some of which, the oriental rugs and the porcelain figurines especially, were delicate and rare. It was puzzling to find his employees in low spirits, and our conversation increasingly strained. Mr Lambton barely answered my comments on our surroundings.

'I have sent the cats to the kitchen,' he said, in reply to Francis's inquiry, 'so that Miss Milsom should not be disturbed by them.' I reassured him – too eagerly, for I was becoming nervous – and Francis put in, 'I will let them out when I take Aunt Anne round the garden.' As Mademoiselle turned from silencing Sybilla's demand for cake, he went on, 'She is taking tea with us for a treat, she'll be going to bed soon – ' upon which his sister, frowning, announced, 'No – stay – ' and we all laughed. Still I could not bring myself to ask for my host, although we were now on easier terms.

It was not until Francis and I were walking in the garden that I raised the subject. He stared up at me; then he said, 'But did you not get his letter? He is in Paris.'

'I have had no letter.'

'That's odd. But he will be back soon. This is the other pond. Isn't it dark? The sun never shines here.'

'Did Mr Quarrendon write to me in Suffolk?'

'I expect so,' said Francis in a dismissive tone, adding, 'I am sorry, Aunt Anne, that I did not mention it. I thought you had heard from him.'

More than ever before, I was struck by his adult manner; he spoke as if we were of an age. I remembered Lucretia Mary saying that few children of eleven were as advanced as I made out Francis to be. His light-brown hair, long eyes and sharply cut features recalled those of his twin, of whom I hesitated to speak until he did. After some further talk of the missing letter, there was a pause. Then he said, 'Edwin died in an accident – did you know?'

'Your Mamma told me how it happened when she wrote from Vevey. You must have thought it strange, and unkind, that I did not come out to you then. But Miss Trevy was ill, and I could not leave her to the servants.'

Silently, we walked away from the pond into the sunshine. 'And then Mamma died – ' said Francis, as one recalling a long past event.

'I was coming out to you, when I heard that Mr Quarrendon had brought you here. I wrote to him at once,' I said, putting my hand on his shoulder.

'I know, he told me.'

'Dear child – how can I help you?'

He looked up at me. 'It is very nice having you here.'

'But your uncle,' I burst out. 'Does he – can you be happy with him?'

Francis considered. 'He is very kind,' he said at last. 'And clever. You should see his library. What do you think of his paintings?'

'I am no expert. But I suppose he has talent.'

'I like them,' said Francis decisively, 'because they are painted in that special way. Mamma used to take me to look at those famous pictures in Paris, but I couldn't – ' he paused – 'appreciate them. Uncle Neville gave up painting animals a long time ago. He only paints flowers now.'

Once more, I was silenced, trying, in vain, to envisage a strange personality. Then it was time to go to my room. There I found Neville Quarrendon's letter. In a minutely neat hand, he expressed his regret that he had had to leave for Paris in connection with Cecilia's will, her former residence there having created 'a somewhat complicated situation'. The formality of this communication provided no clue to the writer's character. Odd – kind – talented – very likely; the words merely enhanced what amounted to an enigma. I turned to inspect my surroundings.

Both bedroom and sitting-room looked out over the concealed pond; beyond, stretched a prospect of meadows and
the faint, far-off gleam of the Severn. Such possessions as I
had brought with me were nicely disposed; my clothes had
been put away as if the maid responsible knew my habits.
Pleasantly faded chintzes, a few pieces of Dresden china,
an oak bureau and a Brittany cupboard combined to make
a setting reminiscent of home. Uneasiness and bewilder-
ment faded away as I put on the dress of wine-coloured
crepe which had been laid out on the chaise-longue.
Fastening my mother's garnet necklace (what would my
parents have thought of my present circumstances?) I
paused for a last look in the mirror – and faced a familiar
situation.

I had sometimes been told that I was 'still' – the adverb
had become rather daunting – handsome. Good proportions, grey eyes, clear colouring and dark-brown hair
added up to what might be thus described; but there
always had been, and always would be, something lacking
in an appearance which satisfied most dressmakers while
failing to impress other observers, whether male or female.
Lucretia Mary used to tell me that I was too severely
gowned; that was before middle-age enforced this present
style.

Suddenly, my spirits rose. Neville Quarrendon's absence,
his employees' depression, anxiety for the children – all
yielded to a looking forward. I had been challenged; rising
to an occasion caused readiness to be amused, curious and
hopeful. I determined to 'pump' both governess and tutor
that very evening. The slang phrase recurred as Mr
Lambton escorted me into the dining-room.

He said that Mademoiselle Hébert had asked to be
excused, having retired with a headache. I did not tell him
that a glimpse of her on my way downstairs had indicated
that she was in no state to join us. During the course of an
excellent meal we spoke of Francis's progress, which his
tutor described as quite remarkable; he smiled as he told
me of a historical tale on which his pupil had been en-

gaged for some weeks, adding, 'I hope that you will encourage him to go on with it.'

By this time, we had reached the dessert, of which Mr Lambton partook freely, as of the port accompanying it. (He had eaten very little so far.) When I said, 'Surely your approval will carry more weight with him than mine?' he flushed, looked away and filled up his glass. After waiting for the servants to withdraw, he muttered, 'I don't know – I can't understand it – ' as if in soliloquy.

I was prevented from further inquiry by Francis's appearance. To my question about his writing, he replied, 'Oh, well – it has to be fitted in with so many other things that I don't get on very fast. But it may be better than the last one, I never finished that. This is about the Crusades. There are no love-scenes.'

'How is that?'

'I don't know about them, Aunt Anne, except in other – I mean, printed – books. In *Ivanhoe*, for instance, Rebecca won't have anything to do with de Bois Guilbert – and one can't blame her, really.'

'Perhaps you would read it to me, some time?'

'Oh, I'd like to, thank you. How I've planned it is like this – ' and he launched into an outline of the tale, while Mr Lambton, gloomily draining his glass, gazed at his plate. Presently he drew out his watch, indicating that his pupil's time was up, and as the door shut asked me to take wine with him. I did so, hoping for a further confidence. He began, 'You have not met Mr Quarrendon, I think?' I shook my head, and he added abruptly, 'I have a favour to ask of you.'

'Pray do so.'

'Would you speak to him for me?'

'For you? Are you afraid of him?'

There was a short silence. 'Afraid – I don't know – ' said the young man, running his hand through his hair, which, already dishevelled, now stood up in a blond aureole. 'I suppose one might be afraid of a person one admires. He was – wonderful to me – ' and to my horror, his eyes filled with tears.

'I think you must explain,' I ventured at last.

'I am to leave! He has given me a month's notice – and a year's salary.'

'With no reason?'

After another pause, Mr Lambton blew his nose and gruffly announced, 'Miss Milsom – forgive me. There is a reason. But it is not one I can speak of to a lady who is almost a stranger.' He then got up, offered me his arm and escorted me into the drawing-room. Here, after drawing a chair nearer the hearth, he rang for coffee, which we drank in silence.

Deciding that he must make the next move, I got out my company work, and became as quietly absorbed as if we had spent many evenings in this manner, while my companion paced up and down. At last he said, 'You must think me discourteous. The fact is, I am – overthrown.'

He now appeared not entirely sober. As I looked at him, trying to think of the right phrase, he went on, 'You play the piano, I believe – would you care to do so?' and opened the instrument.

'If that is what you wish.'

'Here is some music.'

I sat down to play – not very well, in the circumstances – aware only of the tutor's brooding presence behind me. This ridiculous and somewhat taxing scene lasted for what seemed a long time. I then rose and resumed my work. He burst out, 'I will tell you. He may listen to you.'

At this point, the tea-tray was brought in. Mr Lambton seized a slice of bread and butter, crammed it into his mouth and went over to the piano. He struck a few chords and then ceased, his hands on the keys. The pose, if it was one, failed of effect. I had some difficulty in keeping what is known as a straight face while waiting for his next remark.

The last thing I expected was an autobiographical discourse. Mr Lambton told me about his upbringing in a

Hampshire vicarage, his recently widowed mother, his two unmarried sisters, his successful career at Cambridge (this, modestly enough) and his apparent suitability for, and happiness in, the post from which he had been dismissed. He then got up and, standing above me, said, 'What do you think of Mademoiselle?'

'She seems rather reserved.'

'Does she strike you as attractive – personable?'

'Quite personable. Her looks are somewhat blurred. Perhaps she has had bad news?'

'She has indeed. She also has been dismissed.'

'I am sorry to hear it.'

'Unjustly – as I was.' After a short silence he went on, 'Mr Quarrendon has accused us of beginning' – his voice sank – 'a *flirtation.*'

With some difficulty I fought back a laugh at the disgusted emphasis of the last word, before asking, 'Did he not believe your denial?' As he shook his head I pursued, 'On what grounds did he base this accusation?'

'Mademoiselle had other bad news, from her home. The death of a brother-in-law. I found her in tears and was trying to console her, when Mr Quarrendon came into the schoolroom. We were alone. My hand was on her shoulder.'

'But you explained?'

'Of course.'

'What did he say?'

'That he had already observed a familiarity he considered undesirable. Now – Miss Milsom – I appeal to you. She is a thoroughly good woman, some ten years older than myself. A flirtation – can you imagine it?'

'Such a situation has been known. I suppose Mr Quarrendon is a rather rigid, old-fashioned sort of employer?'

'He is a brilliant, experienced man of the world. But you'll see that for yourself.'

'When?' I said sharply.

Mr Lambton shrugged his shoulders. 'He is inclined to be unpredictable. He comes and goes. I thought he trusted me. But nothing she or I could say – ' He broke off and turned away.

'It would be difficult for me to interfere between three people I barely know. My speaking for you might make matters worse. I feel, from what you tell me, that Mr Quarrendon has a suspicious nature.'

'So you refuse to help?'

'No. But I should get to know him. When is he likely to return?'

'Soon. It must be soon,' said the young man shakily. 'Why should I have to go through – but that's my concern.'

'Surely he will give you a recommendation?'

'He has promised to do so. I was happy here – devoted, not only to Francis, but to him, himself. To please him mattered more to me than any tuition. And that of Francis is child's play, not really difficult at all. You know his abilities.'

'But I do not know his uncle.'

'Miss Milsom – I beg you – '

'Mr Lambton – give me a little time.'

As I rose and folded up my work he held out his hand. 'Good night, then.'

'I repeat – if I can help, I will. I promise nothing.'

He tried to speak, and failed. So I left him.

A week passed, and then another, with no news from Neville Quarrendon. Fifteen days after my installation at Pond House Francis received a letter from his uncle, charmingly illustrated with drawings of the plants and birds in the Bois. He read it aloud to me first, and then showed me, his tutor and Mademoiselle the sketches; his pride in being the recipient of this missive, in which there was no mention of the writer's return, was freely expressed. 'I expect he'll write to you next,' he said kindly, and ran off to exhibit his prize in the nursery. Meanwhile, trying to cheer up Mr Lambton, I was partially successful. With poor Mademoiselle Hébert I could do nothing.

3

Next day, I was desired to intervene in the problem of Sybilla's hair. Her nurse, a comely young woman from the village, was much distressed that it did not curl, and put it into papers every night; in the morning these were found neatly arranged on the railing of her cot. When reproached, Sybilla, who was allowed to take one or more of her dolls to bed with her, would reply that Susy, or Ally, or Marmy was the culprit. Accused of telling stories, she appeared genuinely amazed, and repeated, 'No – her – naughty – ' shaking the doll in question, with the result that her ash-fair locks hung limply about her face for the next twelve hours.

'Can't you speak to her, Miss?' Nurse began, when I came to hear Sybilla say her prayers. 'What's the use of asking God to make her a good girl when she behaves so? The only person she ever listens to is Mamsell. But I don't like to worry her.'

At this point the governess entered the nursery and was acclaimed by Sybilla demanding a story. I said, 'Mademoiselle can't tell stories to little girls who tear off their curl-papers,' upon which Sybilla looked grave but unconvinced. Mademoiselle knelt down by her cot and said, 'Keep them – and in the morning Sybilla will look so pretty,' smiling across at me.

Sybilla was not pretty in the accepted sense. Pale, green-eyed, with pointed features, she knew how to cajole, and began to do so now, murmuring, 'Good – prayers – ' folding her hands and looking upwards like the heroine of a Sunday-school tale.

As Mademoiselle and I left the nursery together I said something about her influence with the child. We were standing by a sun-drenched window – and suddenly, I saw her as if for the first time.

She had been beautiful; and she was extremely well-dressed. In fact, she did not look like any governess I had ever seen. A worn, graceful, elegant woman of about my own age faced me, still smiling over Sybilla's coaxing ways. She murmured, 'I shall regret to leave her,' with a gentle dignity that emboldened me to say, 'Perhaps you will not have to.'

'But I shall, I know it,' she replied, her dark eyes widening, as if to gaze into a future to which she had been long resigned. 'You, Mademoiselle,' she went on, 'have promised to speak to the Master. That will not do anything for me – for Mr Lambton, perhaps, yes.'

As we stood looking at one another, she put her hand up to her coronet of hair – it was black, with threads of grey – and seemed to be considering some deeper confidence. Then she turned and walked away, her head bent, her gown flowing out behind her; it was plainly moulded, no longer new, and entirely suited to her position; yet I guessed it to be the work of a skilled dressmaker. For the next few days she seemed to be avoiding me.

So did Mr Lambton; and I began to appreciate an isolation which enabled me to explore, unaccompanied, the amenities of the house and garden, whenever Francis was at lessons or in bed. I was glad when the tutor offered letter-writing as an excuse for retiring to his own room after dinner; my surroundings grew upon me – the library especially.

Here, the bookshelves lining the walls were constructed in a Puginesque style, with crockets, niches and carvings. The niches contained terracotta figures of saints and prophets. At each end of the room stood a pair of pedestals supporting busts of Roman emperors; the heads were of pale-yellow marble, the draperies of porphyry. The effect was curiously lifelike; sometimes, in the lamplight, all four, staring at one another with lidless eyes, seemed to be about to move.

Neville Quarrendon's range of reading was a wide one. Modern novels, French and Italian poetry, some English verse and collections of old plays were flanked by magnificently illustrated sets of Bewick, Audubon and lesser known writers on animals and birds. The furniture was of the conventional leather and mahogany type, but for a small marquetry bureau that must have belonged to the late Mrs Quarrendon, of whom there were no portraits here or elsewhere. She had left no other trace. In the drawing-room, the undraped piano, bronze velvet curtains, brocaded chairs and sombre carpets showed a masculine taste; the spreading plants, reflected in gilt mirrors, added to an atmosphere which excluded the least hint of femininity.

Wandering from one room to another, and failing to extract any further information about their owner, I began to see Neville Quarrendon as a character whose eventual appearance was almost certain to be disappointing. Out of doors, he ceased to exist. On the downs and in the woods I had a sense of personal possession; these walks, whether taken alone or with the children, became increasingly enjoyable. Pond House, while remote, had a rich, varied setting; it provided an adventurous idleness which brought each day to an end with surprising speed.

One brilliantly fine afternoon Francis told me that he and Mr Lambton were to spend his half-holiday fishing.

'In the Severn?'

'No, in Sir Charles's pool. He lets us go down there whenever we like,' said Francis, adding some further details about this absentee landlord, whose estate lay within half a mile of Pond House. It was decided that I should accompany them for a little way and then leave to walk in the woods, 'Or wherever you like,' Francis went on, 'as long as you don't disturb the game. His keeper sells it, so that Sir Charles can spend the money at Monte Carlo.'

Turning into the woods before we reached the pool, I fell asleep in a grove of wild anemones. Waking rather dazed, I walked along a ride into a blaze of light.

I was standing at the foot of a slope. At the top was a

large, long, cream-coloured building. Then, slowly, I realized that I was looking at the kind of house that is described as a mansion.

I had seen many drawings and prints of such places – but never one so serenely dominating. Golden in the sunshine, commanding a sweep of meadow and wood, it crowned a height exactly suited to its proportions. These culminated in a façade flanked by pillared wings. The great central portico supported the family arms; above them, a row of statues and urns indicated a continental inspiration, carried out in the local stone. The combination of English material and Italianate design was so perfect as to compel a search for some incongruity, some lapse into pretension or false grandeur. None could be seen. As I drew nearer, mounting the slope to stare and wonder – for how could anyone, owning such splendour, leave it empty? – I received an impression of simplicity and charm. It was as if this noble structure had once enclosed a home, a place to be happy in, with children and friends and servants – a private world.

Eventually, having found a way round the outer buildings, I made a circle and so faced the pool, or rather lake, where Francis and Mr Lambton were sitting with their rods on the far side. A small island lay between us.

When I joined them the tutor replied to my inquiries at length. Limmerston Hall dated from the 1780s; the interior decorations were by Wyatt and a Tuscan stucco artist, the pictures needed cleaning, and Sir Charles Craik intended to sell it and them, but so far had failed to get the price he wanted. We then rowed over to the island and unpacked our picnic tea; from there I had another view of this deserted pleasure-dome, its neglected gardens and dried-up fountains.

For several days I thought often of Limmerston Hall; yet I shrank from revisiting it, lest my first sight should prove to have exaggerated its fascination. When I did so, it exercised a different spell. I began to picture myself living there, submerged in a visionary existence. Then came the thought that I might somehow obtain leave to see it from within. At last, hovering near the lodge, I came upon an aproned woman, who asked me, civilly enough, if I had lost my way. We fell into talk of the Hall, and of her husband, who was part guardian and part gamekeeper there. Another meeting, and some manœuvring on my part with them both, led her to offer me a 'look round' the rooms. 'They're sadly shabby,' she said. 'I do my best, but there – in the olden days there was thirty servants and a groom of the chambers and a housekeeper dressed like a lady in black satin with a gold watch and all. But till Sir Charles sells – and he's asking high – it must remain so.'

On the day that I was to make this visit both Francis and Sybilla were sent to bed in darkened rooms with hay fever; so I was confined to the house, sitting in a thread of light to read aloud, in turn with Mademoiselle. A week went by before escape came, on just such a sunshiny afternoon as that of my first sight of the Hall.

Fearing disillusionment, I made my way slowly, and so stopped in the lane to read Lucretia Mary's last letter. It contained news of Herbert's return from Canada in the near future. I thrust the crumpled sheets into my pocket, suddenly aware that I had barely given him a thought since leaving London.

As I entered the Hall by a back way Mrs Grant poured out a flood of talk, of which I heard little or nothing. The shutters had been drawn aside, and the rooms were filled with sunlight.

Dimly aware of pastel elegance in one, of darkly gleaming vistas in another, of shell-like alcoves, riotously painted ceilings, and furniture that combined glitter with fragility, and solidity with grace, I walked about in the glare, hemmed in by shapes and colours that were rather oppressive.

I turned to Mrs Grant. She was gone. Then I heard her voice, and her husband's, in the passage; they were arguing, in agitation: anger, perhaps. I passed through the nearest double doors into what I afterwards knew as the

Blue Saloon. It was very large, reaching its climax in a marble chimney-piece of some elaboration. A tall man leant against the carvings of fruit and flowers. He was smiling. He did not move.

I stood aghast. For I knew him. As we continued to look at one another, I became doubtful. Yet the likeness was there – startling, unmistakable – changed only by the passing of the years.

4

Shortly after my eighteenth birthday my parents took me
to Florence. They intended to settle there for some time
before making the continental tour which was to 'finish'
my education. Six weeks later, my father became seriously
ill; he and my mother returned to England, leaving me in
the care of two expatriate sisters, the younger of whom,
Eliza Trevy, later became my companion. For the next
three months I stayed in their house on the Arno. Twice a
week, one of them escorted me down the Via Tornabuoni
for my Italian lesson.

A few days after my parents' departure, my teacher's
discourse on the *Inferno* was interrupted by the entrance
of her brother Gianni who, I was later informed, had been
watching me for some time. With his sister's connivance
and, sometimes, her chaperonage, he began an elaborate
and subtle approach in such a way as to make me feel that
I had become the heroine of a romance. He was in
business, and therefore not received by the Misses Trevy
and their circle. When I told him that my parents would
never allow our marriage, he replied that he would
eventually bring them round; in the meantime, why
should we not be happy together?

Gianni Severini's looks were of the classic ebony-and-
ivory type often seen in northern Italy. Years later, I realized, and could not but admire, the carefully planned
stages of his love-making. Crude seduction was not his
aim; he intended gradually to subjugate me until I threw
myself into his arms and became his mistress. The preliminaries took place in an atmosphere and against a
background of such enchantment as I had never known.
My role was that of the recalcitrant siren, his of the
despairing yet stubborn aspirant. So I lived in a paradise,

shadowed, every now and then, by quarrels and tears *(les beaux jours quand on était si malheureux,* in fact), of which the Trevy sisters had not a suspicion. Then a business crisis called Gianni to Rome; a week before he was due to return I was summoned to my father's death-bed. I wrote once, and received a passionately ambiguous reply.

My dreams of Gianni seldom varied. Standing at the top of the Via Tornabuoni, I saw his dark figure – he had an odd, swaying walk – coming nearer; then, under the light from the fountain, his eyes and his smile. That memory, those dreams, became part of a secret life. It was revived as I entered the Blue Saloon of Limmerston Hall.

For Gianni was standing there – masterful, serene, with greying hair, his outlines a little thickened. Only his clothes were of the kind never worn by Italians of the middle class.

That difference, and a further scrutiny, showed me that I was facing Sir Charles Craik – and that an explanation must be made. Yet the likeness was so extraordinary that I could not speak till moving forward jolted me into reality. I said, 'Please forgive me. I ought not to be here. But the caretakers thought that I might be given leave to see the house.'

'Why should you not see it? I ought to have warned Grant of my arrival. But I did not expect to return so soon.' His voice was deep and rather grating; again, I seemed to be listening to one from the past. He went on, 'You admire all this?' apparently amused by my confusion.

I admitted that I had not yet been able to take in my surroundings. 'There is such a lot to see,' I added lamely.

'Quite enough. This is your first visit, then?'

'Yes – and again, I must apologize.'

He shook his head. The shock of his appearance, and his bland assumption that this meeting was in no way unusual, prevented me from introducing myself. When he offered to show me round, I murmured something about getting back and coming another day. 'That is,' I went on, 'if you are still here.'

He did not answer at once. Then he said, 'Getting back – where?'

'To Pond House.'

His look changed from one of contemplation to sudden interest. 'Are you – is it Miss Milsom?'

Rather surprised that he should have heard of me, I said, 'I ought to have told you. I am there to look after my nephew and niece.'

'Of course!'

This odd reply silenced me once more. At last I went on, 'I hope you will not blame the Grants for my – for this intrusion.'

'Why should I? If it comes to that, I also am an intruder.'

'In your own house?'

He stared, then burst out laughing. 'I see! We have been talking at cross-purposes. Craik is still abroad, and likely to remain there. I am Neville Quarrendon.'

Colouring up is not a habit of mine; yet I felt myself getting uncomfortably red, and more than ever at a loss. As I stood there, abashed, this final surprise and his look of genial tolerance brought back the past so painfully that speech became impossible. Neville Quarrendon said, 'Craik and I are old friends. He has asked me to cast an eye over this place from time to time. I did not expect to find you here – ' and held out his hand.

During the next quarter of an hour I submitted to a pleasant domination that guided me towards the front entrance. Pausing to speak to Mrs Grant in the pillared atrium, Mr Quarrendon drew my attention to an enormous gilded vase, taller than himself and twice as broad, and told me that it had been the subject of a fierce dispute between Wyatt and Sir Charles's eighteenth-century ancestor, who had brought it back from Vienna against the architect's advice. As he stood beside it, smiling to himself, his profile and his poise were so outlined as to give the impression of a conscious pose; then I saw that he was no longer aware of me or of Mrs Grant, and had become absorbed in recollection. At last he roused himself and said, 'Come – I will drive you back – ' ushering me through the great double doors. In the sweep Grant was standing by a dog-cart.

Mr Quarrendon said nothing more until we had passed the lodge. Glancing over his shoulder, he began, 'Craik is a grass-widower. His only son is insane, and lives, with his keepers, in the Dower House, over there. You cannot see it – ' as I turned – 'It will go with the Hall, when that is sold.'

'And the poor young man?'

'His father will establish him somewhere or other, I imagine.'

'Sir Charles will never come back?'

'Never.'

'I suppose he will sell it easily enough?'

He turned and looked at me; his expression was faintly hostile. 'He is asking too much. It's a barrack.'

'A beautiful one.'

'You think so?'

'Do not you?'

He made a movement of impatience. After another silence he said abruptly, 'I understand from Mademoiselle that the children are on the mend. I hope you have not found them troublesome.'

I then discovered that he had reached Pond House a few minutes after I left it, and gone on to the Hall almost immediately, having found out all that had happened in his absence. We separated on arrival, and did not meet again till dinner-time.

The household was transformed within a few minutes of his installation. The children ran past my door, calling to him to come into the garden. Presently, looking out, I saw them making for the orchard; Sybilla was perched on her uncle's shoulder.

When I began to dress I observed that my most

elaborate gown, hitherto worn only in London, had been laid out, together with a new pair of gloves still in their silver paper. Then I heard Mr Lambton say, 'He will expect Miss Sybilla to come down to dessert this first evening,' her nurse's reply and the sound of their footsteps hastening away.

Both tutor and governess were waiting when I entered the drawing-room. Some time passed before we were joined by Mr Quarrendon, urbanely apologizing for the delay. Glancing about him, he went on, 'Where are the cats?'

Mr Lambton looked at Mademoiselle; she shook her head. The tutor said, 'They are usually in the kitchen at this hour, sir. Shall I ring for them to be brought in?'

'Pray do so,' his employer replied, 'or, better still, fetch them yourself, if you will be so good.' Turning to me, he added, 'If they displease you, they shall be sent back again.'

'I like cats,' I said hastily. 'But I have not seen these for several days.'

'That is because they take to the servants' quarters in my absence. Here they are – thank you – ' as Mr Lambton ushered in two Persians and a tabby.

'I could not persuade them into this part of the house, sir,' he began, 'but now that you are here – '

He was interrupted by the announcement of dinner, a longer and more elaborate meal than usual. Tutor and governess were subdued; their employer then drew them into the conversation so adroitly that neither seemed aware that they were being put at their ease. Mr Quarrendon gave them a dramatic account of what he described as my formidable reception of his excuses. 'I thought', he went on, 'that Craik had sold the place, and that Miss Milsom was in possession. I was quite alarmed.'

'So was I,' I put in.

'Do not believe it. When I suggested that we should make a tour of the rooms, I was rejected.'

'But I do want to see them – ' I began. 'Only not then – '

As he turned to smile at me I broke off, adding, 'I am sure they are as wonderful as all the rest.'

Mr Lambton, encouraged by this rallying – and also, perhaps, by several glasses of wine – said, 'That Georgian style is too flat – and too cold, sir, do you not think so?' in the tone of one connoisseur appealing to another.

Mr Quarrendon leant back, half-shutting his eyes. 'Cold – ' he repeated, as if hearing the word for the first time in this connection.

It then became clear that Mr Lambton was as the weaned child playing in the cockatrice's den; only in this case the cockatrice had not lost its powers. He continued, 'Surely, sir, the Jacobean, or – let me see – the Gothic – '

'Wyatt', Mr Quarrendon gently interposed, 'has used the Gothic in the library of the Hall.'

'Well, sir – I'm no expert. But the picturesque – '

'Ah! Yes. That is generally preferred. I must be out of touch in these matters.'

'No, sir, indeed – '

'You are perfectly right to dismiss what you don't care for,' said Mr Quarrendon pleasantly. 'Now, last week I found myself admiring another earlier manner, that of the Tuileries. I was watching the Empress drive out – ' turning to Mademoiselle – 'She is exquisite still.'

'How was she dressed?'

'She flashed by too quickly for me to catch more than a glimpse of that new colour – magenta, is it? There was no cheering. They don't like her, and never will,' Mr Quarrendon replied, and launched into a light-hearted account of Napoleon III's mistakes. His acerbity made me uneasy, and puzzled the other two; he seemed to be skating over a surface of which the depths were hidden from us all.

When the children came in, his manner changed. He took Sybilla on his knee, gave her a bonbon and Francis half a glass of port, remarking, 'That is the '54,' as if to a contemporary. Presently his attention wandered, and they were dismissed, turning to gaze at him as they reached the door.

The process of leaving the gentlemen, of their joining us for coffee in the drawing-room, of duets being played by Mademoiselle and me and the entrance of the tea-tray occupied another two hours – not unpleasantly. Yet again I was aware of an undercurrent which eventually swept away Mr Lambton and Mademoiselle and guided me – with the cats – into the library.

Here, Mr Quarrendon's inscrutability was maintained. He inquired after Herbert Graham, and spoke of his work in Canada. All this time, I had managed to prevent myself staring at him. Now the past rose between us. I sat idle, wondering what to say. Mr Quarrendon wandered round the bookshelves; then he came to the fireplace and leant against the chimney-piece. I said, 'I have to thank you for your kindness to Miss Trevy. She will be here very soon.'

As our glances met he dismissed this speech with a smile and a gesture. Then he said, 'That is a beautiful dress.'

'It was laid out for me because you were here.'

'But it was your choice in the first place – and a becoming one.'

'Thank you.'

'Tell me,' he went on, 'you cannot have wished to take up life here, in a strange house. Did you dread the prospect?'

'A little. But finding the children so happy and well established – it made all the difference.'

'I see. Yet I cannot believe that you have given yourself entirely to their interests. You have many of your own.'

The kindness of his look and tone took me aback. I did not want to yield to them; it seemed essential that there should be a barrier between us. I said, 'I could not disregard Cecilia's wishes. And some of my interests are transferable. This library – ' I paused, halted by his steadfast gaze – 'I have made use of it already.'

'So Francis tells me. And that brings me to another point – one which concerns us both. His education.'

Having decided not to raise the matter of Mr Lambton's and Mademoiselle's dismissal till their employer and I had seen a little more of one another, I said nothing. He went on, 'Francis does not know that Lambton is leaving. In any case, it won't affect him.'

'How is that?'

'Have you not observed his *de haut en bas* attitude towards that young man?'

I hesitated – and then found myself plunged into an argument about the tutor's fitness for his position in which I was gradually defeated. I had to admit that Mr Quarrendon knew more about his methods than I did; and it was difficult to resist his assumption that I was swayed by compassion in pleading the tutor's cause. 'As for Mademoiselle,' he went on, 'that is a different question. Forgive me – I have tired you, I can see it. Shall we talk over the whole situation in a few days' time?'

Rather overcome by the experiences of the last eight hours, I agreed. As I turned to say good night he appeared suddenly radiant; and I wondered whether he was rejoicing in his own mastery. The black and white of his evening dress enhanced the impact of his appearance, and further disturbed me.

That night I slept intermittently. Waking to the realization of changed conditions was more disturbing still. I would have liked to leave Pond House unobtrusively and as soon as possible.

5

The distasteful task of defending Mr Lambton against the charge of a flirtatious advance to Mademoiselle had now to be faced. Squeamishness in such a matter was not to be considered. Having resolved to make my plea a formal one, I arranged an appointment with Mr Quarrendon, and entered the library to find him sitting at that incongruously feminine bureau, which was piled with ledgers and papers. The preliminaries were short, as was my request. He said, 'Why do you consider him incapable of such an approach?'

'For two reasons. He strikes me as perfectly truthful. And Mademoiselle, whom I like and respect, is not the kind of person to attract a man so much younger than herself.'

In the pause that followed, his brilliant eyes were fixed on my face.

'She was in tears, I understand?'

'That is so.'

'For the death of a brother-in-law?'

'Yes.'

'Odd – very.'

'Why? She may have been deeply attached to him.'

'I hardly think so.'

'Again, why? How do you know?'

'Because she was an only child. She has no family – no relations.'

Staring back at him, I found nothing to say. He got up, walked over to the window, opened it and gave some direction to the gardener working below. At last I said, 'I don't understand.'

He shut the window, and leaning over the back of his chair, replied, 'You have not been here very long. There are a number of things you may not understand. Mademoiselle's situation is one.'

Gazing helplessly at him, I waited. 'I have known her', he began, 'for some years. I engaged her, partly because she was in straits for money, and also because she seemed suited to the position. I do not know – though I can guess – why she was found in tears. The fact that she lied, so promptly, so glibly, showed me that I had misjudged her, and that she should not remain here. In fact,' he added smiling, 'she made the wrong approach to young Lambton. Her intention was another matter. Pity – sympathy – may lead to something closer.'

'But it did not!' I exclaimed. 'Why should Mr Lambton be dismissed on false grounds?'

'Because – if you will forgive the expression – he is an ass.'

'Your standards are very high.'

'For Francis, yes.'

A long silence fell. Mr Quarrendon, resuming his seat, said coolly. 'I cannot expect to leave this – court – ' as I began to protest he raised his hand; the gesture was so startlingly reminiscent that I shrank back, and he went on, 'without a stain on my character. You find me harsh, and capricious. But why should you concern yourself about two people for whom I have provided? Their references are all that could be wished. If you care to, you can see them.'

Shaking my head, I got up. As I moved away his voice followed me. 'I fear you are displeased.'

'Why did she lie?'

'She may not have had time to think.'

'She is very unhappy,' I said, turning to face him.

'I have no doubt of that – none at all. She has told me, on several occasions, exactly how unhappy she is,' said Mr Quarrendon. His impassive look so daunted me that I left without another word.

I saw him no more that day. He was spending the evening, Francis told me, with the Rector and his wife, in order to discuss a Penny Reading, in which we were all to take

part. 'And I have to recite,' Francis added. 'I thought –
some Byron. Or do you think a piece out of *Marmion*?'

After this point had been discussed I said, 'It's very odd
– but I don't even know where the village is.'

'Limmerston? Oh, it's a long way away, two miles. We
don't often go there. And I'm not allowed to ride. I've
begged and begged, because we learnt, Edwin and I. But
it's in the will. Because of the accident.'

'I remember.'

'Anyway, they're coming to dine tomorrow, Mr and
Mrs Granger, that's the Rector. He's very nice. She's
different. She means to be, well, jolly – but she isn't really.'

As he continued to talk of the Grangers and their
children I reflected that Mr Quarrendon had put me in
my place, perhaps justifiably. Meanwhile, fully to answer
Lucretia Mary's inquiries about him was impossible. For
she knew nothing of that Florentine encounter, of which I
must crush the memory, somehow or other.

This was made easier by an addition to my duties.
Shortly after Mr Quarrendon's arrival I was summoned to
the servants' quarters, where I was told by the butler that
he and his wife, the cook, expected me to order the meals.
'Master desired me to ask you, Miss,' he added. Mrs
Waring then explained that I was to take dinner with Mr
Quarrendon, while Mr Lambton and Mademoiselle had
theirs in the schoolroom unless bidden to join us. Their
employer and I therefore entertained the Grangers alone;
he made it clear to them that my companion would be
arriving within the next few days.

Mrs Granger was plump, pretty, and loquacious to a
point that reduced her husband, who was some ten or
fifteen years her senior, to the uninterrupted enjoyment of
his food. Gradually, Mr Quarrendon halted the flow of
trivialities; we passed from the Penny Reading to Francis's
recitation, so to poetry and finally to book-collecting. 'You
go to London for such matters, I've no doubt,' said the
Rector, gazing wistfully at his host.

'I cannot understand', Mrs Granger put in, 'why people

who write books have to buy so many. Your tales, Mr Quarrendon, and my husband's poetry – '

The Rector objected to this reasoning, and added that he had long ceased to write. 'I suppose', he added, smiling at Mr Quarrendon, 'that I must not ask why you did the same.'

'It was a distraction, no more,' his host replied. 'And now I come to think of it,' he went on, turning to me, 'why did you not continue with those sketches of Provençal life? Pray don't look so horrified. They were charming.'

After an astonished pause I said, 'They were written many years ago. I did not think that more than a few people had ever heard of them.'

'You know Provence well?' the Rector asked.

'We went to live in Avignon, my mother and I, after my father's death. I wrote those stories to please myself.'

'And others,' Mr Quarrendon put in.

'I did not expect them to be accepted. Now, it's as if they had been written by someone else.'

'A romantic young lady?'

'Perhaps. But it's a pity that I could not illustrate them – as others did their tales.'

Mr Quarrendon laughed, and once more guided the talk into other channels.

The remainder of the evening passed pleasantly enough. I wondered how and why he had come to read my youthful effusion, and concluded that his introduction of it was part of a design to draw me into the general subjugation of the household. Later on, Eliza Trevy's comments supported this impression. She found him rather formidable, and added, 'But I should not criticize one who has been so truly hospitable,' and went on to speak as if our stay at Pond House was temporary.

I did not care to disillusion her by referring to the will. She appeared more than usually frail; facing her with the real situation could not, then, be considered; and it was complicated by her dependence on myself.

That our companionship had been transferred to an

unfamiliar setting did not disturb her. After a brief
conference with Mr Quarrendon, we agreed to help him
according to our respective capacities. He intended to take
over Francis's classical education, while advertising for
another tutor; I was to contribute lessons in French and
Italian. Eliza Trevy consented to 'have an eye' to both
children in their leisure hours and to begin Sybilla's in-
struction in the three Rs.

Two days after the departure of tutor and governess –
who left, it appeared, unregretted – our new course of life
began. Having spent the first part of the morning in the
schoolroom, Mr Quarrendon would leave for a property
some miles away, which consisted of a farm and a mill he
was reorganizing on a more profitable basis. On half-
holidays he took Francis with him. So it came about that he
seldom appeared before the afternoon, and was not seen
until dinner-time, which now took place later than
formerly. This did not suit Eliza, who had been ordered to
keep early hours. I therefore suggested that she and I
should dine upstairs and that, if so desired, I would join
Mr Quarrendon for coffee in the library, adding, 'But not
if you are busy.'

'You mean that I shall be expected to send for you when
I happen to feel like it?' he asked, in what I was beginning
to recognize as his teasing manner. 'And if *you* do not feel
like it, what then?'

We were standing at the hall door in full sunlight; as I
moved back into the shade, his hair caught my eye – not
for the first time; its springing outline was like that of a
young man. He said, 'Your unspoken criticisms are rather
alarming.'

'Do you want my approval of everything you do?'

'Naturally.'

'I will try to give it.'

'Then I suggest a little expedition – to Limmerston Hall
– and a walk through the woods.'

We both knew that Francis and Miss Trevy had
arranged a picnic with Sybilla and her nurse and would

41

not be returning for a couple of hours; this knowledge might have accounted for his look of faintly derisive gallantry. 'I should like that,' I said. 'Do you think we might go round the rooms?'

'That was what I had in mind.'

So we set off. As we turned into the lane he said, 'On the way back we might pass by the Dower House. Old Lady Craik destroyed the decorations just before she died. The structure is untouched, however.'

'The Hall in miniature?'

He did not answer at once. Then he said, 'In a sense,' in a manner which put an end to further questioning. It seemed strange that, while unable to keep away from the Hall – he had been there twice since coming home – he refused to talk about it. What with that, and his books and paintings, he was probably thought of as eccentric by many of his neighbours. Also, though courteous, he was not very companionable.

I wondered whether I should ever feel at ease with him. As we walked on in silence he seemed more than usually unapproachable; he helped me over the stile into the woods without looking at me: and his expression was so remote that I could not even thank him. I began to wish that I had not come.

The first clearing we came into was carpeted with wood anemones and white violets; creamy patches of late primroses alternated with ground-ivy, the whole combining in a pattern of evanescent delicacy. As I exclaimed in delight the note of a pigeon was followed by a flutter of wings and the rustling noise of some wild creature stealing away into the trees. My companion said, 'The bluebells are still to come.'

He moved forward; leaning against a tree, he glanced about him. I was standing in the sunlight; he, looking taller than usual, in the shadow. I said, 'I have never seen such violets – do you think I might pick a few?'

'You will spoil your gloves. I can gather them for you,' he said; still he did not look at me. Then he added, 'The best patches are farther on. Sit there – ' indicating the trunk of a fallen tree – 'I will bring them to you.'

He turned a corner; then he reappeared and, kneeling, began to pick the flowers. He was some yards away, when I became aware that we were at the end of a ride. I looked up it, and saw a man – bearded, thick-set, with a stick in his hand – running towards us.

He came on quickly, stumbling every now and then and muttering to himself. It was not Grant. Presumably an underkeeper had seen us enter the wood and was going to question our right to do so. Striding up to me, he paused for breath.

He was standing so close that I could not have got up without touching him – and this seemed inadvisable; for he was speechless, panting with rage. As I gazed at him he gasped out, 'I came here first!' raising the stick above his head. He was a big young man, and the stick was a heavy one.

For a few seconds amazement overcame alarm. His voice, although rough and hoarse, was that of a gentleman. He carried himself well; and his gesture with the stick was rather one of self-protection than of threatening. Then I saw that his eyes, blue and fixed, were bloodshot. He cried out, 'It's mine – all of it! What are you here for?'

As I tried to edge away Mr Quarrendon reached us. The young man turned upon him, still brandishing his stick; then, strengthening his grip, he brought it down.

I screamed, clutching at the slippery moss of the trunk. Mr Quarrendon seized the stick; now they held it between them. Slowly he managed to lower it; still the other's grasp was sustained. Mr Quarrendon said, 'Come, Henry – let go. We are not doing any harm.'

'It's mine – all mine!'

'I know, my dear fellow. Everything here is yours. Give me that, won't you?'

His eyes were fixed on the young man's face. Gradually, that steady gaze had the effect desired. The stick was relinquished and fell to the ground. The other blinked and sniffed; his reddened eyes filled. He said, 'My handkerchief – it's gone.'

'Take mine,' said Mr Quarrendon. Producing it with one hand, he held on to the attacker's arm with the other. 'Here.' The young man shook his head, sobbing. Mr Quarrendon said, 'They'll be wondering where you are. Shall we go back to the Dower House?'

The lunatic stared at him. Then he whirled round, towards me. 'What's *she* doing here?'

Mr Quarrendon stepped between us. 'Oh – nothing – ' he said coolly. 'Just looking at your woods. You don't mind?'

'I've something else here,' said the other. From his hip pocket he drew out a large, old-fashioned pistol, balancing it in his free hand.

'You'll disturb the game,' said Mr Quarrendon. 'You don't want to do that, surely?'

'It's my game!'

'All the more reason to let it alone.'

'She shouldn't be here!'

'She's just going,' said Mr Quarrendon, jerking his head – both hands were occupied – in my direction. I swung myself over the tree-trunk and crouched behind it. The lunatic plunged forward, was held back and guided away. 'Let us go,' said Mr Quarrendon. He sounded less sure of himself; he was looking up the ride.

This change of tone brought on a struggle. I perceived that my companion could easily have knocked down his opponent and held him till help came. He did not do so; snatching the pistol, he threw it behind him. Then he said, 'Come, Henry – we should be on our way.'

There was a crash behind me, and two men burst into the clearing. A few moments later their charge was walking quietly away between them. As they began to move Mr Quarrendon said, 'I shall have to report this to Sir Charles, you know.'

The elder keeper, turning, replied, 'He's that cunning,

sir. You can't be for ever on the watch. And he can run – '
His voice sank into a mumble as they walked towards the
ride.

Mr Quarrendon picked up the pistol and then his hat.
After a short examination, he put the weapon in his
pocket. Brushing the leaves from his hat, he turned to me.
'It wasn't loaded. Do you feel faint? There's a stream
nearby.'

'No. But I must sit down for a moment.' He stood
watching me, as if in doubt. I muttered, 'If you had not
known how to deal with him – I couldn't – ' and broke off,
covering my face with my hands.

He sat down. Then he put his hand on my knee. Gazing
at those long, strong fingers, I began to get back my
breath. He said, 'Gross negligence. I suppose they were
drinking again. I'm sorry.'

'You were so quick.'

'I did not hear him coming till he shouted at you.'

'Poor fellow.'

'You think so?' he said, with a return to his satirical
manner. 'Well – pity, in this case, was akin to courage.'

'I did not show much,' I said, trying to laugh.

'How do you feel now?'

'Oh – perfectly well.'

'Composed?'

'More or less.'

'Then we should return home.'

'But we were to see the Hall. Are they not expecting
us?'

He stood up. Thrusting his hands in his pockets, he
looked down at me. 'Do you really wish to go?'

'Yes – do not you?'

He laughed, helped me up and said, 'And not a hair out
of place. But your hat is a little, a very little, on one side,'
and straightened it.

We stood smiling at one another, as if sharing some
joke. It seemed quite natural that he should turn to pick
up the bunch of violets and anemones he had let drop a

few yards away. He gave it me, and I pushed it into the buttonhole of my jacket. Then we walked on.

Mrs Grant greeted us as we entered the atrium. When we came into the first room, I received another shock. Hearing an exclamation, I turned and saw Mr Quarrendon's face change. His pallor became suffused; his hat fell, unheeded, from his hand. He was very angry.

6

Mr Quarrendon did not refer to his outburst until we were on our way back to Pond House. Walking slowly, as if exhausted, he described the probability of damp spreading over the walls of the Pompeian boudoir. He had left me there in order to speak to Mrs Grant, to whom he had already given instructions; these had been ignored. She did not realize how urgent the matter was. 'Now', he went on, 'the curator of the Belminster art gallery must be sent for. If I had not happened to go in today – ' he broke off, staring in front of him. I made a sympathetic comment. He continued to speak of the fragility of the paintings in that particular room.

While his encounter with a lunatic had left him undisturbed, this barely discernible damage had caused a partial loss of control (Mrs Grant was in tears when we left the Hall) and the revelation was rather alarming. At last I said, 'I hope Sir Charles Craik appreciates your care?'

Mr Quarrendon turned, smiling. I did not like that smile. 'He cares for nothing but money.'

'Has the Hall been on sale for a long time?'

'Too long.'

'Were there many offers?'

'A few. His price is absurd.'

'That's dreadful.' He looked at me suspiciously, and we walked on in silence. Then I said, 'Cannot you reason with him? That is, write and suggest that he asks less?'

'He never answers letters.'

'But when you report those men – then – '

'What men?'

'The guardians of his son. You said that you were going to do so.'

'So I did,' he said absently. 'In fact, it would be useless.

Craik might not even open my letter. However – the paintings can be repaired.'

'So you will not write to him?' He shook his head. 'Suppose that young man escapes again?'

He shrugged his shoulders. Then he said, 'I am very sorry indeed that you should have been frightened. I'll go over there tomorrow, and give them a talking-to. That patch – you saw it?'

'Yes. In such a beautiful room, too. It's a sad pity.'

'You feel that?'

'Naturally.'

'It is unique – the whole place.'

'When I first saw it – ' I paused, a little confused.

'Well?'

'I could almost imagine myself – it sounds foolish – '

'Go on.'

'Living there.'

He laughed. The sound jarred me, and I moved away, walking faster. When he caught me up, it was with some comment on the flowers in the clearing. Neither the Hall nor the inhabitant of the Dower House was mentioned again.

These contrasting aspects eliminated any association of Mr Quarrendon with Gianni Severini; the latter would never have been able to deal calmly with a dangerous lunatic, or have been in the least disturbed by signs of damage to a house which was not his own. So his image sank away; if I ever thought of him, it was in dismissal: while Mr Quarrendon's effect was strengthened, partly because I could not decide whether I liked him or not. My interest in his character was shadowed by an inability either to criticize or to understand it.

I tried to solve the enigma by a further study of the paintings in the hall. He came upon me doing so; I was getting accustomed to being disconcerted in this way. Turning, I saw him dressed for riding, a whip in one hand, his hat in the other. He said, 'I may remove those, and replace them by others.' His manner was purposeful; he

48

appeared to be testing me. I asked to see the other paintings.

He led the way into the library and drew out a portfolio. As I sat down, he said, 'They are of no great merit. I suppose one begins such pursuits as an amusement – and then they become a habit.' He stood in front of me, gazing at the busts at the end of the room, while I began to look at the paintings. All were watercolour studies of wild flowers, but larger and more elaborate than those in the hall. Some had a rather peculiar quality.

Cowslips growing in rough grass surrounded a small, decaying gravestone: that over a cat which had belonged, Mr Quarrendon told me, to the former owner of Pond House. The roots had been so fed as to have produced flowers of unusual size and luxuriance. Another study was of a white convolvulus; it partly covered a tree-trunk, and was spreading round a group of ragged robins, which were about to be strangled in its coils. I said, 'Did you see it growing like that?'

Mr Quarrendon considered. Then he replied, 'Convolvuli grow in many ways.'

'But could such a plant destroy its neighbours, as here?'

'It is possible,' he said, half-shutting his eyes. 'I may have seen something of the kind. You don't care for the idea? It is not very well carried out, I know.'

'I was not criticizing the workmanship,' I said hastily. Turning back to the picture, I perceived a ladybird climbing up a stem and thus also doomed, and added, 'I think I should have wanted to tear up the convolvulus if I had seen it as you did.'

'Rescuing one plant from another?'

'It's only a notion.'

As he replaced the portfolio I went to the door. He said, 'Do you prefer these to the others?'

'They are more accomplished – perhaps more recent?'

'They were done last year. That was just after Craik put the Hall on the market.'

49

In the passage I heard the children calling me and went to them, while searching for a connection between those two statements. None came: and presently this discrepancy was forgotten, in my concern for our Sunday arrangements.

Eliza Trevy objected to the services in Limmerston church; she said that Mr Granger did not observe 'the true apostolic ritual'. When I told her that the village people who formed the bulk of the congregation, would have been antagonized by any form of Puseyism, she replied that her chief anxiety was for Francis – surely he should not be tempted into Low Church practices? He came in while we were talking; she then spoke of the service in a neighbouring parish as more consonant with her principles, and suggested taking him there next Sunday.

'But that would mean leaving Mr Granger – and Tom and Jack,' said Francis. 'We always meet after church, and sometimes I go back with them to the Rectory for lunch.'

'Ah – your playmates,' said Miss Trevy, her face falling.

'We've always done it, ever since I came here,' Francis went on. 'I don't see how I could explain to them if I went somewhere else. And the other clergyman's sermons might be longer.'

'Let us put the question to Mr Quarrendon,' I suggested.

'But he doesn't go himself, at least not often,' Francis objected. 'He told me once that it didn't signify whether a person was High, Low or Broad, and I said I knew I wasn't low, because I'm rather tall for my age – and then he explained.'

Eliza caught my eye. 'It's all very well, dear,' she began, 'that may amuse you – but when it comes to a question of grace – ' and broke off in some distress. She then agreed to consult Mr Quarrendon, when we next spent the evening with him.

I had said nothing to her about our encounter with Henry Craik; and now I had to consider how best to prevent the children going near the Dower House, while concealing the reason for such a prohibition. Mr Quarrendon had pointed out that their approach to the woods could be made by a different route; but it seemed to me that his attitude towards the possibility of another escape by the poor young man was rather casual.

Meanwhile, Eliza's objection to the Limmerston services was dismissed by Francis. 'I don't see', he told me, 'that it really matters. I read in some book of Uncle Neville's – I forget the name – that you can pray anywhere, even out of doors. Not that I should want to do that, because I should be looking at the birds. And that reminds me, Aunt Anne – for our next picnic in the woods you must come with me by the lane passing the house where the madman is. It's most interesting. When shall we? It's not frightening,' he went on. 'He talks to himself. And sometimes he works in the garden.'

'You know about him?'

'Of course, everybody does. He's famous,' said Francis in a slightly superior tone. 'Waring told me about him long before you came here. Mr Lambton said I mustn't go near the house. But you'll let me, won't you?'

'You went there by yourself?'

'No – with Tom and Jack Granger.'

'Your uncle will forbid it – and so do I.'

'Why?' My explanation left him unconvinced. 'It's quite safe. He's got keepers.'

'Mr Granger would be horrified.'

'In his last sermon,' said Francis gravely, 'he talked about being good to the halt and the blind. And *I* think, and so do Tom and Jack, that that includes mad people. If he were to see us watching him, it might cheer him up. He looks very sad sometimes.'

Our argument resulted in another appeal to Mr Quarrendon, combined with Eliza's explanation of her disapproval of the Limmerston ritual. The news of a dangerous lunatic in the vicinity did not disturb her so much as Francis's preference for Broad (she called them Low) church practices. Mr Quarrendon contemplated her inscrutably; then he said, 'I will arrange for you and Francis to attend St Saviour's next Sunday, while Miss Milsom goes to Limmerston as usual.'

'But that will mean two carriages,' she began, and was told that this was perfectly feasible.

Mr Quarrendon went on to say that his talk with Henry Craik's keepers had resulted in the son of one being added to their number. I had to accept this reassurance, with that of his promise to forbid Francis approaching the woods by the Dower House lane. 'This', he added, smiling, 'will of course add to its appeal. But I suppose Francis can be trusted. As to the Granger boys – I am not so sure.'

A few days later I realized that Mr Quarrendon had foreseen the result of Francis's transference to St Saviour's; his nephew's dislike of High Church ritual was definite and outspoken. 'I'm afraid', he told me, 'that I shall never take to it. It's too restless. Of course, it suits Miss Trevy, because – well, she has less to do in the week.'

'I don't quite see – ' I began.

'At Limmerston,' Francis went on, 'there's more time to think. I can work out my plans there – for my writing, for instance.' When I protested, he told me that Mr Granger knew of this attitude and had accepted it, merely adding, 'I don't expect you to listen to me attentively every Sunday. Just give me a hearing now and then.' 'And I shall,' said Francis, 'because I like him very much. He's teaching us croquet on weekdays. It's a splendid game.'

When I next dined with Mr Quarrendon he asked me if Miss Trevy had been distressed by Francis's return to the Limmerston services. He appeared amused and curious. I said that she was very grateful for his consideration.

Without answering, he continued to look at me. The resemblance between his features and those of the marble emperors was so emphasized that I found myself staring back at him in a kind of awe; it then occurred to me that this effect was intended, and I decided to resist it; but my work was in the drawing-room, and to go and get it or ask him to do so was beyond me. Waiting for him to speak, I felt strangely helpless. At last he said, 'You have known Miss Trevy for many years, I understand?'

This opening seemed like an oblique approach – but to what, I could not imagine. I said, 'Ever since childhood. She was my parents' friend.'

'She is devoted to you.'

'I owe her a great deal. She came to the rescue when they died. Without her, I should have had to go to an aunt, with whom I had nothing in common.'

'Have you much in common with Miss Trevy?'

'I think so – yes.'

'Her Puseyism, for instance?'

'I respect it, naturally.'

'You do not share it, however,' he said, smiling. 'Why has she not converted you?'

'In Suffolk we went to the same church. Here, it is only right, surely, that I should attend the local services, with the children.'

'This question of ritual – you find it trivial?'

'Not exactly.'

'Miss Trevy's feelings concern you more than her principles?'

'I suppose they do.'

'In fact, over all these years, she has not influenced you.'

'She must have done so. She is the only family I have.'

'She shares your tastes?' he went on, his look more than usually piercing.

'We have always been very happy together,' I said evasively, almost sure now that it was not my dear old friend in whom he was interested.

'In fact, she rejoices in your company – and you accept hers.'

'I am very fond of her.'

'So I see.'

'You find her negligible?' I asked after a pause.

'Not more than most people.'

This reply silenced me; yet I wanted him to go on talking. At last I began, 'You must not think that I don't

53

appreciate the changes you have been forced to make in your life since my sister's death. A whole household descending on you – two young children – two strange women – '

'I am interested in the children. As to the women – one, I find very strange indeed,' he said, reverting to his coolly derisive manner. As I looked away he went on, 'I don't object to being puzzled. You are difficult to know, that's all.'

I glanced up at him. He seemed to have come nearer; yet he had not moved. A long silence fell, while I watched him, thankful that he no longer watched me. I could have returned to the drawing-room, and so resumed my work; I sat on, irresolute and oppressed. Mr Quarrendon said, 'Let us have some music. Will you play to me?'

As I took my place at the instrument he lit the candles, sat down some distance away and said, 'Do you object to cigars?'

I shook my head and began to play, vaguely aware that my performance was a poor one. Yet I could not stop. The scent of his cigar was subtly pleasing. There seemed no reason why the evening should ever come to an end. I became hypnotized by the music, partly because I was playing the same pieces over and over again. Glancing beyond the piano, I saw a cat move from an armchair towards the hearth, and that broke the spell – if it was one. As I got up Mr Quarrendon took it on his knee. He said, 'Please go on – ' and I obeyed.

That bluish smoke began to creep nearer. I became aware that he was standing behind me. Pausing, I said, 'You will make me nervous.'

'I do not think so. But if you are tired – ?'

'I am not playing very well.'

'So you wish to conclude?'

'It's late – isn't it?'

I stood up, and we faced one another. He said, 'You have been very patient. Will you play to me again, another evening?'

'Of course.'

'I will ring for tea.'

'Thank you – I don't want any.'

'But I do.'

We sat in silence till the tray had been placed between us. Mr Quarrendon said, 'Please join me.'

I did so, observing that he knew I took a little cream and no sugar. He said, 'It is all rather absurd, you know.'

'What is?'

'Chaperonage – Puseyism – ritual. Don't you think so?'

'I'm not sure.'

'You are determined not to commit yourself.'

'I must think about it.'

'You have always taken such things for granted.'

'Perhaps. But now I must say good night.'

We parted after the usual commonplaces. All next day, and for several days, he and I hardly met, and when we did we were not alone. Having assumed that we would be spending another evening together quite soon, I began to wonder if I had displeased or wearied him, and so found myself constantly thinking rather of his manner than of his conversation – and recalling his hands as they moved over the tea-tray. To interest him seemed essential. Not to do so would be to fall below a standard as yet undefined.

7

Sybilla's demands to come down to breakfast with Francis and the grown-ups became so insistent that I suspected him of having described this meal as a feast she was too young to share. She interrupted my bed-time reading of a Bible story with, 'Tomorrow, breakfast down – ' in the tone of one announcing a long-settled plan. Francis, suddenly appearing in the doorway, said, 'You're not old enough – ' upon which she sprang from my lap and dashed at him, sobbing, 'Naughty boy!' and beating at his legs with clenched fists. Francis gazed down at her, remarked, 'She's getting spoilt, I'm afraid,' and left the nursery.

When she had said her prayers and been settled for the night I pursued him into the garden and taxed him with provoking her. He replied, 'She nearly always minded Mademoiselle. With Miss Trevy she takes advantage, it's only natural.'

'But did you put this idea into her head?'

'Well, of course breakfast is the best meal of the day. She may have heard me saying so.'

'She comes down at tea-time.'

'Only on Sundays. In her mind, you see, that doesn't count – not now. The fact is,' he went on, taking up a stone and aiming at a tree-trunk, 'Miss Trevy can't quite manage her.'

'Then I must. But if you make it difficult – '

'Good heavens – she has Nurse, hasn't she? When I was her age – '

'Francis – please do not use those expressions.'

'I'm sorry, Aunt Anne. There – I got it just on that knot.'

'And you must not tease your little sister.'

'I only do occasionally.'

'Why do so at all?'

'Well – it is usual,' said Francis in a reasonable voice. 'But I'll leave her alone, if that's what you want.'

'Cannot you help to amuse her now and then?'

After a pause, he said, 'Edwin and I sometimes did – ' in a tone which put an end to further discussion. We walked on in silence until we were summoned indoors for tea, a meal seldom attended by Mr Quarrendon. Some hours later, I asked him whether he had come nearer to finding a tutor.

He shook his head. 'I can manage his lessons for the moment. Miss Trevy tells me that she would consent to be permanently responsible for Sybilla's – with your help.'

'Permanently?'

I was standing at the foot of the staircase. He was on his way up to dress for dinner. Glancing down at me, he said, 'You told me that Miss Trevy was all the family you had, do you remember?'

'Yes. With the children.'

'That amounts to quite a large family,' he said smiling, and departed, leaving me, as so often before, at a loss.

Next day, during a walk – with Francis, who had run ahead of us – he asked me if I had hesitated about accepting his invitation to Pond House. 'Hardly at all,' I said. 'I cannot imagine my life without Francis and Sybilla.'

'When my half-brother George married your sister,' he began, 'I wondered what you were like. If I had come to the wedding – but that did not arise.'

'And then he was sent abroad. It's strange that we did not meet when I stayed with them.'

'I never did,' he said shortly. 'Both my half-brothers and I were at odds with one another, always. But that's ancient history – the usual family embroglio.'

At this point Francis joined us. Later, when I raised the question of Mr Quarrendon's relations with his half-brothers, there was no response. Meanwhile, I observed that the children neither wearied nor irritated him, and began to hope that it would be a long time before he selected a tutor; an addition to our little group would have spoilt its harmony.

Mr Quarrendon then told me that he was planning a small evening party. It was to take place after the Penny Reading, to which he would not be contributing. 'As I have no gifts of that kind,' he added, 'I am relying on you and Francis. You don't object?' I said that I would do my best, and Eliza and I began to practise some piano duets together.

As the failure of a Penny Reading is unheard of – for as long as the performers oblige, so the audience is bound to applaud – I had no qualms. Nor, in the event, would they have been justified. Mr Granger's sea-shanties and Francis's recitations were vociferously encored, while our duets received the tribute of tolerant politeness; as did the other items.

Mr Quarrendon's appearance as steward and announcer struck a note of incongruity. In an ill-lit village hall, filled with smock-frocked men, shawled women and awestruck children, he gave the impression of having descended from another planet. His calm geniality was rather intimidating. Hearing one matron describe him to another as real blood gentry, I detected a hint of alarm. In the eyes of the village he was still a stranger – an odd one. This view, I presently understood, was the result of his refusing to hunt or shoot with his neighbours. He was neither disliked, nor yet quite acceptable. The approach of his equals, as shown at the party, seemed to combine caution with curiosity.

While we waited in the drawing-room for supper to be announced Mr Quarrendon introduced me to his guests. Before we sat down I noticed that one of these, Mrs Lang (escorted by her son, a spectacled and gangling young man) was making special claims for his attention, on the grounds that they were cousins. She taxed him with neglect – why had he not brought me to call? – and during the first course leant across the table to talk to me, as if to emphasize her intimacy with the host, who had placed her on his right hand; the Grangers' only daughter, a girl of eighteen, was on his left.

I sat between a Colonel Hay and Mr Granger's curate, an elderly invalid, who, refusing most of the dishes, explained his predicament between attacks of coughing. 'I ought not to be here at all,' he said. 'Late nights, you know –' it was not yet nine o'clock – 'but I have been promised a glimpse of our host's library – a rare treat for an amateur bibliophile like myself.' He then turned to his other neighbour, Mrs Hay, and repeated this statement at length, after which she began conversation with a grey-bearded Mr Courtenay, presently known to me as a bachelor and amateur ornithologist who collected antique prayer-books.

While observing the rest of the party – another middle-aged couple the Portman-Sinclairs, the Grangers, and their sons, who sat, with Francis, at a separate table – I became aware that Susan Granger, a pretty creature, had absorbed herself in Mr Quarrendon's talk. She was on the point of turning her back on her other neighbour when he said, 'But I must not take up all your attention –' and gave his to Mrs Lang, who began, in a penetrating voice, to advertise her knowledge of his background. A gaunt blonde, she wore several bracelets and two necklaces; these made a tinkling accompaniment to her demands.

'But Neville, you must remember the Greys. *She* was a Hunter, almost a connection of ours, well, actually a third cousin, and *he* – do you not recollect his getting quite bald all of a sudden? I'm afraid we made sad fun of him. Surely you have not forgotten the Greys?'

'Was that the couple who bred Angoras?'

'No, no – that was the Arbuthnots. She has three grandchildren, two boys and, let me see, one surely must be a girl, I think so – well, they keep bees now, you know.'

'Pray take some more salmi, Arabella.'

'Thank you. We stayed with them, did we not, Claude?'

– leaning across the table – 'Claude! Tell your cousin Neville about the Arbuthnots.'

The young man hesitated, flushing. Mr Quarrendon said, 'As I have now hopelessly confused the Arbuthnots with the Greys, I will spare you.'

'You will be saying next', Mrs Lang pursued, 'that you don't remember old Mrs Snape.'

'Who lived near the millrace?'

'My dear Neville! That was her eldest nephew, the one who threw himself into the quarry, the disused quarry of course, otherwise – '

'We seem to have had some rather eccentric acquaintances.'

'Ah! that was in Somerset. When your father became Vicar of – Clinch Hatton, was it? – things were very different.'

'You mean no one commits suicide in the Midlands, whereas, in the West Country – '

'I don't mean anything of the kind,' said Mrs Lang, clashing her bracelets. 'You misunderstand me. In Clinch Hatton, so I heard – but this is between ourselves – ' and as her voice sank. Mr Quarrendon, glancing down the table, caught my eye. His look was one of appraisal, as if he were gauging his cousin's effect on the rest of the company, most of whom were unwillingly subordinate to the sound of her voice. I guessed that he wished me to distract them, and presently I succeeded in doing so.

We did not have to wait long for the gentlemen to join us in the drawing-room. Susan Granger had withdrawn to a window-seat near the door, presumably in order to attract Mr Quarrendon's attention as he came in; he was preceded by Claude Lang, who leant over her, in the hope, it seemed, of her making room for him. She at once joined me and the Portman-Sinclairs, a solid, handsome couple, at the tea-table. Falling upon the bread and butter, they began to tell me about their bulbs. Mr Courtenay then approached us, and after a brief preliminary began, 'Bearded tits are extremely rare in this neighbourhood.

61

But I saw two yesterday. They are nesting. I can only hope that the lesser redpolls' – turning to Francis, who was listening, wide-eyed – 'will not frighten them away.'

'Talking of birds,' said Mrs Portman-Sinclair, 'those wretched swallows have been at my rose-bushes again. We have nets, and even a scarecrow – but they nip off the buds just the same. You have no idea, Miss Milsom, what one has to cope with.'

The St Saviour rector, Mr Blow, now one of our group, put in timidly, 'I believe cuckoos are very destructive – ' upon which Mr Courtenay, with a cold look, made his way to Mr Quarrendon, followed by Claude Lang and the invalid curate. They seemed to be discussing books; Mr Courtenay produced a small, squat volume from his pocket, and they were moving towards the library when Mrs Lang called out, 'Neville! Are we not to have a little music? Surely Miss Milsom will play for us again?'

Her emphasis on the last word was not unfriendly; but I felt myself being regimented. Susan Granger said, 'Oh, please do – ' and I remembered that neither of her songs had been encored by the villagers. I offered to accompany her; and so the music began.

Later, under cover of a piano duet between Mrs Hay and Mrs Portman-Sinclair, Mr Quarrendon asked me if I knew anything of ornithology. 'Courtenay', he went on, 'has a number of books on the subject – and is now writing one.'

'I fear I know nothing of birds.'

'Then you will be the next victim. Tree-pipits – avocets – he usually begins with a likeness, taken by himself in Norfolk, of a great-crested grebe.'

'Oh dear.'

'I will try to protect you.'

'But I do like birds,' I protested. 'In my own garden there is a bird-bath – and we always put out food for them in cold weather.'

'A handful of breadcrumbs and a bird-bath will not shield you from Courtenay's willow-warblers.'

Stifling a laugh – for the music had reached its dying fall – I said, 'Perhaps I had better stick to flowers.'

'How is your Latin?'

'Non-existent.'

'Then it would be wiser to take over the birds. Why not start with a chaffinch? I can show you one before Courtenay's next call. Believe me, he has his eye on you.' At this point the music ceased, Mr Quarrendon moved to the piano and I was joined by both his cousins.

Mrs Lang had been watching us; her questions and comments suggested that she suspected me of having what she no doubt thought of as designs on Mr Quarrendon. After I had parried her approach she described her rockery.

I began to wonder whether my own neighbours had shown as limited a range of interests as those I was now trying to entertain. Having hitherto thought of birds and flowers as no more than decorative adjuncts to country life, I was disconcerted by this obsession with ornithology and gardening. Mr Quarrendon seemed to rise above these competitive interchanges, partly because Susan Granger's unconscious flattery amused and touched him; while not amounting to a pursuit, it prevented her attending to anyone else, and at one moment produced a revolt against Claude Lang's advances. I heard her say, 'No, I don't – I've already told you so – ' in answer to some plea or question, as she turned away from him.

That a very young girl should be attracted by a middle-aged man was quite natural; so I told myself, trying to quench an unreasonable irritation. In this gathering, the host stood out, much as he had in the village hall. He could not but be conspicuous; yet he seemed unaware of the general undercurrent of rivalry for his notice. In order not to share in it, I went up to bed as the last guest departed.

Mr Courtenay called a few days later. I found him and Francis in the library, looking through a volume of Audubon. 'Ah! Miss Milsom, I am fortunate to find you,' he began. 'I have brought the sketches of which I spoke the other night. And I have to consult my friend Quarrendon about an item in this catalogue, a Charles II Common Prayer. Frankly, I do not think it is worth the sum named.'

'How much is it, sir, please?' Francis asked.

'Fifteen guineas. I must admit, I am greatly tempted.'

'Uncle Neville has a lot of very old books,' said Francis, rising to put away the Audubon, 'older even than that. I'll show you one, it's in Latin – ' and he came back from the bookshelf with a dimly gilded folio.

'Be careful, my boy – '

'It's all right, sir. My uncle lets me look at all his books. This one has pictures of people being burnt.'

'But this is Foxe's *Commentarii* – a second printing!' Mr Courtenay exclaimed.

'Yes – I've read some of it in English.'

As Mr Courtenay spread the book over his knees a photograph slid out and fell to the ground. Francis, picking it up, said, 'Why, that's my twin, Edwin. I didn't know it was there. He died, you know, in Switzerland.'

I now became aware of Mr Quarrendon's presence. He said, 'Good day, Courtenay. Give that to me, Francis, please – ' holding out his hand. 'You should be in the schoolroom,' he went on. 'Go up – I will come to you presently.' As the door shut he turned to me. 'Your sister sent me this – afterwards. You know it?'

As I took the photograph he continued to look at me. 'I never saw it before.'

'Most distressing – ' Mr Courtenay interposed.

'He rode out alone,' Mr Quarrendon began, 'and was found, some hours later, at the foot of a crag, not a steep one, that he and his brother had often climbed. This likeness was taken a few days earlier, quite near the scene of the accident.' He put the photograph in the drawer of his desk, adding, 'And now, Courtenay – you will stay to luncheon, of course. Is that Goldenberg's catalogue? I can guess what you are after. I received it this morning.'

Having heard that Mr Courtenay was a rich man, I found his hesitation about the Prayer Book rather surprising. This attitude contrasted with his talk of hunting until, during luncheon, he spoke of spending the next season in Ireland in order to economize over his favourite sport. Mr Quarrendon's refusal to join him was so quietly made that he continued to urge this plan, adding, 'For such a rider as yourself, it's a great chance – won't you consider it?'

'No.'

After a short silence Mr Courtenay resumed, 'Now why, my dear fellow?'

'You know my views.'

'Foxes are vermin. They must be put down.'

'No doubt. But not by me.'

The tone of this riposte was crushing. Mr Courtenay stared, frowned at his plate and turning to me, said, 'Do you agree?'

'I don't care to kill animals – myself, that is. I know it must be done. After all, we have just been eating one.'

'Ah! that suprême was excellent. But now, Quarrendon – you are not a crank, I trust?'

'It depends upon how you understand the word.'

'I'll tell you who is,' the other began, 'and that's Craik. What was he about, asking a king's ransom for the Hall? However, I have reason to know that he has thought better of it. I ran into his agent yesterday.'

A long silence fell. I then saw that Mr Quarrendon had drawn himself up and was staring at the bowl of roses in the centre of the table as if it held some secret. Mr Courtenay went on, 'If I were to cut down on other things, my collection, for instance, I might run to it myself. It's a fine place.'

Still Mr Quarrendon said nothing. Unable, now, to stop looking at him, I saw his pallor change to lividity; the skin of his face seemed to have tightened. At last, dragging out the words, he said, 'So he has lowered his price. Is that – what you mean?'

'Not exactly. Robinson thinks that he may do so.'

Mr Quarrendon signed to Waring to fill up his glass. He drank the wine slowly, then he said, 'In fact – the situation has not changed.'

'All I meant was that it may,' Mr Courtenay replied, apparently unaware of the effect he was making.

'I see.'

It then seemed to me essential to distract Mr Courtenay and I did so, hardly knowing what I said. Mr Quarrendon did not join in the conversation. An occasional glance showed me that his impassivity was being regained by an effort of will. When, finally, he had to reply to his guest, he spoke briefly. His manner was courteous; yet there was something about it which indicated that Mr Courtenay had better leave.

Half an hour later, he was gone. Without a word or a look in my direction, Mr Quarrendon disappeared. I walked out into the garden, towards the orchard. There I sat down. Some time passed before I realized that I was hatless and that it had begun to rain.

8

His distress troubled and bewildered me. It showed that
his feeling for Limmerston Hall was of the kind that
visualized, however remotely, its possession; and as long as
it remained on the market he would be tormented by the
hope that its price might one day descend to his level.

In view of this desire for an almost unattainable object,
the agreeable and interesting life he had provided for the
children and me now seemed burdensome and mysterious.
Yet I could not withdraw; responsibility and affection for
them bound me to their guardian. So I told myself that his
eccentricities were none of my business; as long as he did
his duty by Francis and Sybilla – and there was no doubt
of that – this obsession need not matter. Nevertheless, the
more I considered it the more I dwelt on his attitude,
although I was as far as at any time from understanding
him.

I became aware that he was looking down at me. I stared
at him. He held out his hands, and I got up. As he said,
'This is no place to be – will you not come in?' and I
obeyed, I saw that he was watching me. I said something
about a headache driving me out of doors. He sent me up
to rest; and so we parted.

During the next few days a further study of his pictures
re-created his abhorrence of outdoor sports. This produced
another enigma. A would-be protector of wild animals, he
had chosen to portray both their cruelty and that of those
who killed them. In these strange paintings neither group
was spared; and he had made his home in a hunting
county. His flower pieces were equally puzzling; for in
many of them he showed nature to be predatory and
merciless to a point that verged on the perverse.

All these musings resulted in an increased awareness of

his appearance; of his way of moving, and the sound of his voice. He had described me as difficult to know; I might have replied that he was, in that respect, incalculable; adjustment to his company now became a task. Yet it was not one to be avoided. Curiosity led me on.

When we next dined together Mr Quarrendon spoke of his early years; every now and then he appealed to Waring, who had served his family when they were both young men. As soon as we were alone he began to peel an apple for me; then he said, 'We were too much indulged, my half-brothers and I. My father was one of those rich parsons, and my stepmother added her fortune to his. She survived him by a few years and then left everything that was not settled on me to her own sons. The younger one, Simon, killed in a hunting accident soon after we came down from Oxford, had bequeathed all he possessed to his mistress. I was disappointed – but not surprised.'

'Was it then that you gave up hunting?'

'No – earlier. Who told you that I hunted?'

'Herbert Graham.'

'Ah! yes, Mrs Price's brother. She – Lucretia Mary, is it? – is unhappily married, I understand?'

'Her husband is not very – satisfactory.'

Mr Quarrendon leant back, a twist of peel dangling from his knife. 'What is your notion of a satisfactory husband? He leaves her alone, doesn't he?'

'You have been married. Why ask me?'

'My marriage was rather a brief affair. My wife left me after a year and died, in childbirth, six months later. Oh – ' as I began to speak – 'it was not my child. She ran off with the father.' Getting up, he set the plate of sliced apple before me.

'I should not have spoken as I did. All I knew was that you had been married.'

'It's an old story. Meanwhile, you have not answered me. As a husband, I failed. How does one succeed?'

'You are not serious. It's an absurd question. I know nothing of married life.'

68

'And you refused to try it with Herbert Graham.'

'I did not refuse him. We were engaged. It was broken off.'

'I see.'

'We disagreed on a point that I suspect means little or nothing to you.'

'Really?'

'Yes. My religion.'

There was a short silence. Then he said, 'Graham must have changed. Has he become a free-thinker?'

'Yes.'

'That's odd. He was always an orthodox sort of fellow.'

'No longer.'

'If it had not been so,' said Mr Quarrendon slowly, 'I should have been the loser – of your company.' As I got up he went on, 'It is for me to apologize,' and followed me into the drawing-room. I took up my work and sat down. He said gently, 'Would you like me to read to you?'

'If you please.'

When he came back from the library with a pile of books, I said, 'You never suggested this before.'

'I did not think of it. Will you choose?'

'I would rather you did.'

After a little searching he began, ' "But if thou needs wilt hunt, be ruled by me – " ' and stopped at ' "For misery is trodden on by many, And being low, never reliev'd by any." ' He continued with other passages from that poem and from the plays and then, laying aside the book, said, 'Let us try something modern.' When he ended I looked up. 'Well – what do you think of it?'

'It's very strange. Not quite like poetry. Will you read it again?'

After he had done so he handed me the book. I said, 'I see what one is meant to feel. But all my sympathies are with the Duke.'

'Indeed?'

'Yes. I think the Duchess – and after all, she was not to be the last – must have been a most irritating person.'

'Oh – why?'

'Well – "a heart too soon made glad, too easily impressed." I know the kind, I've met them.'

He burst out laughing. 'You really think that?'

'Yes. And here – "all and each Would draw from her the approving speech." How dull.'

'What about the poor fellow who broke off the bough of cherries for her? He must have meant well, at least.'

'I dare say. But the Duke describes him as an officious fool, nevertheless.'

'Miss Milsom! You appal me.'

'I suppose I'm old-fashioned.'

'On the contrary, you are far too advanced.'

'Please read some more.'

I had never before felt so at ease with him. As he appeared to conclude I said, 'It was not very kind of you to deprive the village of such reading.'

'I don't think they would have cared for anything I chose.'

'Not the villagers, perhaps. But your friends – '

'Friends?'

As I dropped my work he stood up and leant against the chimney-piece. 'Do you, then,' I said at last, 'despise them?'

'Despise – no. It is rather the other way round.'

'They come to your house.'

'Some conventions must be observed. Oh – by the way – I leave here the day after tomorrow. I should have told you.'

I stared at him. 'For long?'

'I can't tell. I hope not.'

Slowly, aware that he was watching me, I began to fold up my work. Then he said, 'Your presence here makes it possible for me to go. I am very grateful.'

'If necessary,' I began, 'could I – might I write to you? About the children?'

'You want to know where I am going?'

'Only on account of Francis and Sybilla.'

70

Thrusting his hands in his pockets, he walked away. Then he said, 'When I asked you to come here, I assumed that you would be entirely responsible for them in my absence. You did not object.'

'No. But –'

'Now, you do. Is that reasonable?'

'Of course it is!' I exclaimed. 'If either of them fell ill, would you not want to hear from me?'

'I shall have no fixed address.' As I went towards the door he added, 'You do not believe me.'

I turned. 'Mr Quarrendon – please understand that it is your wards who are concerned – not myself.'

He gazed at me in silence. Then he said, 'I am sorry to have displeased you.'

Searching for an answer, I found none. He opened the door for me, and returning to the fireplace, lit a cigar. I stood looking at him; he did not look at me. Then I went out.

9

'It was so very thoughtful of him,' said Lucretia Mary. 'Few men in his position would have realized that you must miss your friends. Do you not agree, Herbert?'

'He was rather unsociable when we were at Oxford,' Herbert replied. 'He never seemed to care for the popularity he might have had. And now – ' turning to me with a smile – 'I must admit that I am disappointed in the old fellow.'

'Oh dear, why?' said his sister.

'I wanted to see him. His asking us to stay and then going off like that – '

'He was concerned for Anne, my dear. Now – are you really happy and settled here? And Miss Trevy?'

'I think we both are,' I said, beginning to rearrange the tea-things in order to appear preoccupied. 'She is resting at the moment. I fear she is no stronger. That business with her teeth has pulled her down, and at her age – ' I continued to talk on these lines until Lucretia and Herbert broke in with further inquiries about life at Pond House. As Herbert got up to wait on us I perceived the change in his appearance.

He was growing stout and had become rather bald. His look of solid prosperity was caused by a high colour and the beginnings of a double chin. He was well set up and suitably dressed; but his moustache was a little too long, and he had developed a habit of fiddling with it, as if he knew this. His smiles and laughter were more frequent than formerly. Of course I was glad to see him and for us all to be together again.

As he continued to speak of his and Mr Quarrendon's Oxford days Lucretia Mary said something about the younger half-brother. 'Simon Quarrendon was a dull dog,'

Herbert replied, 'and melancholy. His making a will just before he broke his neck out hunting struck me as significant. It was as if he did not want to live.'

'That must have been dreadful for Mr Quarrendon.'

'They did not suit. There was some feeling, too, about that Mrs Clark, the grass-widow who inherited Simon's patrimony. She was a Frenchwoman and, well, not altogether – ' Herbert paused, cut himself a slice of cake and concluded, 'It is all a long time ago and best forgotten.'

(I was going over Mr Quarrendon's parting words. 'You are still angry with me?' 'No – only puzzled.' 'If I have to be away for more than a week, I will let you know,' he said, taking my hand. I withdrew it. 'There's no need for that, you have told me so.' 'Are you reproaching me?' 'No.' 'I think you are.' 'I have not the right to do so.' 'Is that why you will not shake hands?' The faintly derisive tone, now so familiar, made me put out mine; he took both in his. 'You know,' he said, looking down at them, 'I don't wish to be mysterious. I promise to tell you, eventually, why and where I am going.' 'It's the children – ' I began, as he smiled and released me. 'Of course, you are concerned only for them. Goodbye, Miss Milsom.' A moment later I watched the carriage drive away.)

'No,' Herbert was saying, 'I do not think that we were exactly wild – thank you, I am ready for another cup – but Quarrendon, Neville, that is, was different. His looks, now. They were quite striking, as indeed they still are. Do you not think so, Anne?'

'Perhaps – yes,' I said with rising irritation.

'I wish we could meet,' Lucretia put in. 'He must be a most interesting man.'

'A man of moods,' her brother replied in an omniscient tone. 'One never knew what he was thinking. At least, I generally did. But then I have always been a student of human nature. I do not judge. I observe – and conclude.'

I said, 'Suppose you conclude wrongly?' before I could stop myself.

Herbert smiled. 'I take my time,' he replied, 'and plenty

of it. I *have* been mistaken – but not often. As to Quarrendon, now – '

'I am afraid this room is too hot,' I began, getting up to open the window. I was forestalled by Herbert, who resumed, 'People would turn to stare at him in the street – and of course he was rallied about it by the men. But did he care? Hah! Not a bit of it.' Sitting down, he helped himself to a tea-cake. 'These are excellent. I must remember to compliment your good lady – Mrs Waring, is it? And that reminds me. As our host gave you leave to ask his neighbours to call, may I put in a word for the Portman-Sinclairs? I wrote to them of my visit. I could go over there. But I think they should come here – without little Miss Augusta.'

'Is that the daughter?'

'It is indeed. They are in some distress about her. They wish to consult me. I see that I have surprised you. But we are old friends.'

Gazing at me, he prepared for questions. I said that I would write to the Portman-Sinclairs and suggested going round the garden. When Lucretia had gone upstairs to rest I joined him by the pond. He began, 'You look very well, my dear Anne, quite blooming. And that reassures me. I have been concerned for you.'

In order not to ask him why, I spoke of the garden and so led him into the orchard. Herbert, leaning against a tree and looking upwards, began, 'Our friendship – may I call it that? – is based on mutual confidence. At least, I hope so.'

'Of course.'

'It is therefore necessary that I should speak with the utmost frankness about Augusta Portman-Sinclair.'

'Please do.'

'Although she has not yet reached the age of nineteen,' Herbert announced, 'she has made up her mind about the most important aspect of her life – her religion. You may think it strange that I, of all people, should have been consulted on this point. But here, I must diverge.'

He then described, at considerable length, his abjuration

75

of free-thinking for a return to the Church of England. After some twenty minutes or more, I suggested that we should sit down. As we did so he continued with an analysis of his change of heart. 'Or rather, of intellect,' he added. 'I see that I have taken you aback. Let me explain.'

'If you are happier – '

'Happiness', Herbert interrupted, 'is not so much in question as right thinking. I am a clear-headed sort of person, as I believe you know. But I will enlarge – ' and he proceeded to do so.

Presently, roused from what was very nearly a doze, I gathered that he was waiting for me to speak and said, 'I am very glad for you.'

Smiling tolerantly at this feeble comment, Herbert swept into his major theme. Augusta Portman-Sinclair had announced her intention of 'going over' to the Church of Rome. He was now required to reason with her, as one who had 'been through the fires of spiritual conflict'. 'Also,' he added, 'I have, I am told, a *light touch*' – with annihilating heaviness – 'in the case of young persons. It is a gift, no more.'

'Should she not consult a clergyman?'

'My dear Anne, let me outline the situation.'

(It was very natural that Mr Quarrendon should have been admired when he was young. Perhaps his appearance still impressed some people. I remembered Susan Granger gazing at him; but then a girl of that age would be easily affected.)

'And so you see,' Herbert was saying, 'a professional consultant would not, if you will forgive the slang term, quite fill the bill.'

'Is she pretty?'

'Pretty? Why do you ask?'

'Because I have never seen her.'

'And I fail to see the connection. It is too feminine for my poor understanding,' said Herbert archly. 'Youth is generally pleasing.'

'I did not mean to change the subject.'

'Then I will briefly sum up the position.'

(He had probably gone abroad. That might have something to do with his having no fixed address. It was rather pleasant to feel free of him.)

'And so I must, as they say, lend a hand. I am, after all, her godfather.'

'I will write to the Portman-Sinclairs at once,' I said, getting up.

'I will add a word. She will expect it,' replied Herbert, offering me his arm. As we reached the house the children ran out to greet us.

Later, I wondered why I had chosen to write in the library. The envelopes were not in their usual pigeon-hole, and as I pulled out a drawer to find one I saw Edwin's photograph. Then some writing on the back caught my eye. In a sprawling, uneducated hand were the words, 'No. 1. Good plais.'

A Swiss photographer might have so spelt the last word; but surely he would have written in French or German. As I sent off my note and went up to change for dinner the inconsistency was forgotten.

Next day it rained, and Lucretia and I were left alone by Herbert, who set out for a walk under a green umbrella. She then spoke of his renewed faith, adding, 'I am so happy for you both. Now what I most hoped for will come about. But you must give him a little time.'

'I will give him all the time in the world. But you know, our parting was not only based on religious grounds. I felt that he was weary of the engagement and glad to be released.'

'Oh! no – well – the dear fellow was thoroughly upset. It was all very distressing. Now he wants *everything* to be as it was.'

'Has he told you so?'

'Not exactly,' said Lucretia after a pause. 'But I know that he would have sought you out, wherever you were.'

'I was very glad to see him again.'

Lucretia put down her work. 'You have been here such a short time, and yet you are changed. I suppose – Mr Quarrendon –' She broke off, gazing at me.

'You mean that you suspect me of having fallen in love with him.'

'Dear Anne – I cannot judge. I do wish I could have met him.'

'You probably will. Whether you take to him or not, don't concern yourself for me. We get on well – and he is no more in love with me than I with him.'

'Herbert admires him as much as in the old days,' said Lucretia rather sadly. 'He seems to – to dominate.'

'I think he does. But he is strange – baffling.'

'You like him?'

'He is very good company. Yet there is a sort of blankness. I can't describe it. In fact, I cannot make him out.'

'And you are always trying to do so?'

'I promise you, Lucretia, that I am heart-whole. Please believe that.'

'Oh, I do, I do. But then – Herbert –' Again she hesitated, looking away.

'I see that you are determined to marry me to one of them, whatever their wishes or my own,' I said, and she laughed.

After a short silence, she began, 'I suppose he is very handsome?'

'Unusual, certainly.'

'Clean-shaven?'

'Yes.'

'And pale, with black hair?'

'It is getting grey. He is no longer young, nor does he appear so.'

Lucretia's face fell. I got up, and putting my arm round her shoulders, said, 'You must not worry. I am happy here.'

'I don't believe it!' she burst out. 'No, listen. Half the time you are thinking of something else. Herbert felt that. He finds you altered.'

'Naturally, my mind is on the children. I never had such a charge until now.'

'Oh, yes – I see,' Lucretia murmured. We then began to discuss the Portman-Sinclairs' visit. We were no longer at ease with one another; and I was to blame.

It was difficult to reply suitably when she reverted to her brother's return to the faith. I could not tell her that his glib announcements had been rather distasteful. She went on, 'Were you not thankful for it?' in a slightly reproachful tone.

'Yes.'

'I know that you have always been reserved on such matters. Herbert is more outspoken.'

'We differ in that, as in other things.'

'It was not always so.'

'Perhaps we have both changed,' I suggested, and with a sigh she agreed.

During the next few days Herbert and Lucretia fell into the habit of discussing Mr Quarrendon; they both delighted in these conversations. I did not; the only aspect of them which interested me was Herbert's account of his friend's appreciation of the architecture of the last century. 'I never could think, and cannot now, what he saw in that style,' Herbert concluded. 'Take Limmerston Hall, for instance. I shall not easily forget his anger when I said that throwing out a few bow-windows and a glass-covered porch would lessen the monotony of the façade.'

'It is not his house. Why should he mind?' Lucretia asked.

'He looks on it as a work of art. "My dear fellow," I said, "you might be speaking of some great painting, a Carlo Dolci, or even a Sassoferrato." He gave me a look, and walked out of the room.'

Murmuring some excuse about Francis's lessons, I did the same. I returned to find Herbert's forthcoming interview with the Portman-Sinclairs being discussed, and suggested their staying on to luncheon.

They did so in deepest gloom. Herbert's plan of a talk

with Augusta had been destroyed by her running away from home. Her father was speechless; his wife's round, rosy face became flattened and pale as she spoke of the note left by their only child. ' "I will not be shaken in my resolve," it said, "I have gone to the Precious Blood in the Bayswater Road." And all she took with her was a handbag!'

'She had better stay there till she comes to her senses,' said her husband gruffly.

'A Romanist convent, Theodore! How can you?'

'My dear friend,' Herbert put in, 'this is merely a gesture of defiance.'

'Would you like my brother to see her?' Lucretia suggested.

'The only person who has ever really influenced her is Mr Quarrendon,' said Mrs Portman-Sinclair, turning to me, 'Do you expect him back shortly?'

I replied evasively. The poor mother then renewed her objurgations against the Church of Rome, and tearfully accepted our sympathy.

The departure of these guests was followed by a visit from Mrs Lang, agog to discuss what she described as Augusta's shocking behaviour. 'They have always spoilt her, and this is the result,' she announced, adding that she had long foreseen an outbreak of the kind.

It then became clear that she had another object in view. During a tour of the garden she drew me aside to ask where her cousin had gone; my reply produced a shake of the head and a hissing indrawal of breath. 'I thought so,' she said. 'It is most inconsiderate, but at his age, habit – well! You must let me know if there is anything I can *do*. I said to my husband – he is quite well again and so disappointed not to have met you, but the greenhouse being on his hands just now, however, we agreed that Neville is becoming more and more unaccountable, and that you, a comparative stranger after all, might be glad of a talk every now and then and so call whenever you feel it necessary.'

I thanked and reassured her. Looking sharply at me, she began another discourse embodying hints about Mr Quarrendon's 'undesirable' activities. This attack was halted by a summons to tea. During that meal she held the floor. As her carriage disappeared Lucretia and I exchanged glances and burst out laughing.

Francis, joining us, said admiringly, 'Mrs Lang must be very strong. She can talk almost without stopping. Do you suppose', he went on in a thoughtful tone, 'that if she were telling a story, it would go on and on? I mean, most stories have an end. Perhaps hers might not?'

'You should ask her to tell you one,' Herbert suggested.

'Yes! Just before bed-time,' Francis replied, and they walked away together. Herbert was at his best with both children; they never tired of his company.

As we went indoors Lucretia spoke of the Portman-Sinclairs' plight; she seemed to find my response inadequate. 'It is such a terrible thing to have happened,' she added, and I agreed. Aware that a cursory reply would disappoint her, I went on, 'If I had only met the girl – ' and paused. Lucretia glanced at me reproachfully, as if to imply that I was not really interested in the moral issue. Silent criticisms are generally unanswerable; and this one defeated me.

While dressing for dinner I was visited by the new housemaid, one of Mrs Waring's apparently endless supply of young relatives, now in charge of my room. She had been sent to find out whether her preparations were to my taste. 'Perfectly,' I said, 'except for this gown, which arrived only yesterday,' and told her to put out one several years old.

That the other dress should not be worn until Mr Quarrendon's return had occurred to me some days ago, for he often noticed such things. I took it out of the cupboard, changed into it – and put it back again. If Alice saw me so attired she would think me unreasonable and capricious, and that would be a pity. She was Mrs Waring's favourite niece and an excellent worker.

We sat over dessert longer than usual. Herbert, unable

to emerge from his reminiscent mood, recalled Simon Quarrendon's friendship with Mrs Clark and her inheritance of his fortune. Lucretia, ignoring my efforts to change the subject, asked for details. He replied, 'None of us knew anything about her husband, except that she had divorced him. She was very good-looking. After Simon Quarrendon was killed she reverted to her maiden name – what was it, now? There would have been a scandal if Neville had not gone down. Some of us thought he might marry her, but nothing came of it.'

'Do you mean,' said Lucretia, 'that there was a – a connection?'

'I fear so. Wild oats, you know,' Herbert replied.

I interrupted with a question about the port, to which Herbert, who considered himself a judge of wine, replied at length. He broke off to exclaim, 'I remember – Hébert! That was her name. But as to this port, now – '

Some minutes passed before I was able to say that I must look in on Eliza Trevy, who had gone to bed earlier than usual with an attack of neuralgia.

I stood looking at myself in my dressing-table mirror: and saw nothing. So Mr Quarrendon had dismissed Mademoiselle Hébert in order to continue their relationship abroad. It was rather the deception than the act that disgusted me. His affairs were no concern of mine. But to have spoken to me, and so casually, of Simon Quarrendon's mistress now seemed grossly indelicate. And two young children were the wards of a man who had, it was obvious, superseded his half-brother in the favours of a person he then took into his household. I remembered his saying that he found most people negligible; clearly, both she and I came into that category.

The rest of the evening was spent over a game of three-handed whist. In the course of the next few days I was able to think more calmly about Mr Quarrendon's behaviour and to decide on my own. A telegraphic message from Dover announcing his return at the end of the week convinced me that he had been with Mademoiselle Hébert.

Two days before his arrival we took a picnic to the downs. Below these was a stretch of woodland, and here, almost without knowing it, I found myself walking with Herbert. Unable, now, to make up my mind about Mr Quarrendon, whom I might, after all, have misjudged, I reverted to the new dress. I had been pleased with it; in recollection it seemed over-trimmed. Alteration was another problem, not one easily solved. Lucretia Mary must be consulted.

Herbert was talking about his future; his business required a London house; and he had a plan for buying another in Berkshire or Surrey. 'And so,' he added, 'I hope that we shall see a great deal of one another.'

I replied, 'That would be very nice,' and returned to the question of a dress I had begun to dislike. My taste in such matters had changed: perhaps improved. As we came to a fallen tree-trunk I was reminded of that other walk, and the lunatic. Herbert waited for me to sit down; then he took his place beside me. He had stopped speaking. For some time we were both silent. It was a still, warm day; the scent of the pines crept over the clearing.

'Well, my dear Anne? What is your answer?'

'My answer?'

'I await it eagerly – and with hope.'

I stared at him. He put his hand on mine. 'I believe that we could be very happy together – do you not think so?'

In the pause that followed I was still, to my deep embarrassment, unable to detach my mind from the picture of the retrimmed gown. At last I said, 'What do you mean?'

Herbert removed his hand. He said coldly, 'I thought I had made myself clear.' He then got up and, brushing a shred of moss from his trouser-leg, walked away. Appalled, I gazed after him.

10

'You see,' said Francis, 'it was to be a surprise until the actual day. But without Mr Graham that's not possible. He was working with us – secretly.' Pointing to the busts of the emperors, he added, 'He was going to help us move one of those for the last scene. But as he and Mrs Price left before I could remind him, I must ask Waring.'

'I don't think your uncle would like it being moved.'

'Jack and Tom will be very disappointed.'

'Why not choose something more manageable?'

'Well, we might. They're coming over for a rehearsal this afternoon.'

'When is your entertainment to be?'

'Any evening that suits Uncle Neville. I must say, Mr Graham leaving all of a sudden has set us back.'

'You have kept it wonderfully secret.'

'We had to tell Mrs Price. She was going to lend us her red necklace and one of her shawls.'

'And Miss Trevy?'

'She will play the piano while we are changing the scenes. As you seemed rather busy,' Francis went on, 'we didn't bother you.'

'I had to entertain my – the visitors,' I said hastily.

'I know. I say, Aunt Anne – must we ask Mr and Mrs Lang? Jack and Tom want it to be just for their family, and you and Uncle Neville and the servants here. What do you think?'

'Let your uncle decide.'

'Mr Graham thought that the Langs ought to be asked. He said we were to make a regular celebration of it, because he had a surprise of his own. He was going to announce it after the entertainment. What could it have been?'

'I cannot imagine,' I said, looking away.

'He might write a letter about it. Do you think he will?'

'I don't know, Francis. But let us go all over the house to choose something instead of the bust. Then you can tell Tom and Jack what you have settled.'

As we did so I began once more to consider my letter of apology to Herbert. This task was made more painful by the recollection of his and the children's happiness together and of my own inexplicable heedlessness and discourtesy. Also, I must try to make up to Francis for Herbert's and Lucretia's departure.

She knew that he had been refused, but not that I had unwittingly insulted him. I was fond of Herbert, all the more because, after that shameful scene in the wood, he had behaved with dignity and kindness. I could only hope that he would eventually forgive me. Having proposed marriage as a suitable arrangement, it had not occurred to him to renew his courtship; if he had, I might have been forewarned and so have behaved less rudely. His having counted on being accepted deeply distressed me; it was dreadful to think of his plans being spoilt and of his humiliation. I decided to put off writing to him until after Mr Quarrendon's return; only then would it be possible to give my whole mind to the renewal of our relationship.

He was due to arrive at Belminster by the last train, which meant that he would not reach Pond House till nearly midnight. As the weather was cold and stormy, a fire had been lit in the library – and there I fell asleep. I was woken by the sound of his carriage wheels.

I stood up; then I heard his voice in the passage. 'Bring some sandwiches – and the white Burgundy.'

He came in; we shook hands. 'It is good to see you,' he began. 'I was afraid you would have gone to bed.' Gazing at him, I could not answer.

He might have been travel-stained and fatigued: but it was not that. His drawn face and sunken eyes were ghastly. The ghost of Banquo could not have appeared more ravaged.

He sat down by the fire and leant back. As soon as the wine and food had been set before him I moved to the door.

'Please – do not go. I am a little tired. But I should be grateful for your company.'

I came back to the hearth and sat down. He said, as if to himself, ' "Shut up your doors, my lord; 'tis a wild night. My Regan counsels well; come out o' the storm." '

I muttered something about it having rained all day. Stretching out his hands to the blaze, he continued, 'I must apologize. But I seem to have been travelling for weeks.'

'You had a rough crossing?'

He looked faintly amused. 'I had indeed. Several days ago.'

'The telegraphic message was from Dover.'

'You guessed that I had been abroad? Wait – ' as I began to speak – 'You need not tell me that it is no concern of yours. You made that clear before I left.' After a pause, he went on, 'I am thankful to be here – under any conditions.'

Suddenly, my anger returned. This was not how I had meant to greet him. I said, 'It is late. I will bid you good night – ' and moved away again.

'You are still vexed with me.'

'We cannot discuss that now. In any case, what does it matter?'

'I think it does. Pray take one of these – ' holding out the dish.

'Mr Quarrendon – I must ask you to excuse me.'

'Give me five minutes.'

'Why should I?'

'Because you owe me an explanation.'

'Not at this moment.'

'Are you not perhaps a little unjust?'

The cool, half-mocking manner was too much for me. Turning, I said, 'The explanation should come from you. But I don't need one.'

'No?'

'No! Herbert – ' I broke off, struggling to control my voice.

'Ah! yes, Herbert Graham. Is he, are they, still here?' I shook my head. 'I expected to find them. I hope they had a pleasant visit. You and he renewed old times?'

'We did. Herbert spoke of your Oxford days.'

'That sounds rather dull.'

'Not at all. I was interested.'

In the pause that followed he seemed to be waiting for me to explain. Angrier, now, rather with myself than with him, I reached for the door-handle.

'Something troubles you. What is it?'

'Nothing. I must go.'

'Of course – if you insist.'

The gentle courtesy of his tone was unendurable. 'I know now!' I burst out. 'Herbert – he has told me.'

'What?'

'That you and she – that Mademoiselle Hébert – ' Once more, I had to stop. This time, the silence was a long one.

'I see,' he said slowly. 'You thought I was with her. That is not so. However – '

'I don't wish to hear about an affair that – that – '

'Years ago, before I married,' he interrupted calmly, 'she was my mistress. I have not seen her since she left this house. I can prove it.'

'I've no doubt you can!'

'Miss Milsom – please. Sit down.' I then became aware that he had gone over to the bureau. He came back holding out a letter. 'Here', he said in the same quiet tone, 'is the only communication I have received from Mademoiselle Hébert since she – since I dismissed her. I must ask you to read it.'

On the envelope was her writing: above it, a hieroglyphic postmark. 'What – where is this?'

'St Petersburg. She has a post there with a family I used to know. Read the letter.'

It was no more than a note: one that any ex-employee might have written. Rather formally, Mademoiselle Hébert stated that she was well placed, luxuriously installed – and grateful. I gave back letter and envelope without looking up. Then I left the room.

That night I slept as if stunned. At breakfast, Francis told me that Mr Quarrendon would be away all day, returning in time to dress for dinner. Looking at his happy face, I ceased to dwell on the fact that I had made a fool of myself. His and Sybilla's connection with a discarded mistress, and the suspicion that Mademoiselle Hébert had been reinstated in that position until my arrival, was my only concern.

Before going to dress I rang for Waring, told him that I should be dining upstairs and added, 'If Mr Quarrendon asks for me, please tell him so.'

'Master returned an hour ago, Miss, and has gone to bed,' he said mournfully. 'He looks dreadful.'

'Should you send for the doctor?'

'He won't hear of that, Miss. I was to bring up some soup and a glass of the Marsala, that's all he'll take. We've known him be this way before,' he went on in a more cheerful tone. 'It's rest he needs. Going into Belminster all today – but I'll serve you and Miss Trevy at the usual hour –' and he went out.

Next day Francis and I returned from picking cowslips in the orchard to see Mr Quarrendon at the front door, looking almost as usual.

'Are you quite well again?' Francis began; barely waiting for an answer, he went on, 'Look, aren't these big ones? We're going to make cowslip tea and have a feast and decorate the nursery, so will you come?'

As Mr Quarrendon glanced down at his nephew his expression struck me as peculiar. He always took such trouble about the welfare of both children that I had assumed he was fond of them. Now, remembering Herbert's description of his withdrawal from their Oxford contemporaries, I became aware that he was looking through Francis and replying to his chatter as if from a long way off.

When Francis ran indoors his uncle briefly acknowledged my inquiries and continued, 'I understand that the repairs to the wall-painting at the Hall are finished. Would you care to come and see them?' As I hesitated he went on, 'I thought of dining early and driving there before the light fades. Will you give me that pleasure?' His manner was disarming, and I consented.

During the nursery feast the date for Francis's entertainment was settled. 'The things we're doing will be secret till the day,' he explained. 'Then we'll give out the programmes. I do really think it's going to be quite good – as long as you don't expect too much.'

'My standards are rather high,' said Mr Quarrendon, and Eliza added, 'I'm sure it will be a great success, dear child.'

'Well, I hope so. It's a pity Susan will be away. I *think* Jack and Tom will be all right.'

'How do they feel about it?' I asked.

'Oh, absolutely confident. It's a pity they can only rehearse on half-holidays from Belminster. May I go now? Here, Syb – ' lifting her down – 'I shall want you.'

'Master Francis!' Nurse exclaimed, 'I said she was not to stay up.'

'She won't. It's not a long entertainment. I'll send her up as soon as we've rehearsed it – ' and he led her away.

The rest of the afternoon passed rather slowly. After a hurried meal Mr Quarrendon and I drove to Limmerston Hall. As we passed the lodge he said, 'Before I went away I made you a promise. I am going to keep it as soon as we have seen these repairs.'

When he had done so he expressed himself satisfied, adding, 'I must apologize for dragging you out at this hour. But I have been occupied all day, and I wanted to see what had been done immediately.'

I said something about Francis and the Granger boys disturbing his conference in the library with an elderly man I had seen crossing the hall, and was reassured.

Leading the way through the Blue Saloon, he said, 'When we first met, you thought I owned this place.'

'Was that not a natural mistake?'

'Very much so. But we can't talk here. Let us go into the garden.'

Dusk was falling as we came out on to the terrace. It faced a sloping water-course, lined with dwarf cypresses, that had once emerged from below a fountain some fifty feet above and had been controlled by a group of nymphs and river-gods on sea-horses. Now, deprived of their function, they looked down at us as if in protest. Glancing upwards, Mr Quarrendon appeared absorbed, while I watched him in growing curiosity. He led me to a seat opposite that scene of dereliction, and leaning forward, his chin on his hands, began, 'I was not in France. I went to Monte Carlo.'

'To see Sir Charles Craik?'

'There was no other way. I told you that he never answered letters.'

'I remember.'

'You may also remember that his agent told Courtenay he might be going to sell.'

'And is he?'

'Not at a lower price than formerly.'

'Will Mr Courtenay – ' Intimidated by the enforced calm of his manner, I paused. He said abruptly, 'Courtenay won't buy. That was why I went back.'

'Went back?'

'From Dover.'

'You mean – you crossed to England and then returned to Monaco?'

'Yes.'

'So that was why you were worn out – exhausted.'

'I should have told you all this before.'

'Now that you are telling me – ' Searching for the right phrase, I broke off again.

'Well?'

'I don't quite understand.'

'The journeys were tedious – no more. I went back because I thought I might persuade Craik to change his mind. I failed.'

He rose and walked away. Then, staring up at those bereft stone deities, he said in a harsh, grating tone, 'No wonder young Craik is insane. His father is mad in a different way, that's all.'

'Because he will not sell at a reasonable price?'

'Reasonable! Apart from what he's asking, thousands would have to be spent on this place. And every year, more – more. Can't you see what is happening?'

'Yes – yes.'

'Well? Why don't you say it?' he went on, speaking with bitter passion. 'Craik did. I've no doubt Robinson would.'

'Robinson?'

'His agent. "Limmerston? Isn't your own place good enough for you?" '

'Mr Quarrendon – I have not said it. And I shall not.'

'Then you are unlike most women.'

In the ensuing silence I became aware that the moon had risen. Steely light fell over the dried-up water-course, touched the beard of a river-god and illumined his attendants' desolation. The cypresses should have been pruned long ago; their outlines were grotesque, even a little sinister.

Mr Quarrendon resumed, 'But that's over. I can wait.'

'You think that eventually Sir Charles will lower his price?'

'Possibly. Anything may happen.'

He now appeared serene, and as one having come to a decision. It occurred to me that he might be thinking of expectations from some relative. Nevertheless, his feeling for the Hall had taken on monstrous proportions; failing to conceal it, he had succumbed. Everything was subordinated to this desire. Nothing – no one else – concerned him. I felt myself utterly alone. I said, 'Let us go – ' and getting up, burst into tears.

He did not ask me what the matter was; if he had, I could not have told him. He took my arm, and leading me back to the seat, remained beside me. As I mopped my eyes he said, 'What can I do for you? What would you like?'

'I should not have come here. It has all been a mistake.'

'Let me take you home.'

'What I mean is – I should never have come to Pond House. I did so because of the children, and because Cecilia wished it.'

'And now, having done so, you are unhappy?'

'I don't know. Not all the time. But while you were away something happened – something that I should have prevented.'

'And that has upset you?' I nodded. 'Won't you tell me what it was?'

My rather disingenuous account of Herbert's offer was received in silence. At last Mr Quarrendon said, 'Perhaps he assumed too much. Does he expect you to change your mind?'

'It's not that – I haven't told you!' I burst out. 'I insulted him – and I have not even apologized.'

'For refusing him? Surely – '

'For something much worse! I shall never forgive myself.'

'But what can you have done?'

I looked away, drew a deep breath and blew my nose. Then the full story of that disgraceful scene in the wood was told. After all, my problem must distract him, however briefly, from his own cares.

Waiting for the verdict brought relief; I was no longer isolated. At last he said, 'You really did not hear – you were not listening?'

'No.'

I glanced up at him. As if to get a clearer view of me, he moved away, his eyes fixed on my face. Then he burst out laughing. He began to speak: laughter overcame him.

After a moment's dazed indignation, the absurdity of

93

the incident I had so solemnly described came home to me. I said, 'I know – but how am I to write to him?'

He got up. Taking my hands, he shook his head in comical despair – and we laughed together.

Mr Quarrendon seemed to guess that I should feel embarrassed by the recollection of our talk in the garden of Limmerston Hall. I wished that I had not given way to tears; and to have described the offer of one man to another was in bad taste, to say the least. During the next few days I saw almost nothing of him. Several times he went into Belminster – on business, Francis told me, adding, 'That was his lawyer who came over the other day. I have to work by myself a good deal now, but I like that.'

As a result of these expeditions Mr Quarrendon came home late and dined alone. I could not decide whether his avoidance of my company was intentional: and presently came to the conclusion that he still resented my references to Mademoiselle Hébert. But now, all that mattered was that she had been eliminated. If he and I were estranged, I could only wait for his mood of withdrawal to pass; meanwhile, he appeared more than usually enigmatic and preoccupied.

On the morning of Francis's entertainment Mrs Waring consulted me about her share in the proceedings. If she, her husband and the kitchen-maid all attended it, how could dinner be properly cooked and served? 'Master will expect one hot course, at least,' she went on, 'and it seems to me, Miss, that a casseroled dish isn't quite suitable for the Rector and Mrs Granger, let alone yourselves? When I suggested that she should apply to Mr Quarrendon, she pointed out that he did not like to be worried about such things. So I had to approach him.

As soon as I heard him return I went into the library. The door was ajar; he sat at a table by the window, painting a bunch of wild flowers – purple orchids, eyebright, bugloss, and others I knew but could not name. He did not hear me; I stood looking at him.

It was possible, then, to understand the nature of his power, if only because he was not consciously exercising it. Absorbed and amused – he was smiling – he rather resembled a scientist working on a formula than an amateur artist indulging his hobby. I had observed this ability to give himself up to whatever he was doing in other ways. Listening and commenting, he seemed to cast a spell; and this impression was enhanced, as now, by his appearance. (He was not handsome in the accepted sense; but such looks as his are apt to draw the eye and remain in the mind.) Leaning back to contemplate his work, he seemed dissatisfied. Then he glanced aside, saw me, got up and said, 'There's something wrong here. Can you tell me what it is?' as if we were in the middle of a conversation.

His assumption that we were still on friendly terms so affected me that I was unable immediately to take in the painting. I then saw that it was different from his other work and said so, adding, 'Perhaps that is because it is in oils. I have only seen your watercolours.'

'It is dull,' he said abruptly. 'How do you find it different?'

'I know nothing about these things. It seems to me – peaceful. That is not the same as being dull, surely?'

'Peaceful – well, perhaps. I was aiming at another manner. But that sounds rather pretentious.'

For some minutes we stood gazing at the unfinished study in silence. Then I said, 'I like it very much – partly because the flowers are indoors. When I was a little girl, I used to arrange such bunches for my nursery.'

'You think I should go on with it?'

'Certainly.'

'It's an experiment,' he said in a discontented tone. 'Such flowers as these should remain wild – growing – spreading – ' and he began to clean his palette, frowning a little.

'Spreading mischief?' I suggested, and he laughed. Then he said, 'You did not like my other paintings.'

'I did. It was the ones in your books I found rather alarming.'

'So did others. I suppose that was the intention.'

'Not really?'

'It's a long time ago – years before I came here,' he said absently. 'I was surprised at anyone wanting to publish those tales, and that children should like them. I was young – and rather aimless. But now, what have you been doing these last days?'

I put forward Mrs Waring's problem. He said, 'A cold spread – anything. Tell her not to make a piece of work about it.'

We were now joined by Francis. With rising colour, he laid a sheet of paper on the table, announced, 'It's the programme,' and went out. His uncle and I studied it together.

'It seems reasonably short,' he said, 'if elaborate. "Some Animal Studies" – what can they be?'

'The whole programme is planned for your especial pleasure, I'm sure of that.'

'So I must not criticize?'

'Francis, and the other two, think more of your praise than of mine or the Grangers'.'

'No doubt it will be a success. It might even be amusing,' he said coolly.

And so it proved. The Granger boys, dressed as pages, opened the programme with a duet – 'It Was A Lover and His Lass'. Tom, the elder, was extremely good-looking, and Jack only a little less so. Their self-possession was no doubt the result of frequent choir-practices; evidently they were accustomed to performances of this kind. I wondered whether Francis had gauged their limitations in acting.

It became clear that he had done so with his rendering of the Animal Studies – the 'poor Wat' verses, *Les Deux Pigeons* and the 'sequestered stag' speech from *As You Like It* – chosen, obviously, to impress his uncle. Mr

Quarrendon's reception of this tribute was that of a critic listening to a professional: kindly but detached. It contrasted strongly with the undiscriminating enjoyment of the Rector and Mrs Granger and the enraptured applause ('Fancy Master Francis remembering it all!') of the staff.

After a musical interlude the curtains parted to reveal Francis as Brian de Bois Guilbert and Tom as Rebecca in the tower duologue – with this difference, that as the wicked knight advanced upon her, Rebecca hurled herself from the battlements. Peering over them, de Bois Guilbert exclaimed, 'There! She's gone!' and Jack closed the curtains.

Other songs and recitations led up to the final and most ambitious item, a *tableau vivant* entitled 'Married and Single'. On one side of the divided stage Tom, in a dirty apron and torn sunbonnet, nursed Sybilla, who was bedaubed with tears and snatching at a crust in a setting of degraded poverty, while Francis, in rags, huddled over an empty hearth. On the other, Jack, splendidly attired in a brocade dressing-gown, sat at ease with a bottle of wine at his elbow in an apartment crowded with ornaments.

Prolonged applause and bursts of laughter greeted this warning against the married state. Eliza then drew the curtains and hurried back to the piano for the National Anthem. The performers joined the audience and Sybilla, loudly protesting, was borne away by Nurse.

Some twenty minutes later we were all at supper. Francis, too wrought up to eat, received our congratulations with radiant modesty. Yes, he had planned the whole affair. 'But it's so lucky that they' – indicating his friends – 'can sing. I can't manage a note, myself.'

'Is that your own view of marriage?' the Rector asked.

'Oh yes, sir, it's all our view, we agreed about it beforehand.'

'And so none of you will marry?' Mr Quarrendon pursued.

'As a matter of fact, I shall,' said Jack, laying down his knife and fork. 'Because I must have a wife to look after my house.'

'You can have servants,' his brother pointed out.

'One can't depend on them. They give notice, and then where are you?' Jack replied.

'Then you get others,' Francis put in.

'It's not so easy. After all, a wife *has* to stay, whether she likes it or not.'

'Yes, but think of her always being about – ' 'And interfering – ' the misogynists protested, to which Jack replied that *his* wife would be properly trained.

'By yourself?' Mr Quarrendon asked.

'Yes, sir.'

'Have you anyone in mind?'

'Well, no – not these holidays.'

'Whom can you mean?' his mother demanded.

'You'd never have the patience,' Francis exclaimed. 'Besides, when you're grown up, you'll feel differently. You won't have time, for one thing, not if you're going to be a lawyer.'

'I've changed my mind about that, I'm going to farm.'

'Really!' his brother cried. 'You can't even milk a cow.'

'My wife will,' was the imperturbable answer.

Peals of laughter from the grown-ups ended this discussion. Unmoved, the actors continued their meal; Francis, urged by Eliza ('You must be tired out, dear boy,'), helped himself to chicken mayonnaise together with plum cake, and accepted a glass of port. Healths were drunk, the Grangers prepared to leave and Francis was again congratulated. 'Which bit did you like best, Uncle Neville?' he asked.

'The tableau was impressive. But I am very much drawn to that particular fable.'

'I thought you would be, I said so!' Francis exclaimed. As so often, they seemed on a level. Mr Quarrendon's attitude of calm appraisal stimulated his nephew to a point I found rather alarming, until, lighting our bedroom candles, Francis remarked, 'I wanted to put in some of my own writing, then I changed my mind.'

'How was that?' Mr Quarrendon inquired.

Francis flushed. 'Well – it wouldn't have been quite – I don't know – '

'Up to the standard of Shakespeare and La Fontaine?'

'I thought not. But I had a bit ready.'

'That will be for another time?' I suggested.

'We'll have to see,' Francis replied. 'Sybilla was all right, wasn't she? Tom managed to stop her smiling and waving, but it was anxious work – ' and he ran upstairs.

Next day, the effects of Francis's efforts on his lessons resulted in his spending all that afternoon in the school-room. Leaving him to struggle with a passage in the *Aeneid*, Mr Quarrendon finished his flower-painting and then disappeared. Francis, a blotted exercise-book under his arm, joined me as I was going out and suggested that we should approach his uncle together. 'I saw him going down to the lower pond,' he added, and there we found him, standing above the circle of black water. He looked through the translation and passed it with a nod.

Francis, glancing at me as if for support, said, 'Jack and Tom want me to go out with them tomorrow – ferreting.'

Mr Quarrendon handed back the exercise-book and contemplated his nephew in silence. Francis went on, 'They asked me once before, but I didn't go.'

'Why not?'

'I thought you wouldn't like me to. But rabbits are a sort of vermin.'

'So I believe.' After a pause Mr Quarrendon added, 'There are many kinds of vermin. The question is, which should be destroyed first.'

'I suppose – the ones that do most harm.'

'Naturally.'

'I'm afraid', said Francis in a slightly embarrassed tone, 'that I don't know which those are.'

'Human beings can do irretrievable harm.'

'I know, but – if you kill them – '

'Well?'

'It's murder.' Again Francis broke off, his eyes on his uncle's impassive face. 'Everyone,' he said at last, 'I mean, a lot of people, have to kill animals that are a nuisance.'

'In that case it is known as putting down.'

'Well – may I go, then?'

'If you wish.'

'You don't mind?'

In the ensuing silence Francis began to look puzzled, then uneasy. Mr Quarrendon said, 'Let us go in,' glancing at me, and we walked through the trees into the sunshine.

Nothing more was said until, passing through the hall, Francis caught sight of the flower-painting. 'So you finished it after all,' he began. 'I thought you weren't going to. It's not like the others, is it? There's no story.'

'Should there be one?'

'No – but generally, in your pictures, something's going to happen. And then you guess, at least I do.'

'So you don't approve?'

'Oh, approve, that's another thing,' said Francis hastily. 'I don't know about pictures. I like the ones in your books best.'

'If you want a free day tomorrow, you had better copy out that passage again,' said his uncle, and as Francis withdrew he turned to me. 'I have to ask you something,' he said, and opened the door into the library. 'Herbert Graham', he went on, 'wishes me to dine with him when I am next in London. I shall be there the day after tomorrow. He says that he needs my help in a matter that concerns his future. Suppose he wants me to plead with you for him – what am I to say?'

'I have already told him, in my letter, that I – that it's no use,' I said after a pause.

'And that is final?'

'Yes.'

As I sat down he walked over to the window. Then he said, 'Forgive me – but I must know something of your plans. Do you intend to give up your life to Francis and Sybilla?'

'I hoped – that is, I was going to ask you, if they could come to stay with me sometimes.'

'That might be arranged. But their home is here.'

'Do you mean – that you don't want me to share it?' I said after another silence.

'My dear Miss Milsom – of course not. They need you. Are you unhappy here?'

'No. But sometimes I feel – ' It was impossible to continue.

He said gently, 'Please tell me. You feel – ?'

'Like an intruder.'

'You are wrong. What can I have done that estranges you?'

'Nothing. The situation – ' Again I hesitated; at last I managed to say, 'It's rather an odd one.'

'I suppose it is. Meanwhile, I understand from Graham that he has renewed his faith. So that difficulty does not arise.'

'No.'

'Come, tell me,' he said briskly, sitting down. 'He bores you – is that it?'

'He would if I married him.'

Mr Quarrendon laughed; then, leaning back, he said, 'We will have tea together in here, shall we?' and rang the bell.

We talked of trivial matters for a little while, then of my life in Provence and of his in Paris. As an art student there he had been happy, until he realized that he was an amateur and would never be anything else. 'Then,' he went on, 'I wandered over Europe, trying not to paint and wondering what I was good for. Like most young men of that calibre, I began to think of myself as a writer. Later on, I drifted, spending more than I could afford, in the sort of company I despised. You can imagine it – the liaisons, the stupidities – ' He broke off with a shrug and a smile.

'It did not last?'

'I became weary of it. So I married. As my wife wanted to live in Italy, we took a great barrack of a place in Rome.

It was not a good arrangement, for either of us. She was very young – pious – strictly brought up. I was not the right kind of husband for her, then or later.'

'And so it came to an end,' I said after a pause.

'She divorced me.'

'I thought – at least, you told me – that she ran away.'

He had been staring at the tea-table. As he looked up he seemed to return from the past. 'I beg your pardon – I should have mentioned it. That was my first marriage. It is all so long ago, you see. One forgets – and it is not a very interesting story.'

Considerably taken aback, I tried to think of a suitable comment. He said, 'May I have some more tea?' and I took his cup, returning it in silence. He went on, 'I sound callous. Yet I was sorry for her – poor Sigrid.'

'She was not English?'

'Norwegian.'

'But why – you must have been in love with her?'

'Oh – ' He put the cup down, frowning as if in an effort at recollection. 'Yes, well – her parents – but whatever I say will displease you.'

'You mean, they insisted on the marriage?'

'Up to a point. She threatened – all sorts of nonsense. After we parted she married again.'

'And then?' I said rather faintly.

'Then, let me think, yes, I came home and married Leila. That, as you know, did not last either. It was my fault, I suppose.'

'You have been unlucky.'

He laughed. 'It is kind of you to put it in that way. But no – she was. She could not help herself. In those days, Craik was the sort of man few women can resist.'

'You don't mean – Sir Charles Craik?' He nodded. 'But you have just seen him – you – ' I stopped as he stood up, smiling down at me.

'You think I should have called him out – on the terrace at Monte Carlo?'

'Seriously – '

'Ah, seriously, that's another thing, as Francis would say. In fact, he did me a favour.'

'And the child?'

'She is at a convent school, I believe. I have never seen her.'

The ensuing silence seemed to enclose us in an intimacy hitherto unknown to me; so that when he asked me whether I had been happy in Provence, I spoke of my mother's difficult nature as to an old friend, adding, 'But it was so beautiful there that whenever I was free to walk or ride about the countryside, nothing else mattered. There was a great castle on a hill near Vaison-la-Romaine that I tried to sketch.'

'You gave it up?'

'I had no talent.'

'Neither have I, for that kind of thing. I still persist, however – ' and he went over to the bureau, returning with a half-finished watercolour of the fountain at Limmerston Hall.

I gazed at it in wonder. Nereids, river-gods and sea-horses appeared out of a mist, their beauty romanticized and enhanced. Glancing from them to Mr Quarrendon, I saw him look at his work as one dismissing the unattainable. Then he put the sketch away, and we began to talk of other things.

On the way upstairs I heard sounds of altercation in the nursery; laughter from Sybilla, punctuated by Eliza's expostulations. I went in to find the pupil under the table and the teacher on her knees. Sybilla's cries of 'No!' had a curiously muffled sound. Before I had time to intervene Mr Quarrendon joined us.

Standing in the doorway, he said, 'Come out at once,' and Eliza began, 'I really don't know what's come over her.' He put her aside with a gesture as Sybilla emerged, her mouth full of paper, which she let fall to announce, 'Syb's a dog – ' and, barking, advanced on all fours.

Mr Quarrendon picked her up and carried her into the night nursery. As he dropped her into her cot and turned away, she began to scream; having shut and locked the door, he said to Eliza, 'She should stay there for a little while, do you not agree?' in the tone of one expert conferring with another.

Later that day, Eliza said, 'If it happens again, I am to send for him. But it would never do to depend on him – in any way – would it?'

Avoiding her glance, I said something about my dependence on her, and left the room.

12

'I must ask Handford what he uses for these,' said Mrs Lang, gazing at a group of polyanthus. 'Perhaps it is their being near the pond that makes them so large.'

I hesitated to approach Mr Quarrendon's rather formidable gardener; she swept on with inquiries about the children, adding, 'I hear that they and the Granger boys were up at all hours the other night, reciting poetry. Neville used not to encourage that kind of thing, I have often told him that Francis should be put to school.'

'He will be, next year. But as he is now so advanced – '

'At that age one can be *too clever*,' Mrs Lang interrupted. 'I had to hold Claude back at one time, I remember telling Neville so when he and that foolish little Leila, if they had only had a child, well, it doesn't bear thinking of – ' and she launched into condemnation of Mr Quarrendon's second wife.

I gathered that she did not know of his first marriage; nor was she aware that he kept in touch with Sir Charles Craik. As I realized that I had been his only confidant in the matter, the thought of a divorced man being in charge of two young children recurred. Surely Cecilia would not have made him their guardian if she had known of that unfortunate episode.

' – and so,' Mrs Lang continued, 'I am bound to admit that there is nothing amiss, nor' – with a smile – 'can there be, as long as you are here.'

'That was my sister's wish.'

'I know, it was an excellent plan, and of course Neville's share of her inheritance is adequate, but then his being passed over at least partially, for both his half-brothers, that *was* hard, it embittered him. Oh – ' as I began to speak – 'it was all years ago and he is not poor, but he should have been quite wealthy. As it is, the boy will be very rich when he comes of age and one can only hope that he will look after his sister.'

Later that day, I began to think about the will, of which the terms, apart from my own responsibilities, had faded from my mind. Francis's obligations would be heavy: his training was therefore a matter of some concern, and his future held many pitfalls. I assumed that Mr Quarrendon was preparing for these by his rather peculiar form of discipline.

Francis's admiration for his uncle led him to study the ultra-modern authors of which he had heard Mr Quarrendon speak; so it was that, entering the library, I found him deep in a volume of poetry. 'Uncle Neville will be back from London in time for tea,' he said, 'and I want to show him that I do understand some of these. This one about the poisoner is quite easy – and that about the man going to be executed. But this is different – ' and he handed me the book.

'Your uncle read me that poem,' I said. 'The Duke is telling the agent who has come to arrange his second marriage that his last wife bored and irritated him. He treated her unkindly, and she died.'

'And he's had several wives before her?'

'Obviously,' said Mr Quarrendon. As Francis came towards him he sat down, smiling at me over his nephew's head. He looked tired and depressed but not ill. 'What do you make of Mr Browning's poetry?' he went on.

'Some of it is like a person talking,' Francis began. 'I suppose the Duke was a sort of Bluebeard, I mean if he'd had so many wives and got rid of all of them.'

'What makes you think that?'

'Well – "my *last* Duchess" – how many do you think there were?'

'If they existed, might they not have died in their beds?'

'*I* think he murdered them,' said Francis firmly. 'After all, Italians – '

'You use that expression very freely,' his uncle interrupted. 'Ring the bell for tea, if you please.'

'Can I have it with you?' Hardly waiting for consent, Francis continued, 'In the old days, people got murdered quite easily. It's different now, of course.'

'Quite different.'

There was a pause. I said, 'If the Duke had been a murderer, Mr Browning would have hinted at it, surely?'

'What about those other wives?' Francis persisted. 'I must say, it looks very suspicious.'

'In fact, you are convinced,' said his uncle.

'Well, there's such a lot about murder in these poems, he seems specially interested in it.' As I began to pour out, Francis let the book fall; moving to wait on us, he tripped over it and upset a plate of ratafias.

Mr Quarrendon threw him an icy glance. As Francis began to pick them up, he leant back and shut his eyes. He said, 'You may finish your tea. Then leave us. You still have some work to do, I suppose?'

'A little, yes,' Francis replied, adding, 'I'll go now – shall I?' There was no answer. He looked from one to the other of us, and went out.

It was not the moment to begin another conversation: still less to comment on Mr Quarrendon's severity. Clearly, Francis's clumsiness, slight though it was, had exacerbated him. This aspect of their relationship was distressing, if only because it exemplified a coldness which Francis, not easily intimidated, was constantly trying to overcome. I could but hope that Mr Quarrendon's undoubted appreciation of his quality might develop into a warmer feeling; yet I had begun to wonder whether he was capable of more than a casual kindliness towards anyone, myself included.

After a short silence he said, 'I have something here that I hope will please you,' and placed a small packet before me. It contained a worn leather case in which was a gilt filigree brooch set with topazes and seed pearls: an antique piece of unusual beauty. He acknowledged my praise with 'It is Spanish. I thought it would look well with that new evening gown of yours.'

I pinned it on and went to the mirror over the chimney-piece. As I turned to thank him again, he said, 'Now, tell me what has been happening. Are you not perhaps a little tired? Have the children been too much for you?'

'No, indeed,' I said hastily. 'I have been trying to keep up with your – with some of those rather difficult writers. But I'm not tired.'

'Tell me about them.'

That subject led to others of a more personal nature. Presently I found myself talking of the past – my own – and being drawn on to speak of elements in it I had hitherto considered uninteresting to anyone but Lucretia Mary. I said nothing of that long-ago Florentine romance; it was revived as I broke off to look at my companion, and waited for him to speak again. He said, 'Your attitude towards yourself surprises me. You seem to think of your life as given up to the care of others. Are you to have none of your own?'

As this was what I had been thinking ever since I came to Pond House, surprise made an immediate reply impossible. When at last I began, 'Oh, but I have – in a way – ' and Mr Quarrendon interrupted with, 'No doubt, but is it enough?' I remained silent, aware that he was looking at me, yet unable to meet his glance. Fortunately, my work was within reach; as I unfolded it, he said, 'Most women put up barriers – but I never knew one who did so as quickly as you.'

'And you have had some experience in that way.'

' – But I am still amazed by their recourse to needlework when they don't intend to answer.'

Waring now came in to remove the tea-things. As the door shut I said, 'I should like more independence, it's true.'

'You had it before you came here.'

'I don't regret leaving my home. I miss it, naturally.'

'And you will not consider sharing one with Graham?'
I shook my head. 'Yet once, you did.'

'That's over.'

'Irrevocably?'

'Yes.'

'He hopes, you know, to make you change your mind.'

'He never will. For me, marriage is out of the question.'

'But why?'

I went on with my work in order to give myself time to speak steadily. Then I said, 'I am thirty-five. As I cannot accept Herbert's offer, I have resigned myself to a single life.'

In the ensuing silence it was not impossible to continue working as if we had been talking of some triviality. Mr Quarrendon said, 'Would you consider marriage with someone else?'

'I might. But I don't think it arises.'

'I have been meaning to ask you – while I was abroad you saw the Portman-Sinclairs, I believe?'

Feeling as if I had fallen from a great height, I managed, after a pause, to assent. He went on, 'She will be home tomorrow. They have gone to fetch her.'

'As a result of your persuasion?'

'She is a little fool. But with such parents, that's inevitable.'

'They must be very grateful to you.'

'I hope to avoid their gratitude.' Turning to light a cigar, he went on, 'You don't mind this? If they call, I shall be out. Neither of them need see you, unless you wish.'

My answer was interrupted by the sound of the dressing-bell. As Mr Quarrendon was dining out, Eliza and I spent a pleasant evening together, until she noticed my brooch and was told of its provenance. Her disapproval was mild but uncompromising.

'You speak as if I were a young girl,' I protested.

'Forgive me, dear. But you are still very personable.'

'Oh – still!'

'Naturally, Mr Quarrendon finds you so.'

'What has that to do with my accepting a present from him?'

'Perhaps I am over-strict,' she said after a pause. 'I should not criticize him.'

'Yet you do.'

'I find him strange – alarming.'

It was the second time that day that my own thoughts had been uttered by another. Some hours afterwards, lying awake, I heard the sound of the carriage. I lit a candle, saw my brooch shining softly on the bedside table, and got up to put it away.

Three days later, I returned from a walk with the children to be greeted by Waring. 'It's Miss Portman-Sinclair. She wanted Master. I told her he was out, but she won't leave.'

'Where is she?'

'In the library, Miss. I did my best, but there – she's a most persistent young lady.'

'I had better see her.'

'If you would, Miss. Should I bring in tea for you?'

'Not till I ring.' As I removed my hat and gloves I tried to recall what else I knew of this apparently unwelcome caller; that she was eighteen, pretty and over-indulged did not create a picture.

When I came in she sprang up and said abruptly, 'I know who you are. Where is he?'

'Please sit down. Mr Quarrendon is not expected back just yet. May I offer you some tea?'

She shook her head. In the pause that followed I heard her breathing. Tears and agitation – anger, perhaps – had ravaged her; yet she was extremely handsome. Dark, wild-eyed, dishevelled, she dominated the scene she was about to make in which my part would be subordinated to hers. That I had a vinaigrette in the pocket of my dress was not much consolation.

Her efforts at self-control having partially succeeded, she

said harshly, 'I am sorry to disturb you. But I shall stay here till he comes.'

'You are not disturbing me. I would like to help you.'

She was now standing with her back towards me, her hands clasped behind her. Her gloves lay on the floor between us. Mechanically, I picked them up and after a short search for a friendly approach, began, 'Mr Quarrendon may not be back for some hours. If you could tell me – '

'I am going to see him,' she burst out, whirling round. 'I must. He promised.'

'To see you?'

'Yes! If I came home.'

'But that was only two days ago.'

'You don't understand! He said he'd come at once. And now – now I know he never will. It was to get me away. It's not fair – ' She put her hands over her face.

I came forward and took her arm; she did not move; her sobs were violent and irregular. It seemed best to stand there without speaking till she became aware of such support as I was able to give. Then she gasped out, 'You don't know – what he's like. I do. But I believed him.'

After a pause I said, 'I am sure he will see you, I will ask him. We'll arrange it.'

She tore herself away. 'Don't! It's no good!'

'Please – please come and sit down. You can stay here as long as you wish.'

Her face convulsed, she stared at me. I led her to a chair and offered her the vinaigrette; she pushed it away. At last she said, 'You mean to be kind. But you don't know about it. He came – to where I was – because my father and mother asked him to. They had a plot against me.' Pausing to blow her nose, she went on, 'I left so as to get away from him. I thought – being a Catholic –, would help. Ever since I was a little girl – Susan and I – ' The sobs broke out again.

'Susan Granger?'

113

'She's my best friend. We used to talk about him. Now she's in love with someone else.'

I sat down opposite her. Then I said, 'When you told your parents that you wished to become a Roman Catholic, were you sincere?'

'I knew they would mind. But I really did want to. I still do.'

'I don't see what that had to do with Mr Quarrendon.'

'He said – if I came home – he'd come and talk to me – and discuss – ' Again she broke down, her face in her hands.

'Perhaps he will.'

'Not he – never!'

'If you are really thinking about changing your religion, you should consult a priest.'

'I did. At the convent. He was silly.'

'But Mr Quarrendon cannot – '

'It's no good trying to explain,' she interrupted. 'You think he's wonderful. But you'll see.'

A long silence fell. It was if a note had been struck inside my head, throbbing, drowning all other sensations. Presently I became aware that she had gone to the window and was gazing out over the lawn. It had been raining; now sunshine poured into the room. She was shivering. At last she said, in a hoarse, thick voice, 'I had better go. I'm sorry.'

'Please take something first. Some tea – a glass of wine?'

She shook her head. Then, clearing her throat, she began, 'Those boys – twins, weren't they?'

'Yes.'

'And one is dead – in an accident?'

'Yes.'

In the pause that followed the drumming increased, then sank away. She turned. 'My gloves – I dropped them.'

'Here they are.'

'Thank you.' She began to put them on, smoothing out the soft, pearl-coloured kid. They must have been costly; but then all her dress, simple though it seemed, was that of a young woman lavishly endowed and careless of a wealth she had always taken for granted. I stood gazing at her, thinking how proud of her – and how anxious – her parents must be. I said, 'Won't you come here again? I would try to help you.'

She laughed. 'You – and he – are in charge of the children, aren't you?'

Determined not to take offence at the sneer in her tone, I said, 'They need not trouble you,' and went on, 'I don't think, truly, that Mr Quarrendon could have meant to deceive or – or mislead you. I am very sorry that you are unhappy.'

She looked at me with sudden curiosity. Then she moved away. I had to draw back to let her pass. Glancing out of the window, I saw the groom bring the dog-cart up to the front door. He got down, touching his hat. She sprang up. As they drove off she seized the whip and slashed at the horse.

A few days later Mr Quarrendon told me that the Portman-Sinclairs were going abroad, taking Susan Granger with them, 'as enlivening company for Augusta,' he added. 'You appear relieved,' he went on. 'Did she threaten to call on you again?' looking down at me with a smile.

We had been spending the evening in the library with Eliza Trevy, whom he had asked to an early dinner, an attention she repaid with much talk of my youthful days. It seemed to me that he had been both courteous and patient to a person with whom he had nothing in common; now, the irony of his tone re-created the chilling aspect of his approach. I said, 'I should think you must be relieved,' and he shrugged his shoulders.

'They are afraid', he then began, 'of fortune-hunters. It is partly because they suspect me of trying to marry her that they have gone away.'

Having shared that suspicion during the last few days, I was silent, trying to readjust my thoughts. His treatment of Augusta, a combination of interest and neglect, had struck me as deliberately calculated to arouse her strongest feelings. Marriage with her would have made him a rich man; and I had been tormented by imagining the effect of such a step on my own position. The relief I now felt was so great as to be overwhelming. Yet his attitude remained, as sometimes before, indefinable; he had retreated into the dark imperturbability that barred him from me. At last I said, 'I suppose your taking the trouble to see her made them think so.'

He stopped, and leant against the bookshelf between the pillared busts; then he said, 'I have no great opinion of that family. But we are neighbours.'

'And friends?'

'They are likeable. He is a good fellow.'

'I don't see', I said, speaking with an effort, 'why they should object to you as a husband for her.'

'No? I don't hunt, for one thing.'

'You are not serious.'

'And then, there was the scandal. Why did my wife leave me? And for a gambler, who lived abroad, in Monaco, of all places. There must have been, I hope you realize, something very undesirable about me, for that to have happened.' As I laughed, he continued, 'I shall never live it down, try how I may.'

'I don't think you try very hard.'

'As I say, neither hunting nor shooting, nor showing an interest in ornithology – well, I'm not exactly a pariah, but nevertheless – '

'Just an eccentric?'

'My aim was, and is, to be – acceptable.'

'Why?'

He looked at me for a moment without speaking. Then he said coldly, 'I have chosen to live here. And I intend to stay.'

'But it's a pleasant life?'

'Pleasant enough. No' – as I bent over my work – 'leave that alone, if you please. Answer me – why are you not happy here?'

'I am – most of the time.'

'And the rest?'

'I don't know.'

'And I must not try to find out?'

'I might not be able to help you.'

'You help me in other ways,' he said in a low voice. 'Not only with the children, you know that.'

'I know very little about you.'

'What, not after all those revelations?'

'You are – guarded,' I said after a pause.

He was silent for some minutes; then he said abruptly, 'Shall I read to you? Or will you play to me?'

'Please read. I don't feel ready to play.' I resumed my needlework as he went over to the bookshelves and returned to say, 'De Musset – does that appeal to you?'

I murmured an assent; leaning back, he began, ' "Si je vous le disais, pourtant, que je vous aime – " ' and continued till he came to ' "chanter sur le clavier vos mains harmonieuses." ' Then he said, 'Singing hands – that's a romantic picture of what may have been an indifferent performance on the part of the lady, don't you think so?'

'I always loved that poem. Please go on.'

He did so, passing to other verses of the same nature. Then, shutting the book, he got up; if I had put out my hand, it would have touched his. He said, 'I have something to ask of you.'

I did not look at him. It seemed a long time before he spoke again.

13

Sybilla put her hands on my knees, and pressing them down as if to release a spring, said, 'Syb wants a pony.'

Aware that this was in the nature of a *ballon d'essai*, I said, 'Why do you?'

She smiled. 'Tann' (her version of my name) 'has a pony. And Nev,' she added.

'Uncle Neville,' Francis interposed in a stern, emphatic tone. 'You can say it perfectly well, if you take the trouble.'

Sybilla, shaking her head, repeated, 'A nice – big – pony.'

'But we have not got one,' I began. 'We only have horses, and they would be much too big for you.'

She replied with a cajoling look, and Francis said, 'Your riding with Uncle Neville has given her the idea.'

'And you told her what a pony was?'

'Well – in a way.'

'I am very sorry, dear Francis, that you miss the exercise. But you know whose wish it was.'

'Because Edwin was out riding when it happened?'

'I think so.'

'You never used to ride,' he pursued, in a slightly re-proachful tone.

I said nothing. During our last talk, Mr Quarrendon's suggestion that I should ride with him had resulted in dazed consent and then in my sending for my habit, with its accessories. I renewed the pursuit in a trepidation soon disposed of by my companion's reassurances and by the flatteries of the groom. This young man, disliked by the household and sometimes the worse for drink, was kept on by his employer in the face of all complaint; a charac-teristic caprice, impossible to overcome. Mr Quarrendon merely said that Cripps understood horses better than Stringham, the coachman, who had served him for many years. His assumption that his word was law produced the expected response from the rest of the staff.

So we rode out together. On Falada, his black mare, he reminded me of an eighteenth-century equestrian portrait, and thus appeared rather formidable. Yet on these occasions he talked more freely and gaily than usual. Sometimes we stopped at the Hall, dismounting to walk through the rooms or sit by the fountain. Eliza Trevy disapproved of these unchaperoned expeditions; then she would break off her mild censure with an affectionate self-deprecation that I heeded as little as her criticism.

It now became necessary to convince Sybilla by taking her to the stables to see the horses. When Francis pointed out that his uncle could easily buy a pony, Stringham came to my aid with, 'Nasty little beasts, young master – wait till you're up to a cob,' and we returned to the front of the house, where Eliza joined us. Here we waited for the arrival of the Langs and the Hays, who were coming to tea. Mr Quarrendon had promised to be there; but when the meal concluded he had not appeared. As he was generally punctilious in such matters, I became uneasy.

The Hays' consumption of cakes, muffins and bread and butter was rather surprising, in view of the fact that both were thin to the point of emaciation. Colonel Hay's successful breeding of cocker spaniels seemed to be his only interest; his description of these animals formed an undercurrent to his wife's account of her grandchildren; this so prevailed that even Mrs Lang was unable to halt her opening discourse on the eldest of them, a six-year-old girl of, it seemed, extraordinary fascination and originality. Excerpts from little Margaret's conversation alternated with sketches of her younger brothers, whose beauty and intelligence were only equalled by their sister's devotion to Mrs Hay, and that lady's resolve to ensure her happiness in all circumstances. When she said, 'You must see the dears, Miss Milsom, I know they would take to you,' I resolved to avoid them, while perceiving that she was equally determined to advertise her talents as a grandmother.

Mrs Lang then intervened with a description of her husband's asthma, curiously linked with her son's garden-planning. Claude Lang, specializing in rock-plants, was well on the way to becoming an authority on the subject through a privately printed booklet, illustrated by himself.

Defeated, the Hays, escorted by Eliza, prepared to leave; and still Mr Quarrendon had not appeared. As soon as we were alone, Mrs Lang described the visit to her which had resulted in his purchase of Pond House, followed by the break-up of his marriage. 'They were always at the Hall in those days,' she added. 'I never liked Sir Charles, he was so absent-minded. He would actually *walk away* while I was talking to him!'

After she left, my anxiety about Mr Quarrendon was momentarily forgotten in an attempt to understand his attitude towards her and his other neighbours. He could have nothing in common with any of them, with the possible exception of the Grangers; yet he sought their company, and even seemed to enjoy it. They neither bored nor irked him; and while his detachment was not perceived by them, it became increasingly obvious to me. I was not so protected; as I came to the conclusion that this frame of mind must, somehow, be achieved, a dog-cart drew up at the front door. Mr Courtenay sprang out of it and came towards me.

He led me indoors, and taking both my hands, said, 'Pray compose yourself, Miss Milsom. There has been an accident. But it is not serious.'

The struggle for breath lasted a few seconds. Then I said, 'Where?' withdrawing my hands. His expression of concern was infuriating.

'He was thrown from his horse. His arm – the left – is broken.'

'Where is he?'

'It happened near my house. I took him in, and sent for Dr Cross. Unfortunately – '

'What do you mean?'

'Miss Milsom – I repeat, it is not dangerous. Painful, naturally. He has sent me to tell you not to alarm yourself.'

'You said – unfortunately – '

'Cross was out. His assistant came, and has set the arm. I should have preferred, as Quarrendon would, his regular practitioner. But all is well. He will be here very shortly.' After a pause, in which we stared blankly at one another, he went on, 'I fear this has been a shock. Please sit down. May I get you a glass of water?'

'No, thank you.'

He drew forward a chair, placed me in it and continued, 'He was passing my lodge gates when it happened. The mare stumbled and fell, throwing him.'

'He ought not to be moved – '

'I have ordered the brougham. He insisted on coming home – and it seemed best to let him do so.' After another silence he added, 'That mare of his – whoever is responsible for her should be dismissed. The shoe of her near fore was so loose that it fell off, and she tripped and came down. But I do not think her knees are seriously injured.'

I got up and went to the window. 'Is he in great pain?'

'The setting of the arm – ' Mr Courtenay broke off. Then he added, 'He is very stoical.'

During the next few minutes the necessary preparations were set in hand, and Waring was summoned. At the sound of the carriage I drew back, and both men went out. I saw nothing until Mr Quarrendon, unsupported, stood opposite me. 'This is a nuisance,' he said. 'If it were not for Courtenay, I should have had to walk home. But the mare will do well, it's no more than a scrape – '

'You should go straight to bed, my dear fellow,' Mr Courtenay interrupted.

'In a moment. Waring – the Marsala. Why don't we all sit down?'

An hour or so later, I became aware that I had drunk three glasses of wine in rapid succession. After telling Francis and Eliza what had happened, I went up to my room, fell asleep and woke to find her standing over me with a tray, on which were brandy, various pills and a plate of biscuits. I refused them all and, dressing hurriedly, joined her for dinner.

Dr Cross arrived some hours after the meal and asked to see me. His bearded, spectacled face towered over mine as he begged me not to be anxious. He added that he had just left his patient – after resetting the arm.

This information silenced me – fortunately; for I had begun to realize that to show too much concern would be inadvisable. I walked away and, sitting down, asked Dr Cross if he had dined; he replied that he must be on his way. It was easier, then, to ask for instructions.

'I have given him a soothing draught. It was not a pleasant business – but it had to be done. Waring is with him.'

Suddenly, the situation became unbearable. I burst out, 'Why had it to be done at all?'

'I will be quite frank with you, Miss Milsom. My assistant is only an apprentice. He should have waited. It was not my fault that I was attending a case twelve miles away. And now I must be going. I will come over tomorrow morning.'

I heard the sound of his carriage wheels as if from a long way off. As I stumbled upstairs the clock struck twelve. Waking, two hours later, from a stunned sleep, I got up and opened the window. Gazing out, I saw the light from Mr Quarrendon's bedroom spread across the drive.

The blinds had been drawn, but not the curtains. For some minutes no movement could be seen; then a solitary figure appeared, walking to and fro. As Mr Quarrendon's predicament became clear I remembered the laudanum tablets left me by Eliza Trevy. He might refuse to take them; yet a rebuff must be risked. He might have rung for Waring; but that seemed unlikely. I walked along the passage and knocked softly as soon as I was sure that he was alone. He did not answer at once; then he said, 'Who is it?' Another pause followed my reply; then he told me to come in.

His bedroom was much larger than I had imagined. The curtains of the four-poster were half drawn and the covers trailing to the ground. He faced me, his back to the window, his dressing-gown hanging from his shoulders. I stood gazing at him in stricken silence; for his flushed cheeks and glittering eyes were those of a young man; as he pushed back his tossed hair and moved forward, the years seemed to fall away from both of us. At last I managed to say, 'Forgive me – but I saw your light. I guessed that you were in pain.'

'So you could not sleep either?'

'I did – then I woke. I thought that these might – that they would help you – ' and I held out the box of pills.

'What are they?'

'Laudanum.'

'That gown is charming.'

'Please – won't you take one?'

'Not yet.'

'I think you should. They are quite harmless.'

He burst out laughing. 'No doubt – but are you?' As I stared at him, drawing back, he went on, 'Give them to me,' and placed a burning hand on mine; my fingers and the box were suddenly enclosed. I could not move without jarring him: and it was obvious that he was in considerable pain. So we stood looking at one another.

'Mr Quarrendon – let me give you one of these, and – and help you to – '

'Come and sit down.'

As he drew me forward I guided him to the chaise-longue at the foot of the bed. He held me at arms' length; the feverish gaiety of his look slowly changed to hardness, then to suspicion. He said, 'Cripps – where is he? What happened to the mare?'

'She is in Mr Courtenay's stables. He said – don't you remember? – that her knees were not damaged.'

'And Cripps?'

'I suppose he is in his cottage. You can send for him in the morning. But now – please rest. Let me get you a glass of water.'

He released my hand; the box of pills fell and rolled away. As I stooped to pick it up he sank on to the chaise-longue. Turning, I saw the sweat break out over his forehead. He said, 'Make some tea. It's there – ' and he pointed to a spirit-lamp on a laden tray under the window.

I lit the flame, filled the kettle from the ewer on the wash-stand and waited, my back towards him. He went on, 'There is only one cup – how shall we manage?'

'Oh, I – I don't want any.'

'I can't drink tea alone. Find something.'

A glance round the room showed me an empty vase on the chimney-piece. As I rinsed it out and put it on the tray he said, 'I'll have that. You take the cup.'

'Very well.'

'Please come here.' As I obeyed he continued, 'When we have drunk our tea – you will stay a little?'

'I will stay until you have taken one of these pills.'

'And then?'

'You will sleep.'

'That is a promise?'

'Yes.'

'Give me your hand.' Looking down at it, he said, 'Long, white, fine – a good hand. A friend's.'

'I hope so, indeed.'

His fingers gripped mine. He said loudly, 'Do you? Friendship makes demands, you know, in certain – certain – I forget the word. What is it?'

'Please don't try to talk. Let us sit here, quietly – '

'Circumstances! That's it. Circumstances alter cases – don't they?'

'Mr Quarrendon – '

'You think I'm delirious. I'm nothing of the kind.'

'You have some fever.

'Are you watching the kettle?'

'Of course.'

'I think you are watching me.'

'First one,' I said smiling, 'then the other.'

He lay down and leant back, his eyes closed. The movement made him wince, and a slight groan escaped him. Then he said, 'Don't stand over me. Sit down.' As the nearest chair was at the other end of the room, I knelt beside him. 'Where's your hand?'

'Here. But the kettle's boiling.'

'Let it boil.'

'I shall not be a moment.'

As I brought him his tea and drew up a stool, he glanced at me sideways. We drank in silence. Then he said, 'Tomorrow – but it's that already. What's the time?'

'Nearly three o'clock. Time for you to take this – ' and I put the pill between his lips.

'Thank you. But you are not a very good tea-maker.'

'I made it weak on purpose. Your usual brew would keep you awake.'

'I don't really want it. It's an excuse.'

'An excuse?'

'To keep you here.'

'I will stay till you feel sleepy.'

After another silence he began, 'You must keep him out of my way. Will you do that?'

'You mean – Cripps?'

'No. The boy.'

'Francis?' He nodded. 'I will see that the children don't worry you.'

'I said, the boy. Not the other one.'

'But you will stay in bed tomorrow?'

'No. All this' – he glanced down at the sling – 'is nothing.'

As I watched, the hectic youthfulness of his look began to fade. I fetched a blanket and laid it over him. Turning his head, he appeared to settle down. He murmured something I could not hear. Bending over him, I whispered, 'I am going now – good night.'

He put out his hand as if in protest. I took it in one of mine, and with the other smoothed back his hair. Then I went to the door; as I looked back it seemed that he was sleeping.

In my own room I sat up till the sun rose, watching his window. As I got into bed the springing thickness of his hair under my hand came back to me. It was as if I had always known how it would feel.

14

Next day, Mr Courtenay called to report on the mare, and on the negligence of the groom. He then asked to see me, and as we entered the library, began, 'If ever there was a case for dismissal, it is this. Quarrendon admits that the fellow is sometimes the worse for drink, but he is keeping him on. However, I don't doubt that you can persuade him he is mistaken.'

'I am afraid I cannot interfere.'

Mr Courtenay looked at me, smiling. 'I find it difficult to believe that, Miss Milsom.'

'I am a guest here, no more.'

'On rather a special basis, surely?'

'My responsibility for my nephew and niece does not extend to Mr Quarrendon's household.'

'Nevertheless, if you choose to use your influence – ' He paused. Both tone and manner were insinuating. He went on, 'Diplomacy – the feminine touch – '

'If I had such gifts,' I interrupted, 'I am not in a position to use them.'

'So you become that drunken fellow's ally.'

'Certainly not.'

'I am merely suggesting that, if the question arises, you should work against him.'

'If my opinion is asked, I shall give it. As an old friend, you have the right to protest.'

He shook his head. 'The atmosphere just now was not very friendly.'

'Mr Quarrendon is still in pain,' I said indignantly. 'He should not be worried.'

'Ah! I see you know how to manage him.'

'Mr Courtenay – I resent that implication.'

'My dear lady, I am only saying that he values your opinion.'

'I hope he does – about the children.'

'Of course. But – ' He broke off with a sigh, as if deprecating my obstinacy.

'Mr Quarrendon will be down for luncheon – so perhaps you will stay?' He refused, much to my relief, leaving me to contemplate what I now realized was the local view of my position at Pond House. It did not please me.

Mr Quarrendon had decided to take luncheon with Eliza and me, Francis having been relegated to the nursery. He appeared haggard but serene. We began the meal without Eliza, who sent a message asking to be excused on the grounds of a sudden attack of neuralgia. As Waring left the room, Mr Quarrendon said, 'I fear I am responsible for that. I met her as I was coming down, and she was so distressed when I told her of your visit to me early this morning that she went back to her room.'

'You told her!' I exclaimed. 'But why?'

'She was so kind as to inquire for my arm, and asked if I had had a bad night. I said that if it had not been for you, I should not have slept at all. As she seemed rather puzzled, I told her what you did for me.' He added with a smile, 'I think it was the tea-making that really upset her. She appears to look on it as the *comble* of something worse than indiscretion – as it were, an orgy.'

'Surely you knew what she would feel! I do wish – but it's done now.'

'She will get over it,' he said calmly. 'As you don't share her views – or do you regret having helped me?'

'Of course not. But she cannot take that kind of thing for granted, as you do.'

'And you?'

'I was never in such a situation before.'

'Making tea for a man in a dressing-gown – drinking it with him – and then drugging him into unconsciousness. Terrible.'

'It sounds absurd – but it could be described in that way,' I said, and there was a short silence.

'You know – ' he began – 'by the way, this mousse is excellent, most thoughtfully planned for a one-armed man – that loose gown which so well became you does not quite fit with your notions. It's a pity they are so narrow.'

'I can't help it if they are,' I said crossly. 'You seem to forget that I shall have to reassure Eliza.'

'Ah yes, poor lady. You have placed her in an impossible position, I'm afraid.'

'I could not have come here without her. If she tries you, I am sorry for it.'

'Well – she won't, as Francis would say, sneak on us. Or will she?'

'I am glad to find you in such good spirits.'

'It must be the laudanum,' he said as Waring came in with the second course. After that, he went to rest while I walked out into the garden.

His certainty of Eliza's discretion was perfectly justified. Yet I could imagine only too well what our neighbours, already alert for a scandal, would have thought if they had heard that Mr Quarrendon and I had been drinking tea in his bedroom at three o'clock in the morning.

I had then to present the case to Eliza. Tearfully, she assured me that no one would ever hear of the episode from her, adding, 'And we must both try to forget it. I appreciate your good intention, it was like you, but – oh dear – if only it had not been – ' and she began to cry again. I managed to soothe her, and also to leave without giving way to irritation. That was not difficult. The next problem called for a modicum of self-control.

Mr Quarrendon's usual composure of manner was shaken, as pain and bad nights were increased, by the massage and manipulation on which Dr Cross insisted and himself administered. He became impatient, censorious and bitter. Waring, who came in for the brunt of these moods, told me that this behaviour recalled his master's youth. 'He was sometimes crotchety then,' he said, 'but it'll pass. If it hadn't been for that Cripps, we'd have none of this trouble.'

Meanwhile Francis, ordered to show up lessons set but not supervised by his uncle, emerged rather troubled than intimidated from their brief sessions. He received Mr Quarrendon's fault-finding calmly, and refused my help in all subjects but that of Italian grammar. Mr Quarrendon, finding us in conference over a list of irregular verbs, was icily critical. As Francis left the library he said, 'I suppose it is useless to ask you not to indulge him.'

'I will do whatever you think best. When he has a tutor – '

'I have changed my mind about that.'

'Then the burden falls on you.'

'You mean, on him – don't you?' he said coldly, sitting down at his desk, where a pile of unopened letters awaited him. As I moved to the door he went on, 'Am I not to be reasoned with – tactfully persuaded?'

'I don't think a tutor necessary – not for these last few months. Between us, we could manage, if you approve.'

'You put it very well. And now, will you open these letters for me?'

Having done so, I waited, almost sure that he still needed me. He pushed the letters aside and said, 'Let us go out, it's too fine to stay indoors.'

I came down to find that we were to be driven – not by Cripps – to Limmerston Hall. As we entered the Blue Saloon a storm began. He glanced out of the window and sat down on the long brocade sofa opposite the fireplace; I did the same. He said, 'Are you frightened of thunder?'

'Not as a rule.'

'What a pity,' he went on, leaning forward, his chin on his hand. 'A whole storm wasted. Lightning – rain – very soon, we shall not be able to hear each other speak, unless we sit rather closer. And your rules might forbid that too.'

I got up, drew forward a chair and placed myself opposite him. 'Is that better?'

'A little.'

We were silent, as the storm raged and the room darkened. Then I began, 'These pictures – are they all family portraits?' He nodded. 'Please tell me about the one over the chimney-piece.'

'That is a Lely – Henrietta Martel, one of Belminster's daughters.'

'She is beautiful.'

'So the Craik of her day must have felt when he ran away with her. The Duke, who had contracted her to someone else, cut her off. She is supposed to have decamped on her wedding day. There's a later portrait of her, over there.'

'That? But it can't be.'

'They had seventeen children,' he said drily, and again we were silent, listening to the storm. I got up and looked at the picture. 'Poor woman. Did they all live, the children?'

'Some ten or so, I believe. When she died, he married an Italian, who went mad. They had a son. The other surviving children were girls.'

'What a sad story.'

'Yes. Nature was cruelly lavish.'

'And the son?'

'He took Holy Orders. In the next generation Nature – or Fate, perhaps – again took charge.'

'The insanity recurred?'

'From time to time.'

I came back and sat beside him. 'I don't believe that Nature is invariably cruel.'

'Nothing is invariable,' he said impatiently. 'Sometimes there must be – elimination. In any case, you and I are talking at cross-purposes, as we did once before in this room.'

'You have made studies of cruelty, and so you take it for granted.'

'That sounds like an accusation.'

'I only meant that you can be harsh.'

'To you?'

'Oh, I don't complain,' I said, smiling. As he stared at me, I saw that his eyes, red-rimmed, had become suffused. He said, 'Everything takes too long. Time crawls. I'm sick of it.'

'I know. Your arm – '

'That's not what I mean!' he burst out. 'You don't understand.'

As this was true, I said nothing. He rose and began to walk up and down. Then he said abruptly, 'It is clearing. Cross will be there. We must go back.'

His silence during the drive seemed to indicate that he was steeling himself for the ordeal with Dr Cross. I saw him no more that day, and after dinner began to practise some music I had sent for from home and which might be new to him, should he wish me to play. Then I heard the drawing-room door shut with a click. As I got up and came towards him, he said, 'I needed your company. Please go on playing.'

'I will, but – Waring told me you did not want any dinner. Won't you have some now?'

He shook his head. 'Later, perhaps. We might have one of those highly improper little feasts – when you have played to me – ' and he sat down in the shadow; the only light came from the candles on the piano.

I continued to play for what seemed a considerable time. When I paused, he bade me go on. His unseen presence was disturbing: for I did not know whether he was watching me, or had fallen into a doze. At last I stopped; he made no sign. I waited; then he said, 'Are you tired?'

'I will play as long as you like. But surely you should take something. I fear you have had a bad day?'

'It might have been worse. This David and Saul arrangement is a pleasant change.'

'Let me ring for Waring.'

'Very well.'

A few minutes later, sitting over wine, fruit and cake, he began, 'Did you see Cross this afternoon?'

'Yes, he asked for me.'

'And so?'

'He thinks you are progressing – as he must have told you. He said that you should be distracted.'

'And here I am, obeying orders. Where shall we drive tomorrow?'

'Oh – anywhere. But Dr Cross did not insist on my accompanying you.'

'Suppose I do, what then?' I did not answer, and he went on, 'But of course we must be chaperoned. Being driven by Stringham doesn't count, I imagine?'

'It's all very well – ' I began, and broke off.

'Very well indeed – for me. But you are not satisfied?'

'Dr Cross seems to forget that I am here to help look after the children. If we took Francis – '

'No.'

There was a short silence. Then I said, 'Would you like me to play again?'

'In a moment. Tell me, how does he compare with the other – Edwin, was it?'

This rather startling change of subject was accompanied by an equally sudden alteration of tone. He spoke as if we were strangers, making conversation. I said something about Francis being the cleverer, and he went on, 'Of the two, which did you prefer?'

'I hardly know, they were so different. I always thought that Edwin was his mother's favourite.'

'Yes,' he said after a pause, 'his death hastened hers. She never got over it.'

This pronouncement seemed to end the conversation. A few minutes later, playing mechanically, I began to wonder what the time was, and whether Eliza had overheard us. The clock striking twelve coincided with the peremptory mew of a cat and Mr Quarrendon getting up to let it in. My hands still on the keys, I turned to see him caressing the creature as it settled down on the sofa. Looking from it to me, he said, 'We could take Minette with us. But I fear she would not care for it.'

'I know I seem foolish. But I was brought up to think more of these matters than a man does.'

'I should hope so, indeed. I don't care for masculine women. Are you breaking up this domestic scene?' – as I closed the piano.

'Don't you think we should?'

'Take some wine with me first.' As I complied he went on, 'You are fortunate.'

'Yes – but why, especially?'

'Because you make yourself indispensable.'

'More than Minette?'

'Differently.'

'I am not as indispensable to Francis as you are. But as he worries you just now, could I not take over his lessons?'

'If you like,' he said absently. 'You think I am harsh with him?'

'It's natural. Children can be taxing. Sybilla – '

'She does not trouble me. You do, sometimes. But I am keeping you up – ' and he moved to open the door.

'Won't you explain?'

'I might displease you.'

'Criticism can be helpful.'

'I was not thinking of criticism.'

'Of what, then?'

'Of your inconsistencies – of the see-saw you make of your life here, between the children and Miss Trevy. Would you remain with them, if she left?'

'She would never do so, unless you made it impossible for her to stay.'

'Don't concern yourself for that. I am thinking of her health. If it broke down, would you install another chaperone?'

'Not without your leave.'

'And if I refused?'

'I don't know,' I said rather helplessly. 'It depends.'

'On what people would say?'

In the pause that followed, a new and surprising aspect of my situation had to be faced. Then I said, 'That would not matter so much to me as being with Francis and Sybilla.'

'And with me?'

'You are their guardian.'

'You mean, you would put up with my company for their sake?'

'I like your company.'

'In any circumstances – unchaperoned?'

'Mr Quarrendon – why do you cross-examine me on a point that may never arise? It is not fair.'

'I might reply with a proverb.'

'It's much too late for proverbs, or anything else.'

'Not even the one about love and war?'

Forced to meet his impassive scrutiny, I found no answer.

Next day, I realized that some kind of revolution was being effected; I could not define it, or make up my mind what my part, if any, would be. During the next few days, the change in the atmosphere of that quiet, easy-going household became painfully apparent, and adaptation to it a bewildering and difficult process.

15

'It's all right,' Francis repeated. 'I thought it wasn't, but now it is. He is not like he was a few days ago. He said I could spend tomorrow afternoon with Jack and Tom – I mean, have my half-holiday with them.'

'At the Vicarage?'

He nodded. 'Of course, it's partly because he wants me out of the way, I know that.'

'But you like going there,' I said rather lamely.

'Now, I do, more than before. I don't want to be a nuisance. When you've both gone out, I shall sail my boats on the lower pond – ' and he began to move away across the lawn.

'Francis – wait. We shall be back soon after tea, and then I will do whatever you like.'

He whirled round. 'Chess – or bezique?'

'Either – both.'

'You're sure Uncle Neville won't want you?'

'Directly I come back we will go up to the schoolroom, and then neither of us will be in the way.'

'You never are,' he said after a pause. 'Trev sometimes is, of course.'

'Francis – you know I don't like that way of speaking.'

'Oh dear – Miss T, then – ' and he ran off.

As I went to put on a more suitable gown, I was waylaid by Mrs Waring, with renewed complaints of Cripps and the seventeen-year-old between-maid, another of her nieces. Having 'spoken sharply' to Miriam, she believed that his attentions were being repulsed; now, she hoped again for his dismissal. My refusal to interfere was greeted by a shake of the head, a significant glance and, 'What this place needs – well, there, gentlemen can't be expected to see to everything, can they, Miss?' I made an evasive reply, and prepared for the daily drive I had begun to dread and yet could not avoid.

Mr Quarrendon had decided to make, with me, a series of calls on the neighbours; their view of our relationship varied. That of the Grangers seemed charitable; I felt that the Langs and Mr Courtenay saw me as invidiously placed. The Portman-Sinclairs, who had just come back from France, were too much elated by Augusta's engagement to an elderly widower to concern themselves with anything else. They had always hoped that his admiration for their treasure would thus develop; and that the encounter and courtship ('At Deauville, was it not strange?') should end in his being accepted occupied all their attention. That Augusta was not there to receive our congratulations did not seem to trouble them.

As we set off for the Rectory, my comments on this news were received in silence; and I became aware that my companion's mood was again one of restrained irritation. Aware that nothing I said would please, I made no further efforts. He then began, 'Francis and I are now on better terms – another example of your powers,' in his ironic manner. His grating tone of voice was hostile; but I had become accustomed to this during the last few days. He went on, 'You do not really care for these expeditions, do you?'

'I like the Grangers, the Rector especially.'

'More than my cousins – or Courtenay?'

'Well – yes. But that is partly because they have not much use for me.'

'And the Hays?'

'Are we going on to them?'

'Don't be alarmed. After the Grangers, we shall have had enough.'

'I happen to know', I said after a moment's thought, 'that the Hays are away. So you could call in safety.'

'As ever – indispensable,' he said, and we sank into a more companionable silence, disturbed, for me, by the recollection of his rating of Cripps.

As I came out of the house, the groom had been standing by the horses' heads. I could not hear what was said, because Mr Quarrendon and Cripps moved away, presumably so that Stringham should not hear either; but it became clear that the master was enraged, while the servant, cringing, dared not defend himself. I was about to get into the victoria when Mr Quarrendon waved him aside and said, 'I shall not tell you again – this is the last time,' and Cripps slouched off. He might have been the worse for drink; I could not be sure.

I was still considering this incident when Mr Quarrendon told Stringham to draw up, so that we could walk in the neighbouring copse before going on to the Rectory. We climbed the slope it surmounted in silence; under the trees, he took his arm out of the sling and put the scarf in his pocket.

It was a sunless, windy day; the clearing in which we stood was chilly, dark, and coloured here and there with patches of wild garlic, cuckoo-pint and solomon's seal, palely gleaming in their depths of green. He looked round, as if in search of something; then he said, 'I once found a butterfly orchid here. Have you ever seen one?'

'Not near my home, it's too bleak.'

He grasped my elbows, drawing me closer. 'Why go back there, ever? Isn't it pleasanter here?' Forcing myself to look at him, I found nothing to say. His hands slid down over my wrists. 'It's ludicrous – absurd – that I should have to bring you here. But where else – ' He broke off, staring at me, and continued, 'Why do you wear a veil?'

'I suppose – to keep my hat on.'

'And behind it, you are on the watch. Protected – safe.' After another silence, he went on, 'Also, there are the children, and your friend. They stand between us.'

'That is not true at all,' I said, attempting a light tone. 'You seem to forget – ' It was impossible to go on.

'What?'

'All those evenings.'

'But you are always listening, waiting, for an interruption. Are you afraid of her "discovering" us, as if we were in a play, or a novel?'

'Of course not. But if you want to get rid of her, I cannot stop you.'

'And if I did?'

I drew my hands away. 'It would be part of a process. I only saw it a few days ago.'

'Won't you explain?'

'First Mr Lambton, then Mademoiselle Hébert – and now Eliza.'

He turned, went over to a patch of flowers and came back with a sprig of cuckoo-pint in his hand. Glancing from it to me, he replied, 'I don't mind her. You do.'

'I am very fond of her.'

'Of course. And she helps with the children.'

'If you object to her being in your house, you should say so.'

'Why should I? There's no time. I'm on the edge.'

'The edge?'

'Of a very deep sea. Tell me, have you ever played the tables? No, I thought not. But come, we've had our walk. Take my arm.' As I did so he said, 'You're trembling. What's the matter?'

'Nothing. It's only – I'm on the wrong side.'

'Impossible.'

'I am thinking of your arm. Let me put back the sling.'

He stopped, appeared to consider and gravely said, 'Yes – perhaps it would be as well. Stringham might wonder how it was that I went into the wood with it bound up, and came out like this.' Giving me the scarf, he added, 'And that would not do at all.'

In order to untie the knot I put back my veil; when I removed my gloves he took them from me, turning them over. 'You know – I never could understand this preference for small hands. Yours are beautiful.'

'They're certainly not small,' I said, moving behind him to adjust the sling. The hair at the back of his head was very thick, tending to curl where it had been cut; I could have touched it without his knowledge.

The scarf slipped – twice – and had to be caught up again. Then it was done. As we faced one another, he held out my gloves. 'I need both hands to put them on for you. But as you have bound one – and so well, too – I am helpless.'

Hurriedly pushing them on, I took his arm. As we moved away he said, 'It's a pity about the butterfly orchid. The roots must have perished.' As we descended the slope he went on, 'Did you realize that Frederick Lang is a *malade imaginaire*? That asthma and his famous delicacy unites them, and makes it impossible for Claude to leave home. But he has his rock-garden. You admired it, of course?'

'I tried to – but the plants are almost invisible,' I said, and he laughed.

The Rectory was surrounded by apple trees; as we drove past them, I saw that the fruit had just begun to ripen. Crowning one of the tallest was a whole cluster; then the sun came out, suddenly lighting up the globes of red and green, and I remembered climbing to reach a similar growth, as a child, at home. Each time I stretched out a hand to shake it down, the branch had swung away, and then towards me, so that it seemed that all I had to do was to persevere.

That situation was being re-created. Compliments, admiration, gallantry, combined into a kind of pursuit, had swung our relationship forward – and then away, into indifference and mockery. Finally, love had been mentioned; yet without the demands which generally accompany such a word. Also, while accusing me of making a seesaw of my life, it was he who kept it going. I had become helpless; he was in control. I had no idea why our walk had been cut short; but then his changes of mood were usually inexplicable. And we had reached the point of performing – there could be no other word for it – before a public represented by the Granger family, who were grouped round the tea-table on the lawn in front of the house.

As they all got up at the approach of the victoria, one of the horses began to fidget and toss his head; Stringham remained on the box, and Mr Quarrendon got out to hand me down. Concerned for his arm, I looked up at him; his answering glance held mine. We were then surrounded by our hosts and their three children, in eager welcome. It had not occurred to me that they would be so glad to see us.

After an exchange of commonplaces the subject of Augusta Portman-Sinclair's engagement was raised. Mr Granger, glancing at his wife, said, 'Yes – most interesting – ' and appeared to wait for her next comment. Susan, looking prettier than I had ever seen her, offered Mr Quarrendon a dish of tea-cakes, apparently unaware that she should have removed the lid for him. While Jack and Tom interchanged glances of conscious weariness, as if preparing to be ineffably bored, Mrs Granger said archly, 'Engagements are in the air just now, are they not, Susan?' Her daughter shook her head, coloured and murmured, 'You may as well tell them, Mamma,' still holding the dish Mr Quarrendon had refused.

'Susan and our dear Claude are going to be married,' Mrs Granger then announced. 'Not just yet – it was only settled yesterday.'

Our congratulations were radiantly received by the three grown-ups; the boys seemed to withdraw from their talk of future plans. Some time passed before a tour of the garden was proposed. Mr Quarrendon then walked ahead with Susan (the Rector was summoned indoors), and I followed them with Mr Granger's wife and sons. As she fell back to speak to the gardener I said, 'I suppose the wedding celebrations will call for several half-holidays?' looking from one to the other.

Stopping to break off a branch of laurel, Jack replied, 'Yes – but we shan't have a minute's peace till it's all over,' and his brother, kicking the gravel, gloomily added, 'The worst time will be when the presents begin to come. Sue and Mamma like that sort of thing, I can't think why.'

'What about parties? There will be plenty of those,' I said, attempting a cheerful tone.

'Plenty,' Tom replied. 'Too many, as far as we're concerned. He's not so bad, we've always known him, it's not like a stranger, but still – marriage!'

'Won't it be rather pleasant having a brother-in-law?'

In his most judicial manner, Jack replied, 'I don't feel very hopeful – do you?' turning to his brother, who shook his head and began to strip the leaves from the branch, scattering them on the grass as we walked along. 'She – ' he said, indicating his sister, 'seems quite pleased. But she hasn't even got a ring, so far.'

'He said he was coming over with it tomorrow,' Jack observed.

'I shall believe that when I see it,' Tom replied.

'Why don't you now?' I asked.

'Well, he's rather an odd sort of fellow, at least I think so. He's always at home, for one thing – gardening.'

'Surely that won't make him forget the ring?'

'It may – ' was the answer, ominously given, and Jack added, 'It'll be a miserable one, even if he does remember it, you can bet on that. Of course,' he went on resignedly, 'we knew she would get married some time or other – but why Claude Lang? He's not even rich.'

'I hope you have not taken against him – ' I began.

'It's marriage I'm against,' said Tom.

'I remember, that came into your entertainment. But your sister will want you all to be friends.'

'Oh, I can manage *that*,' replied Tom, whirling the now leafless stick round his head. 'I can be *friends*' – in contemptuous emphasis – 'with almost anyone.'

'I can't,' said Jack firmly. 'And I don't like the notion of his rock-garden. He might want us to help him with it, you never know.'

'I don't suppose Susan would insist on that,' I put in.

'Wives have to obey their husbands. Since only yesterday she keeps on about what he wants. She's changed, already.'

'Over-excited,' Tom suggested.

'Yes, well, that may not last, but still – ' Jack broke off as Susan and Mr Quarrendon turned back to meet us. Both boys went to feed their rabbits, and we were joined by the Rector and his wife.

For a moment Mr Granger seemed unable to speak. In a tone of enforced calm he then said, 'I shall tell the boys to go indoors and stay there. Young Craik has escaped from his keepers, and cannot be traced. No doubt' – turning to Mr Quarrendon – 'your servants have been warned. Meanwhile, your carriage will be ready in a few minutes.'

'How long – when did this happen?'

'The Limmerston postmaster sent his boy over to tell me. That is all I know.'

Mrs Granger said, 'He is not likely to have reached us – it is all of five miles. Had you not better stay here, Miss Milsom?'

'No – no, thank you. The children – ' As I looked at Mr Quarrendon, he nodded and took my arm. 'We will go together,' he said. 'He is probably wandering in the woods, as he did before. We shall be home within half an hour.'

'Oh, do let us send for Claude!' Susan broke in. 'He will know – he always does.'

'My dear child – ' her mother began, but Susan, turning to us, rushed on, 'Claude has a special gift. If there is ever any danger, it – it comes to him. He'll be able to see. Mamma, let me send Hadham – ' indicating the gardener, who now approached us.

'Before we do anything else,' said Mr Granger, 'Quarrendon and Miss Milsom must be on their way. Hadham and I will help with the horses – ' and he hurried off.

We left in a confusion of agitated farewells. As we drove through the orchard Mr Quarrendon said, 'Keep a good pace, Stringham – but don't lash them on. If they are frightened, we shall only be delayed,' and took my hand.

'Don't be too much alarmed,' he went on. 'They will have been warned long before we get there.'

As I assented, leaning forward, he held me back. A few minutes went by before I was able to say, 'What did Susan mean about Claude Lang? What use can he be?'

'He claims to have second sight.'

'He really thinks he will be able to see where Henry Craik is at this moment?'

'Apparently.'

'How excessively foolish.'

'He is a silly fellow,' said Mr Quarrendon calmly. 'Susan was telling me just now that he had had – what was it? – a divination that she would accept him yesterday. It's as well for him that she subscribes to his delusions. Now' – pressing my hand – 'try not to imagine the worst. Henry Craik will not leave those woods, he never has. You saw, that time, that he was obsessed by them.'

'Yes – but – '

'Sit back, and stop looking at the hedgerows.'

I obeyed, shutting my eyes. As we drove on at a steadily increasing pace, a single thought occupied my mind – that one day, we should be always together, either as now, or in tranquillity. His remark about being on the edge of a deep sea might indicate his contemplating another marriage; it was possible that, two having failed, he should thus visualize a third.

It seemed rather strange that at this particular moment he should begin to describe the future he had planned for Francis – Eton, Oxford, possibly the law – without mentioning Sybilla; yet it was she he preferred, or so I had always believed. (Later on, I decided that he had embarked on this subject so as to distract me.) He concluded with an assessment of his nephew's gifts, when we reached Pond House. The Warings, Nurse and Cripps were standing at the front door. As we got out they rushed forward. Then they all spoke at once.

BOOK II

Ceux qui ont voulu nous réprésenter l'amour et
ses caprices l'ont comparé en tant de sortes à la
mer ... Ils nous ont fait voir que l'un et l'autre
ont une inconstance et une infidélité égales, que
leur biens et leur maux sont sans nombre, que
les navigations les plus heureuses sont exposées
à mille dangers, que les tempêtes et les écueils
sont toujours à craindre, et que souvent même
on fait naufrage dans le port ...

La Rochefoucauld

1

The Belminster Inspector was a very large man. Looming above us, he appeared to dominate the library, almost to darken it. Asked to sit down, he drew out his notebook; then, glancing from Mr Quarrendon to me, he placed himself on the sofa and began, 'As I told you yesterday, sir, the actions of your staff are accounted for. And as they've caught the young man – Craik, is it? – I think we can safely assume what he was up to. But as a complaint will have to be lodged with his father, and better precautions taken, I must have a full statement as to what took place.'

'Certainly, Inspector. We arrived, Miss Milsom and myself, just after it happened. Miss Milsom's friend, Miss Trevy, had gone to afternoon service. Sir Charles Craik lives abroad, and I will of course give you his address. But I must warn you that he seldom answers letters.'

'Dear me, sir, that's bad. It could be actionable.'

'I have already been to the Dower House – ' Mr Quarrendon paused; then, watching the Inspector's pencil, he proceeded more slowly, 'and have arranged for further, indeed very stringent, precautions. If, having inspected those, you are still dissatisfied, I shall myself go to see Sir Charles and insist on the removal of his son to an institution.'

'I don't suppose it need come to that, sir. Now, about the young gentleman – her brother, is it? – who found her. I should see him before I make out my report. But as I don't want him frightened' – turning to me – 'could you stay with us?' As I got up he continued, 'And the little lady, how does she go on, Miss?'

'She seems dazed. The doctor says she must be kept quiet. She can't – she must not be disturbed.'

'No, no, that's only natural. But later – will you be able to find out what she saw?'

After a short silence I managed to say, 'I don't know. She is not quite three years old.'

Mr Quarrendon said, 'My nephew will be of greater help to you at the moment. He is a very intelligent boy. But although we have told him that he is in no way to blame, he is bewildered and agitated. Will you fetch him yourself, Miss Milsom?'

It was not difficult to reassure Francis. He only insisted that his uncle and I should remain while he was questioned. As he sat down, gravely eyeing the Inspector, Mr Quarrendon said, 'This is not a tribunal, Francis. We just want your help about one or two things that have puzzled us. I've already told you that you are not to blame for anything.'

'Well, sir,' the Inspector began, 'you were both in the nursery by yourselves. Where was Nurse, then?'

'She went down to the kitchen – for a minute, she said – but she stayed there.'

'How was that, do you know?'

As Francis hesitated Mr Quarrendon interposed, 'She found herself in the middle of a scene. The between-maid, Miriam, was in hysterics, and she stayed to lend a hand.'

'I see. And you, sir' – glancing at his notes – 'then left your sister alone in the nursery. Why was that?'

'I promised to let her help me sail my boats in the lower pond, that's the big one. Then I remembered I had taken one of them to pieces, so I went to my room to fetch it.'

'How long did that take?'

Francis glanced from me to his uncle; receiving a nod of encouragement, he replied, 'There was a bit I couldn't find – one of the masts – and I started looking for it. I don't know how long I stayed.'

'And then you returned to the nursery?'

'Yes.'

'And the little girl was missing?'

'Yes.'

'So what did you do?'

'I went on mending my boat.'

'Did you wonder at all what had happened to her?'

'I thought she'd gone down to the kitchen. She's not supposed to – but she does sometimes, we both do,' Francis replied, with another glance at his uncle.

'So then you went, with your boat, to this pond?'

'Yes.'

'And found her?'

'Yes.'

'In the water?'

'Yes.'

'Now – ' the Inspector went on, 'we know that you jumped in and dragged her out, like a brave young gentleman. But as you did so, you saw someone?'

'Yes. A man.'

'What like, sir?'

'I don't know – truly. He ran off.'

'His back towards you?'

'I'm not sure.'

'Had he – mind, I don't expect a description – a beard?'

By this time, Francis had reached a state of tension. He looked down, clenching his hands; then he muttered, 'He might have.'

'You're not certain?'

'I can't remember.'

After another silence the Inspector, turning to me, said, 'You see, it is clear that little Miss meant to join her brother. There would have been plenty of time for her to have left the nursery and run down to the pond, I suppose?'

'Yes.'

'Without being seen?'

'If she had been – by the gardener, for instance – he would not have stopped her. Both children run in and out of doors without supervision.'

'Quite so. Well now, sir – what puzzles me is this. Why was your sister in your clothes – a black blouse and

153

breeches? If you had not got there in time, they would have dragged her under the water.'

'We were – playing,' said Francis, after another silence.

'Dressing up?'

'Well – partly.'

'In mourning clothes?'

'They were the ones that had been put away. We don't wear them any more.'

'But you got them out again?'

'Yes.'

'Why?'

'Because we were playing – I told you,' said Francis, and buried his face in his hands. I knelt and put my arm round him. 'Tell us why, dear. Don't be upset. Nobody is angry with you.'

'We were playing – at funerals,' was the gasping answer. Francis then continued more calmly, 'She – Syb – didn't know what the word meant. So I explained, and said we'd both be mutes – you know – and they're always men. We were going to bury one of her dolls in the garden.'

As his sobs burst out, Mr Quarrendon said, 'Come here, Francis, I want to tell you something.' Standing the child between his knees, he went on, 'You know, of course, that Nurse would have forbidden your taking out those clothes. She is strict in these matters, and rightly. But neither I nor your aunt would have objected to your dressing up. So you see that though you behaved rashly' – he smiled – 'you were not in the wrong, as far as we were concerned.'

As Francis nodded and scrubbed at his eyes, the Inspector began, 'It comes to this, Mr Quarrendon. That looney, if you'll pardon the expression, mistook the little girl for a boy up to some mischief. That's one of his notions, his keepers told me.'

'Then it *was* my fault!' Francis exclaimed. 'If we hadn't dressed up – ' and the sobs began again.

'Nonsense – you may have saved your sister's life,' said Mr Quarrendon briskly. 'You got to her before she reached the deep water. If it had not been so – '

'We should both have been drowned,' Francis interposed; he was beginning to recover, and spoke in a faintly gratified tone.

'Can't you swim, then?' asked the Inspector. As Francis shook his head he got up and said, 'It only remains to see if the little girl can tell us any more,' and after briefly thanking us, he was ushered out by Mr Quarrendon, who returned to say, 'Had the fellow a beard, Francis? Try to remember.'

'I think – he had. Yes, I'm almost sure.'

'You had better go upstairs and finish your Latin prose,' said his uncle, guiding him to the door. 'You have behaved very well indeed. I am pleased with you.' He then sat down at his desk, as if to dismiss us both. Later that day Dr Cross gave me leave to question Sybilla.

I had arranged with Nurse, who had been told to let her rest and not talk, that she and I should have a 'treat' alone together. Sybilla decided on a picnic in the potting-shed, a favourite resort, generally forbidden both children by the gardener. There we encamped, with milk, chocolate cake and honey sandwiches, all chosen as being her dolls' preferred fare. I gathered that two of them had been ill. 'Sick,' she explained, pointing to their swathed and prostrate forms.

Although not particularly advanced, as far as her vocabulary was concerned, Sybilla's utterance had always been clear; it was now encumbered by a lisp, so sustained as to give the impression of being deliberately assumed; her sidelong glances as she spoke convinced me that this was the case. Taking up a doll, she repeated the word.

'And Syb has been in bed too – are you quite well now?'

'Mm-m – ' nursing her doll – 'No milk.'

'Surely Nanna gave you some?'

'Marmy didn't have milk.'

'I see, poor Marmy. But when you were in bed, you had – what? Tell me.'

'Bread and butter – egg – jelly.'

'I expect you were glad of that – after all, you had been in the water,' I said in an uninterested tone, beginning to cut the cake.

She said nothing; I held out a slice, which she ate hastily. Then she announced, 'With the boats – ' in a triumphant voice.

'I wonder how you got there. Can you remember?'

She glanced at me and began to feed one of the dolls. I said, 'I expect it was rather cold,' in the same offhand manner.

She nodded, abandoned both doll and cake and demanded a sandwich. Then she said, 'Naughty,' in a detached, contemplative tone.

'Who was? Not Sybilla?'

She shook her head. 'No – *pushed* – ' she replied, with sudden emphasis, and burst out laughing.

'Oh dear – who pushed you?'

Sybilla turned her head away, murmuring something inaudible, and bolted the remains of the sandwich. 'Cake now,' she demanded.

'Here it is. I wonder who pushed you – a man?'

'Mm-mm. Black.'

'In black clothes?'

'No. Syb' – pointing downwards – 'all black. Wasn't naughty – ' with another sidelong glance.

'Of course not. But the man?'

Although she had been screaming and struggling when Francis dragged her out of the pond, no remembrance of that terror now appeared to haunt her. Yet her flushed cheeks looked as if she were sickening for mumps or suffering from toothache; and her hands were swollen. Brushing away the cake-crumbs with an air of distaste, she said loudly, 'Must – *must* – have a pony,' her lisp intensified. 'Cripps', she went on, 'will give a pony – now!' and she got up, treading on both dolls in her progress to the door. She then ran in the direction of the stables.

I caught her up as she stopped at a flowerbed and began to gather a mixed bunch. Holding it out, she said, 'For

156

Cripps – ' extending her other hand to me with a sly smile.

I could only follow her lead, which resulted in the groom's embarrassed reception of the bouquet, presented by Sybilla with looks of adoring love and further requests for a pony, to which he replied, 'We'll have to see – ' as she clung to his hand in fascinated awe; his gipsy darkness was plainly irresistible.

Persuaded to leave, she skipped along, smoothing down her frock and then taking it up, as if about to dance. Springing away, she pointed in the direction of the lower pond, and said, 'In the water – pushed. Francey came too, all black, and so – so – '

'Cold?' I suggested, as she paused. She nodded, suddenly grave. 'A man pushed you?' Another nod. 'Had he' – I swept a hand over my chin – 'hair all round his face – like this?'

'Lots and lots,' Sybilla replied, adding, 'Marmy has lots too,' with an illustrative gesture.

During the next few days, she was constantly escaping to the stables with gifts – flowers, pebbles, broken toys – for Cripps, whose relationship with the unfortunate Miriam had now reached a crisis. He had, it seemed, promised her a walking-out period, culminating in marriage. On the afternoon of the accident they had spent some time in the woods, where he announced that this plan was 'off for good and all', leaving her to return alone.

Miriam now wished to give notice; Cripps, who had stopped drinking, was to remain, and was unwillingly accepted by the rest of the staff. When Mr Quarrendon told me that he was going to transfer him to work on the farm – provided that Bownall, his bailiff, consented – we drove there in the dog-cart to arrange it. 'Without you,' he said, as we set off, 'I should have no moral support. Bownall is something of a dictator. I have told Cripps that unless he reforms, he will be dismissed without a character. If only I can persuade Bownall to take him, this will provide a new start.'

'So you think he really deserves another chance?'

'Well – I don't know. "Use every man after his desert" – and so on. On a lower wage, and with gin at sevenpence a bottle, he may pull himself together.'

'Sybilla will miss him,' I said, and described her latest approaches. He cross-examined me on this point, so minutely that we were still talking of it as we reached the farm, and there was no time for me to consult him about Eliza, whose state of mind had become extremely disturbing.

Against a background of Cotswold stone and pale timber, Bownall's great height and strength were strikingly apparent. When he moved forward – an Old Testament prophet with a Newgate fringe – we were formally greeted, while one of his men took charge of the dog-cart. Preceding him and his employer into a raftered parlour, I sat opposite a mantelpiece crowded with Staffordshire figures and pewter mugs. Bownall stood between us, contemplating his employer as if from a long way off. He said, 'Your arm, sir – you've been sadly, I'm afraid?'

'It's well, or nearly so. I've disposed of the sling, as you see. And how is Mrs Bownall?'

'She should be back from the mill by now. When you and the lady have rested, she'd be obliged if you'd look into the dairy. It's on her mind.'

'Anything wrong?'

'She'll tell you, sir. We'd no wish to worry you when you were poorly. And put about too, as I hear.'

'That business of young Craik is being dealt with,' said Mr Quarrendon hastily. 'But the dairy – tell me what you want done.'

'It's not what *I* want, sir. My duty's with the stock and the pasture – ' Bownall began, breaking off at the entrance of his wife, a small, delicately made woman, who came in carrying a tray with a jug, glasses and the largest cake I had ever seen. After further introductions we settled down to cowslip wine and vast slices of lardy-bread, while the leak in the dairy floor was described at length. 'It's the rats I don't fancy,' Mrs Bownall concluded, as if admitting to a

158

childish weakness. 'Run over my feet, they do, as cool as you please. And Bob – that's our terrier, Miss – he's not what I call the bold sort. When there's more than two at a time, he just turns tail, like.'

'It must be retiled, then?'

'You'll never get that done, sir, not in a twelvemonth,' said Bownall with grim satisfaction. 'Those tiles as was put in last year – I shall ask you to look at 'em, if you will. Rotten already.'

'But surely – Burrows and Harding – '

'That lot? I wouldn't have 'em near the place, not at a gift. Not if they was to come – ' pausing for a sufficiently daunting analogy – 'crawling to me, like so many ants. No, sir. I know my duty.'

'Well, we'll have a look,' said Mr Quarrendon resignedly. 'Something must be done. I can't have your wife frightened.'

Mrs Bownall smiled pityingly. 'If I was that sort, I'd've been out of my mind long ago. It's when they get at the cream-bowls, you see, sir. We've lost two this week, and the cream all over the floor. They're obstinate, that's what it is.'

The discussion spread over rats, tiling and the semi-criminal activities of Burrows and Harding, throughout our tour of dairy, pigsties and barn, concluding in the orchard, where Mr Quarrendon, leaning against a tree, said, 'The herd looks healthy enough, Bownall. You were right about those Herefords.'

'Ah – maybe. But not for long, they won't. Being ill, you never heard about Eli, did you, sir?'

'No – has he been ailing?'

Bownall folded his arms, gazed at the ground and then, fixing his glance on his employer, replied, 'The funeral's on Saturday.'

'Eli Crabbe? Dead? Why didn't you let me know he was ill?'

'All in a minute, it was,' Bownall began, in a tone of melancholy recitative. 'In the cowhouse, under one of those Jerseys you were so proud of. Dead' – raising his hand – 'as a leaf. Well – if a man shall come to fourscore years, I reckon he may be thankful. But then you'll remember, sir, I always said as that Jersey strain wouldn't do here.'

'Come now, Bownall – you're not going to tell me those creatures are unlucky.'

'It's not for me to say, sir. All I know is that Eli Crabbe was the best cowhand as ever worked for me.'

'He will have to be replaced,' said Mr Quarrendon after a pause, 'and that brings me to another matter I had to discuss with you. I intend to send over my former groom, Cripps, to be under you here. You would of course have to train him as milker and plough-hand. But he's quick to learn.'

A long silence followed, during which Bownall's glance soared over our heads, as if seeking inspiration. He then began, 'You are my master, sir, and I must obey you. Whatever you do say, that I do, as being my duty.'

Even I could see that this reply embodied an unshakable resolve not to employ any person put forward by Mr Quarrendon. He, better prepared for such a reception, said amiably, 'If he doesn't suit, you need not keep him. But I wish you to give him a trial.'

'Very well, sir. They were saying at the Silent Woman – no – ' with scrupulous accuracy – 'at the Ring o' Bells, it was – that he's one of these drinking chaps. Often the worse. But there.'

'He has promised to give it up. If he goes back on his word, he won't have another chance.'

'Wine is a mocker, strong drink is raging,' Bownall replied, smoothing his whiskers with an enormous hand.

'I know, I know. But I want him to have the opportunity. Please oblige me,' said Mr Quarrendon, with a slightly desperate look in my direction.

I murmured something corroborative. Bownall, adopting an indulgent tone, remarked that many ladies were soft-hearted. The argument continued on these lines till a neutral ground was established; we left under the impression that Cripps, although doomed, would be allowed to go through the motions of being employed – if only in order to demonstrate Bownall's obedience to his master's caprices – before being ignominiously dismissed.

'Discussions with Bownall make me feel as if I had been put through a wringer,' said Mr Quarrendon as we drove away. 'Yes, yes – I can manage the reins, you must allow me some initiative – and he knows it. I saw that he overawed even you – quite a feat, if I may say so. What do you think – should I force Cripps on him?'

'It might be less trouble to let him stay where he is.'

'In spite of your disapproval? Wait – don't tell me that it is not your affair, I'm tired of that answer. I shall have to see Craik,' he added. 'This state of things must not go on. It's a pity that we cannot visit him together. But of course that would be' – he glanced at me sideways – 'unthinkable.'

'It would, indeed.'

'Because of the children? Or the neighbours?'

'I can't answer rhetorical questions.'

This reply seemed to displease him. When I reverted to the Bownalls, he answered curtly and at random. Further efforts met with the same result, and I began to sink under the weight of his moody domination. Then he put his hand on mine. I could not look at him; his touch, light though it was, held and silenced me. I was trembling as we turned into the drive, to find Waring looking out for us. He said, 'Will you go to Miss Trevy, please Miss? My wife does not know what to do for her – and she won't let us send for the doctor.'

2

It was very distressing to have to lie to Mr Quarrendon: and more distressing still to realize that he did not believe me. Yet partial concealment of the truth was not, I told myself, quite so unscrupulous as deliberate falsehood; and a complete account could not be considered. Debating how best to continue, I looked round the drawing-room where so many pleasant hours had been spent, and felt myself miserably helpless.

The entrance of Waring with tea was a respite; as I stood there, staring at a meal I did not want, Mr Quarrendon drew up a chair for me, sat down and himself began to pour out. He said, 'I think you must tell me a little more. She is ill – that is, nervously overwrought – and wishes to leave. Where does she propose to go?'

'She has relatives in London. I suppose she will go to them.'

'And that leaves you in a difficult situation.'

'She wants me to go with her,' I said, steeling myself for the next question. It was not what I expected.

'Has this sort of attack occurred before?'

'That's what it is, of course!' I exclaimed. 'An attack. But I did not realize – ' and put my hands over my face.

For the memory of Eliza's state was dreadful. Her grey hair, escaping from its chenille net, her features swollen and convulsed, her streaming tears, had been those of one who hardly knows what she is saying. (*But she had said it*: the unbelievable, the monstrous thing.)

'You may persuade her to see a doctor,' Mr Quarrendon was saying. 'Drink your tea. Then we will think what is to be done.'

Accustomed to do what he told me in little ways, I

obeyed. 'She must go,' I began, 'whether she sees a doctor or not. She declares that there is no need for one.'

'She may change her mind.'

'I wish never to see her again!'

'Is not that rather hard?'

'You don't understand.'

He put down his cup and leant back. 'I think I do. It is the accident. She fears that something of the kind may happen again – is that it?' As I nodded, speechless, he went on, 'Don't be too much concerned for young Craik. I leave for Monaco at the end of the week. The arrangements for his removal will take a little time. Till then, you must be on your guard. You can manage that?'

I looked at him – and burst into tears. He got up; putting his hand on my shoulder, he said, 'It has been a bad time for all of us, especially for you. And Miss Trevy has not made it any easier.'

As this was, almost word for word, what I had said to Eliza, I sank under the recollection of her attack. 'The lunatic? Of course not. It's that groom. Don't you understand – can't you see?' and then a flood of exclamatory and meaningless warnings.

Yet they were not quite meaningless – that must be faced. They embodied the delusions of someone gravely afflicted, not with the hysteria of a frail, foolish old lady, but with a kind of insanity. And he, calm, reassuring (and so oddly incurious), must never know what she had said. 'I hate her!' I sobbed out, getting up to walk about the room. 'The sooner she goes – but perhaps it's not her fault – I would not have believed it.'

'Would you like me to see her?'

'No – no! Don't think of it!'

'Very well. She had better leave before I do. Now – sit here by me, and don't cry any more.'

I did so, hardly aware that he had guided me to the sofa. Gradually, I became calmer: then, all at once, resolved. I rose and resumed my place at the table. When I was ready to speak, my voice sounded steady enough. 'I shall stay here. The children need me – and that's all that matters.'

There was a long silence, during which he rejoined me, cut himself a slice of cake and filled up the teapot. Then he said, 'If there is anyone you can think of to replace her, you must tell me.'

'That's ridiculous! At my age, to be shadowed by someone I don't care for – I shouldn't dream of it.'

'So – ' he said slowly, 'we are not to be chaperoned. But as you don't want me to see her, I can only conclude that she has taken a dislike – a violent antipathy – to me.'

'She is in a state of hysteria,' I said after a pause.

'And seeing me might make it worse?'

'Perhaps.'

'But then, if she is not responsible, why are you indignant with her?'

Forcing myself to meet his glance, I muttered something about shock, adding, 'She angered me – I couldn't help myself.'

He continued to look at me. Then he said, 'Do you intend to keep in touch with her after she leaves?'

'I suppose I must.'

'I see. Let us leave it at that. Now – try to eat something – ' and he held out the plate of bread and butter. Once more, I obeyed, and he began to speak of his journey. Nothing else was said about Eliza. Two days later, she was gone.

During our final interview she had been strangely calm; and her acceptance of my resolve to stay unchaperoned surprised me into silence. 'I know', she added, 'that though you have been indiscreet, your relations with Mr Quarrendon are not improper. But neither you nor the children should remain here.'

'You also know that I cannot take them away without his consent, even if I wished it – and I don't.'

'It's only natural', she said after a pause, 'that you should disregard what I say.'

'In this case, certainly.'

'I have never tried to influence you,' she went on, 'because I knew it was useless. Long ago, when you became entangled with that young Severini, all we could do was to arrange for him to leave Florence, so that if your father recovered and you returned, he would no longer be there.'

'You knew – ' I broke off, as she continued, 'You can forgive me that, at least. What I am going to say now' – her voice shook a little – 'you may not forgive.'

'Pray go on. After what you have already said, nothing matters. But there are accusations I will not allow. If they were not evil, they would be ludicrous.'

'You are unaware – you always have been – where men are concerned. You were deceived by Severini. You were mistaken about Mr Graham. And now – '

'That's enough! I won't listen to these baseless, monstrous – '

'I could give you my reasons. But you would dismiss them.'

'I should, indeed,' I replied, and left the room.

Some hours later, I prepared to see her off as if we were on our usual terms. She drew me aside and said, 'You will hear from me very soon. This must not go on.' I did not answer. Francis, gazing after the carriage, remarked, 'It's funny – but I don't think she will be missed,' and I could not reprove him. It was just possible, then, utterly to reject her semi-maniacal foreboding, and to refuse to put it into words, even in my own mind; but the effort made me feel sick.

Dressing for dinner with extra care – for the Grangers and the Langs were expected – I felt an overwhelming exhaustion, and sent Alice downstairs for a glass of wine. I had never done such a thing before; but the circumstances were so unprecedented as to call for a stimulant of some kind.

It promised to be an agreeable evening, partly because the happiness of Claude Lang and Susan Granger enlivened us all – even Frederick Lang, whose hypochondria too often prevailed – and also because Eliza's departure was an immense relief. Mr Quarrendon had never criticized her; but I knew that she irked him.

As our guests heard of her leaving without much interest, I began to hope that my position would not appear invidious, until I realized that Arabella Lang saw it as the preliminary to her cousin's third marriage. Her hints became so broad that I decided to dwell on Mr Quarrendon's absence in Monaco and my plan for taking the children to Suffolk for a visit.

'You must not desert us, Miss Milsom,' she archly began. 'Claude and Susan are counting on you.'

'I might return for the wedding. But before I leave, we must decide on a present,' I said, and so guided the conversation on to future arrangements, reaching those for the honeymoon with dessert.

As we left the dining-room Susan said, 'I want to go to Switzerland, but Claude prefers Italy. What do you think?' turning to me.

'Why not both?' said Mrs Lang.

'Claude does not like leaving his rock-garden for too long at this time of the year,' Susan replied; her mother pointed out that Switzerland was just the place for adding to his collection.

We had taken up our company work and were still discussing these alternatives when the gentlemen came in, and music was proposed. Susan and her mother sat down at the piano; Mr Quarrendon stood behind them, ready to turn over; Frederick Lang and Mr Granger lingered by the bookshelves, while Mrs Lang took up a portfolio of sketches. Presently she beckoned to Claude. 'These are the Swiss views, see how charming – ' and he took his place beside her rather listlessly, half his attention on the players, who broke off with the entrance of the tea-tray. When everyone had been served I joined Claude and his mother, and the duets were resumed.

Suddenly, Claude's whole manner changed. Bending over a watercolour of rock and pine, he took off his spectacles, wiped and replaced them with shaking hands. Then he shut the book with a bang, exclaiming, 'Not there – we must never go there!'

Mrs Granger and Susan stopped playing; the three men turned to gaze at him. His mother said, 'Claude – what can you mean?' and took the portfolio from him.

He snatched it away, pressing it against his chest. Turning from one to the other of us, he said loudly, 'I saw it – there.'

Susan sprang up and came towards him. 'Don't, dearest – ' she began. He flushed, and then, regaining some composure, said, 'It doesn't signify – I'm sorry.'

'My dear boy – ' his mother interposed. 'What? What did you see?'

A long silence fell. Claude, still clutching the portfolio, shook his head, apparently unaware that we were all staring at him. I put my hand on his arm; he looked up, his eyes dilated, his mouth ajar, whether in terror or disgust, I could not tell. 'It's nothing – ' he said slowly, forcing out the words. 'There was blood – that's all.'

Gazing from Susan to Mr Quarrendon, and then at his mother, he looked more than usually foolish; and I began to wonder how Susan, a charming and intelligent girl, could have fallen in love with him. But so it was; she knelt beside him, and took his hand. 'Let us put it away, dear – ' she began, and removed the portfolio, laying it on the table.

'I think we should go home,' said his father in a high, strained voice.

Mr Quarrendon, who had left the room, now reappeared with a glass in his hand. 'Drink this, my dear fellow,' he said gently.

Claude drained the glass mechanically; fumbling at his spectacles, he readjusted them. 'It was all over the rock,' he muttered; then, glancing down at Susan, he said, 'I did see it – really,' as if pleading for her support.

Confused reassurances drowned the poor young man's apologies for his outburst and his plea that the party might continue. That he should describe more fully what he thought he had seen was not suggested; and his father's insistence on departure resulted in a general exodus. As Mr Quarrendon escorted them to the door, I took up the portfolio, and was studying the sketch when he returned. Looking over my shoulder, he said, 'I remember now – I bought that book in Vevey on my last visit to your sister, with a view to using those watercolours as backgrounds for some animal studies of my own.'

'I'm afraid I put it there just before you joined us. It was one of three that I got out without looking at them. But what could he have imagined that he saw?'

'Heaven knows. He did us one service, that of ending a tedious evening.'

'You found it so?'

'I prefer the present situation,' he said, smiling down at me. 'Would you have liked them to stay?'

'I felt so sorry for Susan,' I said evasively. 'Ought she to marry him, do you think?'

'No doubt they will see visions and dream dreams together. But I don't quite discount his gifts, you know. It may be that something did happen there once. You look horrified – don't you believe in second sight?'

'I'm not sure. He is such a silly young man – one cannot take him seriously.'

'Yet you seemed to do so.'

'I did not know what to think. I was troubled for her – and for his parents.'

He walked over to the fireplace. 'If you would allow me a cigar, we might continue the evening more pleasantly.'

'Please smoke. But it's late – and I am rather tired.'

'You won't sleep if you go now,' he said calmly. 'What you need is a posset – ' he rang the bell – 'I'll make you one – ' and as Waring appeared he went on, 'Bring what I need for some bishop.'

'What can that be?' I said, beginning to laugh. 'Something deadly?'

'Better than tea. Are you cold? Shall he light the fire?'

'No. But indeed – '

'You are going to stay. Sit here, where I can see you.'

A few minutes later, occupied with preparations that included lemons, wine, sugar and what looked like powdered spice, he glanced at me through a cloud of scented steam and said, 'What shall we drink to?' holding out a horn beaker with a silver handle.

'Oh – I don't know – success. For you, with Sir Charles Craik, perhaps.'

'That reminds me, they have found a scarf of Henry's near the pond – and incidentally' – drawing at his cigar – 'an empty gin bottle in the clearing. Cripps has admitted to it. But since that afternoon he has kept his promise. Nevertheless – ' he paused to stir the mixture over the spirit-lamp – 'he must go, if only for your sake.'

'Mine? What about poor Miriam, and the Warings?'

'They might trouble you – if he troubled them.'

'And so Cripps is to be thrown on the world?'

'I shall see to something for him. I meant to tell you that I had a word with Francis about the man he saw, but I could not gather very much, except that as he disappeared something dark seemed to be floating out behind him.'

'The scarf?'

'Perhaps. But I was going to suggest that no more questions should be put to him. He gets flurried and says whatever comes into his head, as you may have noticed.'

'Of course. But as Henry Craik's guilt is proved, there's no need.'

'Well, as to guilt – he is hardly responsible.'

'And you really will be able to get him sent away?'

'I think so. His keepers are, naturally, very indignant. They have been trying to make out that someone released him. I saw them this morning. But I shall persuade his father to let them stay on.'

After a pause I said hesitantly, 'You know – I hope very much that you will persuade Sir Charles to something else.'

'What is that?'

'To sell the Hall to you – at a reasonable price.'

He stared at me; then he burst out laughing. 'You see me there, do you – *en prince?*'

'Do not you?'

'Not alone. Such a place – ' once more, he drew on his cigar, so that the smoke rose between us – 'should have a – don't they call it a châtelaine?'

Both voice and expression were so harshly mocking that I was silenced. Yet though I did not want to look at him, I continued to do so. At last he said, 'We might ask Claude Lang for a vision.'

'Of the future of the Hall?'

'Why not? But this conversation is becoming rather silly, don't you think so?'

'Then let us end it,' I said, getting up. He did not move; and I left, feeling that he would stay there, heedless of the hour.

His changes of mood were destructive. For a long time I lay awake, wondering how best to deal with them; it then occurred to me that I might not be called upon to do so; in that case, it would be wiser – but wisdom was now far to seek – to leave Pond House, while keeping in touch with the children in my own home. Yet I could no longer see it as a home, or hope to regain the contentment it had once provided.

3

'My son has been greatly disturbed, and so have we,' Mr Lang was saying, 'by what happened last night. He wished to speak to our host himself, but I persuaded him to let me do so.'

'Will you not wait till he comes back, and join us for luncheon?' I said, leading the way into the library.

'I fear not, Miss Milsom. My present diet forbids these pleasures,' Mr Lang replied with a bleak smile. It was then possible to guess what Claude would look like in middle age – stooping, pale, emaciated and sparsely whiskered.

'Surely we could provide – ' I began.

'You are very kind, but such complications as mine require solitary meals. Last night was an exception; I am paying for it today – As I must not stay, perhaps you would explain to our friend that this gift of my son's has often distressed him, and never more so than when we were celebrating his engagement.'

'He need not apologize for what he could not help,' I replied as we sat down.

'It may well be', said Mr Lang, gazing mournfully at me, 'that you suspect him of entertaining delusions.' As I searched vainly for a tactful answer, he went on, 'He has now described to us *all* that he saw – ' and paused, his spectacled glance still fixed on mine.

'A rock – with blood on it?'

'Worse.'

'Oh – no wonder he was distressed.'

'A tragedy was re-created – need I say more?'

'It is just as you feel. That is, if your son thinks we should know, of course – ' My voice sank into a mumble as Mr Lang shook his head and resumed, 'Certain mysteries are best unexplored.'

'I see.'

'Forgive me, but you do not see – why should you?' Mr Lang then rose, adding, 'I merely wished to beg you not to brood over that breaking up of a pleasant evening. My son is, naturally, concerned for you, and for Mrs Granger. I am on my way to her now. The garden looks well,' he went on, in a high, bright tone as we moved towards the door. 'Ours is undergoing a temporary decline. My wife has great hopes for the Marshal Niels this year, but then she is an incurable optimist. "Sun! Sun!" I said to her, only this morning. Greedy feeders as they are, they also need what Nature alone can provide – but I must not keep the horses standing – ' and having entered his brougham, he drew up the windows. As it disappeared Mr Quarrendon joined me.

He received my account of Mr Lang's mission without comment. Then he said, 'My cousin was rather a pretty girl. I never could understand why she married him. As for Claude, he looks like an unfrocked priest – awkward and haunted.'

'I never saw an unfrocked priest,' I said, with a laugh, adding, 'The odd thing is that that watercolour struck me as familiar, and yet I know I saw it for the first time last night.'

'You may have seen the place on your walks, when you were there.'

'I don't think so. Did you tell Waring to say you were out?'

'I cannot face Frederick Lang two days running, and so relied on you – as usual. I am going to the Hall this afternoon. I thought we might take the children.'

'Both of them?'

'Sybilla need not trouble you. We'll drive there, and I will carry her when it's necessary.'

'Francis has often asked to go there again, since that first time.'

'You were not with us then. Now, it will be a party of pleasure, the last till I return.'

And so it proved, even more for the children than for myself. I had never before seen their uncle so gentle and considerate; he adapted himself to each of them, describing Wyatt's methods to Francis and telling Sybilla stories from the pictures and wall-paintings. Yet his manner with his nephew contrasted with that used towards her. It seemed slightly artificial, as of one entertaining a guest, while with Sybilla he was indulgent and amused.

This aspect of his temperament was reassuring. Any suspicion I might have had about the children being a burden was dissipated. He tended to ignore me, and this added to the sense of ease and familiarity, which increased as we contemplated conversation-pieces, painted ceilings, marble carvings and, finally, the garden, reaching a climax with the neglected fountain. As Mr Quarrendon lifted up Sybilla so that she could touch the beard of a river-god, Francis said, 'It's very sad – isn't it? I don't like to see them with nothing to do. Would it cost a great deal to get the water going again?'

Mr Quarrendon turned; glancing at him over Sybilla's head, he replied, 'Whatever it cost – it must, somehow, be achieved.'

'Soon?'

'That depends on what you mean by the word.'

'Well, I meant a week, or perhaps a fortnight. Shall you ask Sir Charles about it?'

'Not this time.'

'You might, if he was in a good mood.'

Mr Quarrendon smiled: a smile that was almost a grimace. Then, as he put down Sybilla, his hand touched her hair. Springing away, she began to run down the slope. 'She will fall, go to her,' he said abruptly, and as Francis obeyed he looked after him with an expression I could not define. Stepping back, he leant against the outstretched arm of a nereid, and so seemed to take on her stony blankness.

Somehow, the spectacle disturbed me, and I followed the children. At the bottom of the slope I turned and saw him standing there, his arms folded. Some minutes passed before he joined us as we walked towards the battered belvedere and sat on the steps. Sybilla, climbing on to his knee, said, 'A story – ' and he began, in a low voice, a tale of enchantment and sorcery that I guessed was one of his own.

I found myself listening rather to the sound than to the narrative; then, I began to take in a tale of gigantic toads and snakes which ended, as Francis pointed out, somewhat unexpectedly. 'If they weren't destroyed,' he said, 'what happened to the forest people?'

Before his uncle could reply, Sybilla whispered, 'More – again – ' seizing his hand. When I asked him if he meant to frighten us, he replied that he would finish his story differently another time, and got up. Sybilla said, 'Nice, big toads,' and Francis remarked that it was just as well she was too little to be afraid of something she could not imagine, adding, 'Otherwise, I should have called it rather nightmarish,' in a slightly disapproving tone.

'As you are too old to be frightened, all is well,' his uncle replied.

'Oh, of course. But if it was in a book – with pictures – it would be like my Grimms' *Tales*, and I used to dream about them when I was very young. And ghost stories – do you believe in ghosts, Uncle Neville?'

'Certainly. But I have never seen one.'

'I should think there might be some here, don't you?'

'If there were not, it would be necessary to invent them,' said Mr Quarrendon, as we walked between the overgrown yew hedges towards the carriage. He was still carrying Sybilla; she murmured something about toads and snakes as he raised her to his shoulder.

I was on my way upstairs when Miriam asked to speak to me, 'on her own', in other words, without telling the Warings. Suppressing her tears, she begged to be allowed to stay on – would I plead with her aunt on her behalf? 'Of course,' I said, 'that is, if you have parted from Cripps.'

'Oh, I have, Miss, he treated me dreadful – ' and the tears began again.

'When is he leaving?'

'He's gone, Miss. He and his brother are setting up in a public in Belminster.'

'A public-house – whose?'

'They're the landlords, Miss.'

'I did not know he had a brother.'

'Alfred, that's the other one, came back from – some French place, I think it was – last year.' Mopping her eyes, she went on, 'That afternoon in the woods, he frightened me about that man – you know, Miss, him that's shut up. He said I ought to be with him. And then he ran off.'

'To the Dower House?'

'I don't know, I was crying. He had a bottle of gin with him.'

'I see. Well, Miriam, if you promise to have nothing more to do with him – '

Interrupted by an outburst of reassurances and thanks, I was left to wonder how Cripps had raised the sum needed for his new employment. Later that evening I passed on this news to Mr Quarrendon, and suggested that his former groom had released Henry Craik in order to frighten Miriam.

'It is possible,' he said after a short silence. 'In any case, we have seen the last of him.'

'But how has he managed to buy himself a share in that place?'

'His brother owns it.'

'You know him?'

'I am not in the habit of frequenting public-houses,' he said coldly.

'I mean, you knew of his existence?'

'He has been there for some months. There was trouble about a licence for the Belminster races, and I heard of him through Portman-Sinclair, who is on the committee. By the way, Augusta has broken off her engagement. Her parents are in despair.'

This news, and the resultant conjectures, prevailed until Mr Quarrendon abruptly announced that he was leaving early the next morning. As we went into the drawing-room he said, 'Would you like Graham and his sister to come and stay?' I shook my head. 'That's unfortunate – because they have already proposed themselves.'

'I fear that is my fault. In my last letter I told Lucretia that you were going abroad. I suppose she thinks I shall be lonely.'

'Shall you be?' I did not answer, and he went on, 'I cannot hope that I shall be missed.'

'There will be a lot to do,' I said, taking up my work, 'and you will not be long gone.'

'Suppose I never came back – would you be sorry?'

'It does not arise – ' I began.

'You count on my return?'

'Yes.'

'Because of the children?'

'Not only for them.'

'For what, then?'

I put down my work. 'You are attached to this place.'

'And to those in it – to one, especially.'

His smile, and the tone of negligent gallantry, irked me. I said, 'You are attached to something else.'

'What is that, pray?'

'Limmerston Hall.'

For what seemed a long time he looked at me without speaking, while I tried to convince myself that I did not care if I had angered him. When he got up, I resumed my work: but my hands shook so that needle and thread fell and were lost. A side-glance showed me that he was at the window; he drew back the curtains and stood gazing out into the dusk. At last he said, 'Have I made it so plain, then?'

'To me, yes.'

'You find it absurd?'

'Why should I? Such a place should not be abandoned – uncared for.'

He came back and stood over me, looking down. He said, 'I shall not see you in the morning – ' and seemed to be waiting for an answer; then he went on, ' "My gracious Silence" – that well describes you – ' and walked away.

'I seem to remember that the man who said that was a tyrant.'

'An anachronism. As I am.'

'There's no harm in that.'

'No? It's a luxury. You, for instance, are not so foolish as to waste your time reaching for the moon.'

'You might get it – the moon – and then find nothing but dust.'

'That remains to be proved.'

As I got up he took my hand. 'Stay a little. We'll walk in the garden, or sit here, whichever you like.'

'What shall I do about Herbert and Lucretia?'

'Nothing – unless you want to put them off.'

'I cannot do that.'

'And if he asks you to marry him?'

'He will not risk being refused a second time. Now I must go.'

When I moved away he stood looking after me. As I reached my room the hall clock began to strike. I listened – lost count – and shut the door.

Next day, I made out a timetable for all that would have to be done now that I was in sole charge. The children's lessons and amusements were paramount; then came orders for Nurse, the Warings and the gardener; then preparations for Herbert's and Lucretia's stay. (I was a little put out at having had no news of their arrival.)

These activities were pleasantly absorbing, because hope and happiness underlay them; a sense of security made up for Mr Quarrendon's absence and what he called our little feasts. Yet these might be renewed with Herbert and Lucretia, who would be surprised and amused by a more highly evolved *savoir-vivre*; and I began to plan a series of small parties for them with our neighbours.

Throughout the ordered occupations of that first day memory linked up the hours. The lunatic grasping his revolver: candlelight on the piano: Mrs Bownall's cowslip wine: the Hall fountain: the Lely portrait: the Rectory orchard: a four-poster, its coverlet in disarray: two ponds, one blackly shadowed, the other set about with glistening reeds: a silver saucepan, brimming with scented wine: shallow teacups and gilded plates: watercolours of animals and wild flowers: music, talk, laughter, children's voices: and, finally, one voice, harsh, mocking, rallying, then suddenly low and gentle – all these made a mosaic which had become the basis of a life as yet unexplored.

Time passed so quickly that I did not realize how busy I had been till after dinner; and then Francis's French and Italian exercises had to be gone through, and an illustrated alphabet for Sybilla constructed out of some rough drawings of Eliza Trevy's. In the midst of this last piece of work I felt the need of refreshment other than tea; yet to ring for wine for myself alone would not look well; and I reflected that an agreeable habit must have grown on me unawares.

I had arranged the alphabet sketches and got out my colour-box, when I heard the sound of wheels, the unbarring of the front door and Herbert's voice in the hall. As Waring made way for me, Lucretia Mary rushed forward and took me in her arms. 'We came as soon as we could – ' she began, and broke off at a sign from her brother, who turned back to pay the driver of a four-wheeled cab loaded with luggage. I said, 'Your letters must have been delayed, I could have sent for you – ' and she murmured something about having had no time.

Refreshments were then offered and refused, the trunks carried away, and we went into the drawing-room, where Lucretia flung off her wraps and sank into a chair, in what I now saw was a state of exhaustion. 'We could not come before,' she repeated, adding, 'Oh! my dearest Anne – tell me – is all well?'

Astonishment silenced me; as I stared at her, Herbert intervened in the forcibly calm manner of one taking charge in a crisis. 'I think', he said, 'that we should have something – tea or coffee, perhaps. Then, bed. It is very late. But the earlier trains were not possible, as the boys are at home – with chickenpox – and certain arrangements had to be made for them.'

'You left them?'

'What else could we do, my dear Anne? Now we are here, beside you – you and the children – and – ' He paused as I rang the bell and gave the requisite orders. Then he resumed, 'Our plans are made – but they must be discussed in the morning. It only remains to assure you that we will stay until everything has been settled.'

At this point Lucretia burst into tears.

4

The violent attacks of rage that overcome most small children had tormented me until I reached my teens; then, the influence of an exceptionally kind and pious governess helped me to conquer them. But shameful memories of flinging myself on the floor, or banging my head against the wall, still sometimes recurred. They did so now, as Herbert Graham repeated that my welfare was his first, though not his only, consideration.

We had been sitting opposite one another in the library. Now, struggling against anger, horror and disgust, I had to walk up and down before it was possible to reply with a modicum of self-control.

'First of all,' I began, 'what reason could you have for listening to Eliza Trevy? Don't you see that she is no longer responsible for what she says? Even so, it amazes me that she should have come to you and Lucretia, of all people, with her crazy notions. And now you repeat them to me, as if – as if –'

It was not possible to continue without breaking down. Herbert's answer came to me from a long way off, faint yet inescapable. 'I have already told you that though she may exaggerate –'

'Exaggerate!'

'Please let me finish – and try to believe that our concern is for the children, or rather, for Francis and yourself. Her suspicions are based on facts, one being her knowledge of the will, which she studied at Somerset House, as soon as she left here. She then came to us for advice.'

'And you – I thought you were his friend!'

'I don't deny that I was.'

'Yet you dare –' Once more, it was impossible to go on.

'Listen to me, Anne. In your sister's second will – of which you admit you know nothing – Quarrendon stands to inherit Francis's whole fortune, in the event of the boy's death.'

'And what of that? What of it? On those grounds, you and poor Eliza – who, I repeat, is not responsible – accuse him of an attempt on his nephew's life! You insult us both. It's beyond bearing, and I won't bear it!'

'You forbid me to state the case?'

In the pause that followed I began to realize that this was not the way to defend a wronged man. However detestable the charge, it must be heard and dealt with, no matter what the cost. I forced myself to sit down, drew a long breath and, though unable to speak, signed to Herbert to proceed.

'In Cecilia's first will,' he said, 'the fortune, for it is no less, was divided between Francis, his uncle and yourself, on the understanding that after your deaths Francis would be responsible for his sister. By the terms of the second will, he is the sole heir, while you receive a legacy only.'

'And that is why Sybilla was attacked? Your reasoning –'

'Wait. She was mistaken for her brother by this groom, who had been drinking. Both children were dressed up, she in her brother's clothes.'

'Very convincing – a child of two is mistaken for one of eleven! You choose to forget what really happened.'

'My belief is that the groom released young Craik so as to throw all suspicion on him. You will agree that he succeeded.'

'And Eliza came to you with this pack of lies!'

'At the moment, the guilt of the groom cannot be proved. But before coming here I found out that he is sometimes blindly drunk. That explains his attempt on Sybilla, who was in any case disguised. Meanwhile, Francis arrived just in time.'

'You have not yet explained – though I've no doubt you will – what Mr Quarrendon's motives were. He is incapable – but what's the use of talking to you? You are set on this insane, this disgusting attack.'

'You have yourself told me of Quarrendon's desire to purchase Limmerston Hall.'

'And you actually think – you dare to say – that he would commit murder, on a child, his own nephew, for that! Have you and Lucretia both gone mad? It's horrible – I won't listen!'

'There is further evidence against him.'

'Let me hear it – and then we need never see or speak to one another again.'

'First, I must remind you of Edwin's death in Switzerland, then of the will by which Quarrendon would inherit from Francis – and finally, of the scandal caused by his parting from his first wife in Rome.'

'She divorced him! That has nothing to do with what you have just said – and you knew nothing of it at the time.'

'True. But Miss Trevy has now told me that she and her sister, who left Florence for Rome shortly afterwards, heard that a maid of Mrs Quarrendon's was found drowned, and that he was suspected – '

'Suspicion again! Why did Eliza produce this story years later? Why did she not tell me of it when she agreed to come here?'

'She dismissed it as gossip until this other event – and her examination of the wills.'

'In fact, Mr Quarrendon is the villain in a melodrama of Eliza's invention.'

'There remains the mystery of Edwin's death.'

'It was nothing of the kind! He fell while out riding, and was killed.'

'I know', said Herbert, who had grown very pale, 'that that point cannot be proved.'

'So you yourself are guilty of criminal libel – both you and Lucretia. I refuse to hear another word against Mr Quarrendon. And I must ask you to leave this house.'

As he got up and moved away, Lucretia came in. The discussion was then resumed, more fiercely and with many divagations. In the midst of it, luncheon was announced.

After an embarrassing and painful interlude, during which a semblance of sociability prevailed, it was just possible to remain outwardly calm, and so to realize that Herbert and Lucretia must stay on for a few days, whatever their feelings or my own, in view of those of the household. As soon as we were alone, this was agreed. We then separated; they went for a walk, and I stayed indoors with Francis who – perhaps fortunately – was in bed with a cold. This enabled me to remain upstairs until the afternoon; the discussion then continued, during which I gathered that the brother and sister had spent some hours in Belminster before coming on to Pond House.

By this time, the change in Herbert's manner had become very marked. When we first knew each other and I thought myself in love with him, he had been neither pompous nor arch. Now, the gravity of the situation and my enraged response to his accusations re-created that earlier simplicity; and this made it easier to argue coolly, while ignoring Lucretia's support of his attack.

Having decided how best to put forward my views, I asked him to explain his change of attitude towards the friend he had always admired. 'I have known for some time', I concluded, 'that his feeling for the Hall amounts to an obsession. But the conclusion you have come to – on totally inadequate evidence – is fantastic. Nothing can justify it – nothing.'

Herbert paused, glanced at his sister and replied, 'If I were still in the profession which I trained for and practised some fifteen years ago, you would be more likely to listen to me. As it is, any lawyer would tell you that certain people contemplate and sometimes commit horrible crimes for what might be described as trivialities. This desire for Limmerston Hall is that of someone who has lost all sense of proportion. It has become a passion – as you made plain in your letters.'

'In fact, you are suggesting that he is not sane – that's what it amounts to – and you expect me to believe you.'

Once more, Herbert seemed to be considering his reply; he looked as wretched as even I could have wished. Then he said, 'I have known him since we were boys – ' and put his hand over his eyes.

'Does that give you the right to blacken his character?'

'What I am trying to describe is a blankness, a lack of humanity. He has great gifts and much charm. Many people become attached to him – as I did. He does not, perhaps he cannot, respond. It has always been so. He could never feel for anyone, man, woman or child, what he feels for – ' Herbert broke off; then he added, almost inaudibly, 'possessions – in this case, the Hall.'

'Your accusation is based on guesswork. It is monstrously unjust.'

'I was afraid you would think so.'

A long silence fell. More than ever determined to retain some measure of self-control, I began, 'Take one point, one little piece of evidence. If it was Cripps who tried to drown Sybilla, why then does she pursue him? When she heard that he'd left, she cried and would not be comforted. But I suppose you will tell me that that has nothing to do with your – with these ridiculous theories.'

'I can't answer that,' said Herbert slowly. 'I do know, however, that the brother with whom he is now established came here from Switzerland with enough money to rent a public-house, shortly after Edwin's death.'

'On the contrary, he came from France.'

'Who told you so?'

'The between-maid, Miriam.'

'She may have been given this information by the groom.'

'The first and second murderers! You have an answer to everything.'

'Dearest Anne – ' Lucretia began, as I went to the door. There, shaking, I managed to say, 'This must stop. I cannot go on – ' and crossed the hall – to be confronted by Arabella Lang and Susan Granger.

As their smiling faces came towards me on a flood of

apologies for their lateness, I remembered having asked them to meet Herbert and Lucretia. That invitation now seemed to belong to the remote past. I ushered them into the library, made introductions and rang for tea with the mechanical ease generally experienced in dreams.

Some time passed in the preliminaries of eating, drinking and small talk before I took in the excuses being made for Claude. 'And that', Arabella concluded, 'is partly why my little Susie and I are on our own, we just *stole away*, didn't we, dear? Claude must really sometimes let her out of his sight, but it's that rockery, however, she will tell your friends what it means to him. I said to him this morning, "Don't let it become an *obsession*," because that's what it is, I assure you.'

As she swept on, that particular word froze any response Herbert, Lucretia or I could have made. We need not have concerned ourselves. Susan sat dreamily gazing into space, cake and bread and butter disappeared and teacups were refilled until Mrs Lang drew breath. Then Herbert took the floor in his most heavily artificial style, rallying Susan on her engagement and describing his plans for the property he had just acquired in Berkshire.

As Lucretia engaged Susan in talk of her honeymoon, I remembered what I now thought of as Claude's seizure over the portfolio of Swiss views. Its connection with the scenes just gone through was almost comic; no doubt the poor young man would have been gratified if he had known of them.

Meanwhile, this visit, ending in the usual tour of the garden, seemed not wholly intolerable. It was further eased by Herbert's attitudinizing, which began to turn my anger into something like pity. His distress about what he and Lucretia had seen as their duty was genuine; however foolish and enraging, their efforts ought to be patiently endured.

As we reached the orchard Susan drew me aside to ask about Mr Quarrendon's return, adding, 'It's because of Augusta, she's very unhappy, not only about her engagement, though that's bad enough. You see, she doesn't believe in *anything* now. Papa came to talk to her, but she ran out of the room in the middle of what he was saying. She says that Mr Quarrendon is the only person who will understand.'

My rather random answer seemed to satisfy her; and she and Mrs Lang left on the understanding that Mr Quarrendon would call as soon as he came home. The relief of their departure was momentary; for now Lucretia led me away in order to renew her plea for Eliza Trevy; although old and frail, she was not easily deluded. 'I feel', Lucretia went on, 'that you have always discounted her. She is not clever exactly, but – well – '

'No – merely persuasive.'

As Lucretia continued her defence, the memory of Eliza's knowledge of my relationship with Gianni Severini and her machinations for his removal became unpleasantly vivid. But that rather devious acuteness no longer existed; and I still resented her blundering comments on my 'mistake' about men as widely different in character as Herbert and Mr Quarrendon. I broke into Lucretia's timid assertions with, 'No doubt Eliza means well – as you do. It's the only possible excuse for slander. But it's rather ironic that a few moments ago Susan asked me to let Augusta Portman-Sinclair know when Mr Quarrendon can help and advise her. Both those girls think the world of him. I wonder how they would have received your attacks.'

I was about to go indoors when Lucretia burst out, 'If you had accepted Herbert's offer, you would have been ruled by him, and not by – ' breaking off as I turned to look at her.

'I am too old to be ruled by anyone,' I said after a pause, during which we stared at one another in silence.

Next day Herbert told me that he had arranged for a telegraphic message to be sent asking for his and Lucretia's return; he added that he desired my consent to his obtaining further information about Cecilia's second will, which she had signed some three weeks before her death. 'However angry you may be,' he concluded, 'I ought to find out whether Quarrendon was with her at that time.'

Difficult though it was to reply calmly, I managed to say, 'Make any inquiries you like, I can't stop you,' before leaving the room. It then occurred to me that I might forestall and so defeat him by asking Francis whether he remembered the date of his uncle's last visit to Switzerland; I was able to do so in the course of a conversation about the sale of Cecilia's villa. He said, 'Uncle Neville was coming in time for my birthday, but he never did, so we had it without him. It was rather a pity, because he came a week later, and we could easily have put it off.'

I handed on this information to Herbert, adding, 'It will please you to know that he was with Cecilia just before she made the second will. So now your case is complete. The dates fit perfectly.'

'I had hoped – ' he began, and broke off with a look of such misery that I had a twinge of pity. No more was said until he and Lucretia made a final appeal which I rejected with a steadiness that now came quite easily. Twenty-four hours later, they were gone.

Alone, no longer embattled, I began to feel as if I were recovering from a long and painful illness. After getting through the day and its usual duties, I went up to my room, locked the door and knelt down. Presently, the moment came to wait for an answer – and almost at once a great peace, a divine assurance descended. It conveyed to me, with absolute and miraculous certainty, that I had done rightly – loyally – and that all doubts about both defiance and defence must be laid aside. Thus to submit my faulty judgment, and humbly to pour out thankfulness for its acceptance, produced such exhaustion as I had seldom known. I countermanded dinner, threw off my clothes, fell asleep – and woke to find myself lying on the coverlet while sunlight streamed over my face and hands.

5

None of the friends left behind in my former home had been as close or as much prized as Herbert and Lucretia; and now that their grotesque delusions and Eliza's senile treachery had combined to separate us, perhaps for ever, I foresaw a great loneliness. That first parting from him had been painful enough; and though it seemed odd that I had once longed to be his wife, I could not but appreciate his dignity and kindness after the disaster of his second offer and his generous acceptance of my apologies. This response had been made easier by the practical nature of his affections. His plans for marriage appeared to be those of a man who wanted to settle down with a suitable companion; and I possessed the necessary qualifications.

Now, this picture changed. Herbert's attack on Mr Quarrendon was possibly (I could not be sure) that of the rejected aspirant. Both he and Lucretia believed me to be subjugated – blinded. According to their standards, nothing else could account for my remaining unchaperoned at Pond House; and that conviction must have been strengthened by my defence of its owner.

This attitude was all the sadder to contemplate because I had been misjudged, bereft, and thus become more than ever dependent on the enigmatic ruler of the children's lives. True, he sometimes *appeared* inhuman; but I believed that this outward frigidity concealed depths of feeling of which Herbert was incapable, and had never, in all the years of their friendship, perceived. He did not know Mr Quarrendon as I had come to know him; and he had now turned against him through jealousy. Meanwhile, such influence as I had over that inscrutable being might eventually draw us together and show Herbert how wickedly mistaken his suspicions were.

Mr Quarrendon was interested in and dependent on me; our times alone together had become part of his life; his provocative gallantry might mask a warmer feeling and one day produce a more demanding approach. That was all I knew, all I could count on; yet concern for the opinion of others was discarded; the world outside the microcosm of Pond House had become a shadow show, its echoes fading into extinction. A tide was carrying me on, day by day, wave after wave, towards a hidden shore.

The background of this situation was brilliantly vivid, out of doors above all. Flowers, leaves and trees were illumined and magnified. As the delicate growths of spring gave way to the deeper colours of summer, that transformation had a dramatic quality. A group of lilac trees, ranging from dark purple through pale mauve and thence to ivory, was especially conspicuous. Those scented clusters seemed to dominate their surroundings, whether in sunshine or under the vapours from the pond over which they hung and swayed. I never tired of looking at them; cutting off the smaller branches to arrange indoors became an adventure, one to anticipate and yet shrink from in this time of waiting for the master's return.

The letter announcing this event was brief and rather formal. I ought not to have expected a more intimate communication; rereading it, I braced myself for his arriving in a mood which might set some inexplicable barrier between us. Instead of reaching home exhausted and very late, he appeared in time for luncheon, having spent the night at the Belminster Arms. As the children ran out to greet him, he looked at me over their heads with a smile. During the meal he made a number of inquiries about Lucretia, Herbert, our neighbours, my own pursuits and the children in such a manner as to create a comfortingly domestic atmosphere. 'We have still much to say to one another,' he went on, as we left the dining-room. 'Give Francis a half-holiday, and come for a walk as soon as I have looked through my letters.'

'To the Hall?'

'Not this time. Let us make for the downs.'

As we did so, I became aware that he was in good spirits; his genial look emboldened me to ask how he had progressed with Sir Charles.

'Very well, excellently. He was so co-operative as to write, in my presence, a letter to Henry's keepers, and to make arrangements for his removal to one of those *homes*' – he paused on a satirical note – 'where he will endanger no one but himself.'

'So the Dower House will be empty?'

'He has offered it to me for a nominal rent. Would you be happy there?'

'I don't know,' I said after an astonished pause. 'What about the children?'

'There's no doubt that they would be better off here. But you must decide.'

'How can I? I've never set foot in it.'

'Well, the garden is half the size of this one, and the stables are inadequate, to say the least.'

'What you mean is, that you have already made up your mind to stay where you are.'

'I had another idea. But it might not suit. Would you consider setting up there, while keeping an eye on us here?'

We had begun the descent to the woods, and now reached a stile. Removing my arm from his, I sat down. 'Leave Pond House?'

'It would hardly amount to that. We should be seeing you every day – and many evenings. You don't care for the notion?'

I shook my head. He sat down beside me. 'I was thinking', he began, 'of your scruples. I don't share them, as you know. But this seemed the solution to a problem.'

'A problem?'

'Now, really – what would Miss Trevy say, if she could hear you?'

'Oh – yes.'

After a short silence he resumed, 'I don't wish it,

naturally. I was merely aiming at propriety, as you understand the word. Have I offended you?'

'No – that is – I'm not sure. If you wish me to leave –'

'Don't be perverse, it does not become you. I thought you were concerned for – let me see – my cousins, the Hays, the Portman-Sinclairs, Courtenay – by the way, what is the news of Augusta?'

Feeling as if I had been struck on the chest, I waited until I could breathe evenly before replying, 'She has changed her mind again, and they are to be married next month.'

'Who is the unlucky man? I can't remember.'

'A Major Briggs – retired.'

'Through ill-health?'

'I don't know, why?'

'Because he will need all his strength.'

'I suppose it's as well that he is twice her age. But – the Dower House. Perhaps I should go there.'

'Not against your will. And talking of houses, I have disposed of your sister's villa for quite a handsome sum. With your approval, I propose to invest it for Sybilla. As Francis's trustee, I must keep it for him until he comes of age, but I have no doubt he will consent –' and he began to outline the financial aspect too rapidly for me to follow. As figures and estimates whirled over my head, his suggestion about the Dower House prevailed. For perhaps he did wish to get rid of me, as he had got rid of tutor and governess and then, although unwittingly, of Eliza Trevy.

During the rest of the walk I managed to maintain the response he seemed to expect; as we came into the drive he said, 'It was perhaps foolish – unpractical – to suggest your moving. Will you forgive me?'

I replied that there was nothing to forgive, and hurried indoors. Solitude seemed essential; yet we must spend the evening together as if all was well – and I remembered that that had been Lucretia's phrase when she and Herbert appeared in order, as they thought, to rescue me and the children.

That memory was obliterated when we faced one another in the evening light. As I stood gazing at him, the familiar background sank away. I could not bring out whatever commonplace it was that I had prepared. When he spoke, I neither took in the words nor moved. Afterwards, I came to the conclusion that he had intended this to happen.

As we came into the dining-room he paused to look at the vases of lilac I had arranged on the sideboard. Their scent crept towards us; when he sat down his head and shoulders were outlined against a frieze of purple and green.

During the first part of the meal he described his visit to the casino with Sir Charles Craik, whose form of gambling was that of placing the smallest possible sums, regardless of the covert mockery thereby aroused. 'But I did not stay very long,' he went on. 'When I called next day, his daughter was there.' He waited for Waring to withdraw before resuming, 'She had been ill and was convalescing. She has a look of her mother, at least I thought so – ' and he began to peel an orange, smiling to himself.

'Is she pretty?'

'Not yet. One day, perhaps – she is not a gawk nor a tomboy, that's the convent training. He dotes on her.'

'Did you feel – that is, would you rather not have seen her?'

'I was interested – mildly. She did not have very much to say for herself. We hardly interchanged three sentences.'

'And she had no idea who you were?'

'None. She has been told that she was orphaned as a baby and that Craik adopted her, after parting from his wife.'

'Is she, the wife, still alive?'

'I haven't a notion. They parted twenty years ago.'

I was considering an inquiry about the Hall, when the

door opened to admit Waring, who began, 'I beg pardon, sir, but it's Bownall. He says he must see you.'

'Send him in,' said Mr Quarrendon, 'and bring another glass. No – ' as I got up – 'I wish you to stay, if you please.'

In the candlelight the bailiff's height and breadth dominated the room. He accepted a chair and a glass of Madeira with sombre dignity, and then announced, 'It's our Grace, sir, as I've come about. I'd have waited till morning – but it couldn't be.'

'That's all right, Bownall. What has happened?'

'She's run off – to service, at the Belminster Arms. But that's not the worst. They've put her behind the bar.'

'When did she go?'

'This afternoon. She's there now, serving that ragtag and bobtail – '

'How did you know where she was?'

'She left a letter in the dairy. That was so as we wouldn't find it till we come to lock up.'

'But why? Was she unhappy at home?'

'Not so much that,' said Bownall after a pause, 'as unsettled like. Up one minute, down the next.' Staring at the tablecloth, he drained his glass.

'I'm very sorry about this. Have you been to the Arms?'

'No, sir. She'd defy me, and that'd add to the talk. Her mother's been on at me to go, but I came to you. Grace always thought a lot of what you say.'

'What's the reason? Some young man, I suppose?' As Bownall did not answer, Mr Quarrendon went on, 'The best thing would be to speak to the landlord. Do you know him?'

'Haversham, yes, sir. He's Mrs Grant's brother, her as is caretaker at the Hall.'

'What sort of fellow is he?'

'Rough.'

As Mr Quarrendon leant back, he seemed to come to a decision. 'What is behind all this?'

'We never meant her to go into service – not ever. If we had, it'd have been here. You'll understand that, sir.'

'Naturally.'

'And now – in that place – with him in and out – it'll break her mother's heart. If he'd come to us, instead of setting up on his own, I'd've sent him off, orders or no orders.'

'So it's Cripps – is it?'

Bownall bent his head. A long silence fell. Mr Quarrendon got up, refilled the bailiff's glass and, glancing at me, shrugged his shoulders. Then he said, 'What do you want me to do?'

'Send him packing.'

'I don't own the public-house he works for. I'll speak to Grace, if you think it would do any good, and to the Havershams. That fellow', Mr Quarrendon went on, resuming his seat, 'is a nuisance. But the days are over when his sort could be run out of town. I might, I can't promise, get his brother's licence withdrawn. But that would take time.'

Bownall brought a huge fist down on the table, not heavily, but with sinister deliberation. 'If I catch him – '

'Violence won't do, my good Bownall, you know that as well as I do. You'd be up before the Bench, and what good would that be? I'll see Grace tomorrow, and I'll speak to Mrs Haversham.'

Bownall, leaning forward, said huskily, 'I'm obliged to you, sir. I said to the wife as you'd not fail us – ' and got up.

Mr Quarrendon accompanied him to the door; returning, he leant over the back of his chair, his hands hanging down. 'What is it about undesirables that attracts some women?' he began. 'Do you know? I'm sure you were never drawn to one.'

'I was – once.'

'Really? What happened?'

'Nothing – no scandal. Eliza came to the rescue, at least

that's how she would have put it. I was very young, and as foolish as most girls. Much like Grace Bownall.'

'Tell me about it.'

'I would rather not. It was an incident, no more.'

'A romance?'

'Hardly.'

'You were in love?'

'I thought so at the time.'

He sat down, his eyes on my face. 'How does one know? You must have thought yourself in love with Graham, for instance.'

'Oh – Herbert – perhaps.'

'Your tone of dismissal is rather alarming. Have you become unapproachable?'

He was smiling. I managed to say, 'It is possible.'

'And if I tried to find out?'

'You could begin by asking Grace Bownall what she sees in Cripps.'

'The appeal of the undesirable,' he said slowly. 'I suppose there's a strain of it in most men.'

'In many, certainly.'

'Where are you going?'

'Upstairs. I have some exercises to prepare for Francis.'

Following me to the door, he said, 'When you have finished, won't you rejoin me?'

I shook my head. Taking the matches from me, he lit my candle. As he held it out, our fingers touched. 'Why? What have I done?'

'Nothing that you can help.'

'So you will not even look at me.'

I did so; then I turned away. As I began to walk upstairs he said, 'I shall wait for you.' Next day, the thought that he had done so in vain was a kind of satisfaction. Yet with the remembrance of his plan for a settlement on Sybilla came the desire to inform Herbert of what was surely a conclusive refutation.

As I rejected the idea of such a letter, Francis burst into my room, exclaiming, 'Isn't it splendid, Uncle Neville says

I may ride after all! He's getting a cob, I never thought he would, but now he's going to, so we can all go out together.'

After a short silence, I said, 'That will be very nice.'

'Aren't you pleased?'

'Of course.'

'My riding clothes are here. But I may have got too big for them.'

'Yes.'

'Do you think I might try them on?'

'Later – later.'

Francis was staring at me. He cleared his throat, began, 'Shall I ask – ' and broke off. Then he left the room.

6

'May I say,' Mr Courtenay began, 'that this is an occasion? I mean,' he added, measuring out tea-leaves from a lacquered caddy, 'your coming here for the first time. I warn you that I shall be compelled to display some of the little treasures that my friend Quarrendon has seen more than once. Newcomers are victims, as I expect you know.'

'I want to see them very much,' I said, glancing over the tea-table, which had been placed in a trellised arbour, and wondering what we were going to eat; for on it were three covered dishes, one supported by a silver tripod; the others, of Chinese porcelain, were flanked by gilt servers, much like those used for asparagus, but smaller. Mr Courtenay, perceiving my curiosity, smiled, took up the urn, which represented Atlas supporting the world, filled the teapot and took out his watch. 'Two and a half minutes, no more,' he said, placing it on the tray. 'I hope you favour this Russian brand, Miss Milsom. But I think, somehow, that you are rather a fastidious person, am I right?' I murmured something about enjoying novelties, and he pursued, 'Now – will you be so good as to lift that lid, the silver one, while I attend to this? Wait – let me look. Yes; those scones, made from my own wheat, ground this morning, are, I judge, adequately buttered. I have trained my cook not to *soak* them. Take one, and let me know.'

The scone was so small and so hot that I nearly let it fall. As I bit into it as delicately as possible, Mr Courtenay began to pour out; then he said suspiciously, 'You take milk, I suppose?'

'Not with this brew, surely?'

'Well done, indeed! I might have known it. And sugar? No? You are a paragon. What about lemon?'

Entering into the spirit of this esoteric feast, I asked for a very thin slice, and was again congratulated. A porcelain cover was then lifted to reveal a collection of oblong green biscuits; the third dish concealed a round, flat object, glistening redly and dotted with segments of blue and yellow sugar (specially dyed, I was told, through a process found in a seventeenth-century cookery book), which had to be cut with a Turkish dagger – 'because', Mr Courtenay explained, 'that race precedes the Italians in such matters. In fact – pray try one of these pistachio leaves – I have always thought Italian confectionary overrated, except in Sicily. There, they have a feeling, an instinct – but oh dear, the cake is not quite as I had planned. Never mind, we can fall back on this.'

He turned, opened a cupboard concealed in the trellis-work, and produced a black pot with gilt spoons and saucers. 'Rose-leaf jam, from Halicarnassus. Never, my dear lady, buy it anywhere else. The Turkish manufacture is a wretched affair. You would hardly believe it – but when Mrs Lang came to tea, she actually *spread* it, on a scone! I made no comment, of course. But it will be a long time before she is given another chance – ' and he began to spoon out the contents of the jar, adding anxiously, 'You don't find me over-particular? I do like a well-planned tea, I admit.'

'Your cook must be a genius.'

'Hardly – but he is conscientious. Now – we must not talk only of food, or you will think me a gourmand. What has been happening at Pond House? I hear that Cripps has been up to his tricks again.'

'Grace Bownall and our between-maid, Miriam, were brought together. That was Mr Quarrendon's idea. And Cripps has been forbidden the Belminster Arms.'

'He should never have been allowed to set up with his brother. Nasty fellows, both of them. So Grace has returned home?'

'She is coming to work at Pond House. We don't really need an extra maid, but she wished it, and her parents consented.'

'And under your aegis – ' Mr Courtenay broke off with a sly glance.

'The Warings will be responsible for her,' I said hastily.

'And meanwhile, I understand that Quarrendon is looking for another groom?'

'Has he said so?'

'There seems to be no one suitable locally,' Mr Courtenay went on. 'Quarrendon was saying that his nephew must not ride out alone until he has got the feel of that new mount. He is, if I may say so, over-scrupulous on that point. He rejected my coachman's son, as not being sufficiently experienced. But neither you nor he can always ride with the boy.'

'I did not know – ' I began, and stopped, aware of an injured note in my voice.

Mr Courtenay then suggested a tour, first of the library, and then of his hothouse plants. His collections would have interested me more if I had not been increasingly preoccupied, to the point indeed of wishing to get back as quickly as possible. I had left Francis sailing his boats; then he was going to have tea in the garden with Nurse and Sybilla; Mr Quarrendon would not be home till dinner-time. I was so anxious to leave, that one excuse came on top of another; the dog-cart was brought round after what seemed a long wait. On the way, I met Mr Granger setting off on his rounds, and had to give him a lift. So impatience yielded to anxiety – yet why?

When I reached home, Francis was nowhere to be seen. I rang for Waring, who told me that the young Grangers had called for him to go rabbiting with them on the downs. Half an hour later, he appeared. I broke into his account of his friends' ferrets with, 'You should have asked my leave. What about your lessons?'

'I'd finished them. And it's Thursday. I always go out with Jack and Tom on Thursdays.'

His tone was one of mild reproof. I said irritably, 'Of course, I'd forgotten.'

'When I woke up this morning,' he went on, 'I was sure

it was Wednesday, and I did so want it to be Thursday, and then after all, it was. Well – Jack and Tom – '

'Go up to the nursery now. I will come to you later.'

'You mean the schoolroom,' said Francis gently.

'Yes, yes – but go, please – ' and with a puzzled glance he obeyed.

I had joined him and settled down to *Kenilworth*, when he put in. 'That was where we started yesterday, don't you remember?'

'I'm sorry, Francis. My wits are astray, I can't think why.'

'I know, you forgot about Syb's story last night, so I told her one.'

'That was good of you, dear.'

'She didn't like it!' said Francis, with a burst of laughter. 'No – ' as I began to protest – 'I wasn't teasing her, truly. *Kenilworth* being on my mind, I told her about Queen Elizabeth and Sir Walter Raleigh. Fancy not being interested in that! She made quite a fuss. She'll grow up silly, I've often thought so. Not that it matters, she can always get married. But please read, Aunt Anne. It's the bit after they go on the river.'

An hour later I was dressing for dinner with the memory of Sybilla's objections to Sir Walter Raleigh's gesture in my mind; his cloak being thrown down in the mud had re-created the attack made on her.

Dinner was delayed because Mr Quarrendon had been detained at a committee meeting, whose members could not agree about the licences for the Belminster races. He told me that those of the Cripps brothers were to be withdrawn, and went on, 'After that, Courtenay buttonholed me. He is afraid that you did not enjoy your tea-party, as you hurried away before visiting the plantation.'

'But that meant watching for some bird or other, and I had to get back.'

'You were expected?'

'Not exactly. I forgot that Francis was to go out with the Granger boys.'

'He seems to be on your mind.' I said nothing, and he continued, 'Something troubles you. Won't you tell me what it is?'

'I had a letter from Suffolk this morning.'

'Not bad news?'

'No – but I think my maids are wondering about me. I told them that I should be back before very long. I thought – could I perhaps take Francis and Sybilla?'

Waring now reappeared with dessert, Mr Quarrendon sent away the port set before him and ordered a different brand. As the door shut he replied, 'Certainly – but not at the moment. When do you wish to go?'

'There's no hurry,' I said hastily. 'They will understand.'

As he put out his hand for the dish of walnuts I wondered, not for the first time, whether the ring on his little finger had once belonged to a woman. He peeled some nuts, got up and set them before me, one hand on my shoulder. As I stared down at my plate, of which the pattern had become indeterminate, he gave my shoulder a slight pressure and moved away.

Presently, waiting for him in the library, I sat idle; my work had been left upstairs. From a pile of new books I took up the top one, a volume of Madame de Sévigné, and finding it uncut, looked for a paper-knife; that lying near was shaped like a dagger, with a turquoise and coral handle.

The tea-tray appeared; I continued to cut and read; when he came in and stood looking down at me, my hands dropped. He placed a cup of tea and the plate of bread and butter beside me, removing the book and the paper-cutter. Then he handed me the cup; as it clinked and rattled against the saucer I put it back. Now he was holding the knife, swaying it to and fro; its point caught the light. I said, 'Was that always there?'

'Always. I bought it in Rome, many years ago.'

'It is really a dagger – a poniard?'

'Of the fifteenth century. Are you not drinking your tea?'

'I don't want any.'

'Let us go out then, it's a fine night.'

We were crossing the lawn when he turned back and opened the door, so that the light from the lamp in the hall streamed out across the pond and over the seat under the trees. As we sat down he said, 'It's a pity there's no moon. But it would never do to sit in the dark.'

'You think of everything.'

'I have to, in your company.'

'From here, the house looks like a scene on the stage.'

'Yes,' he said after a pause, 'but it is not the right setting.'

'You would prefer the Hall?'

'Not at the moment – and not for you. We should have known each other long ago, in Italy. That's the background for a beautiful woman.'

Only one other person had so described me; and the image of Gianni Severini rose, blurring the black-and-white figure at my side. I said, 'Italy can make fools of silly young women. I was one, I suppose.'

He took my hand. 'Look at me. Yes – you are beautiful. But that's not all.'

'There's Waring, drawing back the curtains. We should go in.'

'Not yet. I want to go on looking at you. Is that too much to ask?'

'It depends.'

'On how I behave? But I don't trust you.'

'What do you mean?'

'You might decide to go indoors. And that – '

A scream rang out from the upper floor. He ran forward, too fast for me to catch up with him. When I reached the hall he had gone. Panting, I stopped at the foot of the staircase. From above came a confused sound of voices. Then he reappeared. 'It was nothing. A nightmare.'

'The children – '

'Fast asleep. It was that girl – Miriam. Mrs Waring is with her.'

'But Francis – '

'Go and look, if you don't believe me.' As I stared up at

him, he went on, 'Wait in the library, I'll be with you in a minute – ' and went into the dining-room, returning with glasses and decanter. I drank, then looked at him; a mist rose between us. My hand was shaking, and I put down the glass. 'I will hold it for you. Lean back.'

I did so; then I said, 'A nightmare. Poor Miriam – ' and drank again.

'The result of too much toasted cheese for supper, I imagine.'

'I thought – it was Francis.'

'Why?'

'Because he is – I can't remember the word.'

'Inclined to nightmares?'

'No.'

In the pause that followed I rejected several other phrases. The word that had escaped me was just ahead; yet it must be grasped, however great the effort, however long the process of concentration. I said, 'Wait – ' and shut my eyes. As giddiness produced further chaos I clenched my hands till my wrists ached. Pain steadied me; now the word was in sight, was held. I repeated it to myself till I was quite sure that it was the right one. 'I know now. Threatened.'

'I don't follow you. Threatened? By whom?'

A long silence fell. 'I think I should go to bed – ' I began, and got up. He led me through the hall and stood watching me as I climbed the stairs.

When I reached my room I went to the mirror. He was there, behind me, his head on one side. Slowly, his smile became a grin. I turned. There was nothing. The candle guttered and went out. Alone in the dark, I began to undress, fumbling with hooks and eyes.

I came down to breakfast to see Mr Courtenay riding past the window. Mr Quarrendon then appeared, followed by Francis, who seemed to be protesting. His uncle said, 'You should be in the schoolroom. In any case, there is nothing to discuss.'

'I just want to know why – '

'I have already said that you are not to ride out with

anyone but myself or Stringham, or, when he is installed, the new groom.'

'But Mr Courtenay asked to take me with him.'

'He is a reckless, in fact a dangerous rider. It's out of the question. Now go upstairs.' As the door shut Mr Quarrendon went on, 'Courtenay keeps early hours. I think he came in the hope of seeing you. His invitation to Francis is not to be considered. He has ridden over hounds more than once, crams his mount, and is what they call jealous in hunting circles.'

'You cannot have seen him doing so.'

'No; but before you came here there was an outcry. Even though he has mended his ways, his offer would amount to – shall I say a threat?' As I looked blankly at him, he went on, 'That's a quotation.'

'I remember now,' I said after a pause. 'I don't know, quite, what was in my mind.'

'But you knew last night?'

'I was frightened. That screaming –'

'Ah! yes – it was a most annoying interruption, at least I thought so.'

'Francis will be very disappointed.'

Mr Quarrendon went to the sideboard, helped himself, and returning, replied, 'I must make it up to him somehow. He can ride over to the farm with me as soon as he has finished his lessons.'

'You will be back for tea?'

'I hardly think so. I promised to go through Bownall's accounts with him.'

'But then I shall not be able to come with you. The Portman-Sinclairs are expected.'

'You can make my excuses to them.'

'Won't it be rather a long visit, I mean for Francis?'

As he leaned back, his look changed from suspicion to one of impatient mockery. 'I will see', he said slowly, 'that he does not wander about the field where the bull is – or fall into the duckpond, though it's quite shallow – or eat more than one slice of Mrs Bownall's lardy-cake, or get tipsy on

208

her cowslip wine. What other dangers – threats – are there?' Silenced and rather angry, I crumbled a piece of toast, avoiding his glance. Then he said, 'He need not come with me if you don't wish it,' and pushed away his plate.

'He should not be tied to my apron-strings.'

'So I have your leave to take him?'

'He is your responsibility. My leave is not in question.'

'My dear girl, of course it is. He shall go or stay, just as you decide.'

The words fell on me like a caress. I could not answer. At last he said, 'Let me know, later on, what you want –' and left the room.

The arduous monotony of the afternoon was enlivened by the Portman-Sinclairs. They brought Augusta and her fiancé, Major Briggs, a tall, bald, heavily moustached personage, who dominated the conversation, contradicted his betrothed, and assaulted her most vulnerable points, as if raising a siege. He described her conversion to the Church of Rome as hysterical, her free-thinking as ridiculous, and their engagement as a solution to both phases. While her parents interchanged nervous looks and vainly tried to change the subject, Augusta remained calm, smiling maliciously at the social havoc thereby created and replying to these attacks with such remarks as 'You think so, do you?' or 'You are embarrassing everyone,' and finally, in sinister tones, 'We shall see how you feel about that after marriage.' This rough-and-tumble relationship seemed to suit her, and was epitomized by her giving the Major a sharp kick on the shin as he handed her into the carriage.

A few minutes later Francis appeared, escorted by one of Bownall's men. After giving me a rapturous account of his visit, he announced, 'Uncle Neville says you are not to wait dinner for him, he may have to go into Belminster,' and I walked slowly indoors.

I had been looking forward to telling Mr Quarrendon about the tea-party, and the thought of a solitary evening was rather daunting. I dined hastily, tried to read, began to practise some new music and went up to bed resenting the aimlessness caused by a disappointment I did not care to acknowledge.

As I reached my room I heard horse-hoofs, looked out, and saw him dismount. He waited for Stringham to lead away the mare; then he was underneath my window. As I opened it and leaned out he said, 'It's early – won't you come down?'

'Have you dined?'

'Inadequately, at the Arms. I had to see Haversham. It was all extremely tedious. I promise not to bore you with it if you will only oblige me.'

I withdrew, lit two more candles, pinned on the brooch he had given me, rearranged my hair and came down to find him standing in the drive. Dropping his whip on the grass, he said, 'I thought you weren't coming. Why did you take so long?' The critical, proprietory tone made me draw back. He seemed to be staring me out of countenance. 'Well – what have you to say for yourself?'

'I meant to go early to bed.'

'You still can, if you insist. But it would be a pity.'

After a short silence I began, 'The Portman-Sinclairs were very sorry to miss you. Major Briggs was with them, and Augusta.'

'I trust he had his riding-crop with him.'

'In a sense, he had. He contradicted her every time she spoke – trod on her toes – told her not to be a silly girl – it was rather extraordinary.'

'Come for a stroll, and tell me about it.' As I took his arm he went on, 'Did you like him?'

'Not really, no. But I think she does – ' and I described Augusta's final gesture.

He burst out laughing. 'The boot, literally, should have been on the other foot. How did her parents take it?'

'They seemed dazed.'

'And you?'

'Oh, I – I filled up the teapot and hoped for the best – I mean, that they would not stay very much longer.'

Sliding his hand over mine, he said, 'And so you are exhausted. It's a shame, I should have been there.'

'That might have made it worse. I have been trying to imagine them as a married couple.'

'They will probably settle down and become perfectly humdrum. But is that what you have been thinking about all this time?'

'Not entirely.'

'About Francis, then?'

'A little.'

We had now reached the wall enclosing the lower garden and were looking out over the slope that led to the village. The moon was rising; far off, I saw the pale streak of the Severn. Taking both my hands, he held me at arms' length. 'Now – if one of those girls screams out, I shall assume that you have arranged it. So you had better listen to me, whatever happens.'

'I am listening.'

'To begin with, are you not getting rather tired of this place? Because I am.'

'If you want to go away – ' I broke off as he drew me nearer.

'I do. But not alone.'

'We can't – ' Again, it was impossible to go on.

'Well?'

'We cannot both leave the children. As it is, my being here alone looks odd. I don't care for that, I have told you so. But I must stay with them, I promised.'

'What devotion.' In the pause that followed he dropped my hands and turned away. 'Do you want me to plead with you?'

'Certainly not.'

'To confess that I can't do without you?'

'I should not believe it.'

'No?' he said harshly. 'Then you might think about this. I could, if I liked, tell you to leave this house. You realize that?'

'Please – don't.'

'Very well. In that case, you must adapt yourself a little.'

'To what? I don't understand.'

'To me, to my wishes.'

'I thought I had done so.'

'Did you, indeed?' he said, leaning back against the wall. 'Think it over – ' and he looked me up and down, smiling. In the moonlight he appeared strangely menacing, much as when I thought I saw him in my dressing-table mirror. 'Come, we'll go in,' he went on. 'You are, of course, concerned with what the servants will be thinking – ' and we returned to the house in silence.

Our good-nights were brief. I lay awake until I heard his footsteps in the passage; they stopped outside my room. Then he walked on. I sat up and listened. His door shut softly. Presently it opened again, and he went past and down the stairs. From the sound, it seemed that he had discarded his riding-boots for slippers.

7

Francis had become increasingly popular in the neighbourhood, especially with Colonel and Mrs Hay, who were in
the habit of asking him to the tea-parties they gave for
their grandchildren. When Mrs Hay told me that my
nephew and her little Margaret were great friends, I replied
suitably, in the hope that his tolerance towards a dull and
over-indulged child would not fail. Shortly afterwards, Mr
Quarrendon and I found the Colonel, who had called when
we were out, talking to Francis about the antiquities of the
Belminster estate. After explaining that the property had
long ago been divided up and sold, he described his rehabilitation of the eighteenth-century folly on the downs,
adding that he had prevented its destruction by a tenant
farmer.

'Do you mean that sort of tower?' Francis asked. 'We
had a picnic there the other day, and I wanted to explore it,
but the door was sealed up. It's just the sort of place I
should like to live in when I have a home of my own.'

'You would be rather lonely,' said Colonel Hay. 'It con-
sists of one small circular room on each floor. That on the
top has not even a window.'

'Anyone living there would be quite independent. You'd
lock yourself in, and no one could get at you,' Francis
replied.

'That might be depressing after a while,' his uncle put in;
as Francis looked doubtful, Colonel Hay said, 'Next time I
go over there, you might like to come with me.'

Francis accepted eagerly. As Mr Quarrendon and the
Colonel walked away he said, 'Do you think he'll remember, Aunt Anne? I want to see inside that place more than
anything. It's like a story – ' his highest form of praise.

'I will remind him. We might visit it together.'

'Thank you. Perhaps another time I could go there alone.'

'So as to get on with your writing?'

'Well, partly. Of course,' he added hastily, 'I don't mean always. But I'm afraid he wouldn't let me have the key. I'd be specially careful. Do you think you could ask him?'

I agreed to do so, and then forgot all about the folly, until I came upon Francis discussing it with his uncle, who said, 'I will tell the Colonel that you are to be relied on. I suppose you know that there's nothing but rubbish inside those places.'

'Oh, I don't care about that, it's just being there.'

When the question of Francis's request recurred, Mr Quarrendon replied rather vaguely, while in my mind the subject sank beneath the weight of other problems.

That of the letters from Herbert and Eliza Trevy came first. For some days I could not bring myself to open them; then a hasty reading convinced me that they were unanswerable, although there was one accusation I was tempted to refute, because it was so insulting. 'Your refusal to suspect him', Herbert wrote, 'places you in a highly invidious position.'

That phrase was haunting; for it touched on Mr Quarrendon's attitude towards Francis, which had always struck me as mysterious. Now it became more so; it was impossible to find out what he felt about his nephew, whom he never discussed. It was as if he had put up a shield against him; and that made for an inexplicable uneasiness.

Meanwhile, neither Herbert nor Eliza was aware of my personal dilemma. For now I faced the fact that Mr Quarrendon was not considering marriage; and it seemed that the alternative to rejecting a dishonourable offer was that of departure from Pond House. I was not as horrified by the contemplation of such a choice as I should have been before I knew him, because our relationship had brought me a profounder knowledge of myself. Yet its outcome was impossible to think of without suspense, secret tears, irrational joy and wild conjecture. To lie awake or walk up and down, muttering, 'What shall I do, what *can* I do?': vainly to seek support from a source that seemed to be drying up: to sustain an outward calm that might at any moment give way: to continue my efforts for the children – all these ordeals, however painful, engendered an almost maniacal energy. As I surmounted one obstacle after another I felt an extraordinary consciousness of power, an intermittent hope. He needed me. I lived in his moods; whether destructive or exhilarating, they were the mainspring of our days.

And now the background of the Hall, inescapable in its beauty and decay, began to obsess me as it absorbed him, whether we visited it or not, dwelt on or avoided it in conversation. At the same time a pleasure-dome, a goal and a trap, it dominated thought and action; as I remembered once negligently remarking that one might well imagine living there, the vision of such an apotheosis began to float before me in a golden haze.

One rainy afternoon, I escaped from it to find Mr Quarrendon at the hall window, his arms folded, looking out. Without turning round, he said, 'I have just had a visit from the Langs. Arabella is concerned – for you.'

In the pause that followed I was aware only of a gilt-framed watercolour, that of a spider orchid; springing out of shadowed grasses, it slowly enlarged itself, sank to a blurred pinpoint and then seemed to move, creeping nearer and nearer. With its retreat my reply came quite naturally. 'I can guess why. She wanted to put the general view.'

'The spokeswoman?'

'I suppose so.'

'Because she meant well?'

'Possibly. But the general view does not affect me.'

He turned. 'It should. The present situation won't do.'

'There's no alternative,' I said loudly, and sat down, staring at the carpet. Its colours were harsh; I seemed to be looking at them for the first time.

'You are not as happy here as you were at first,' he presently began, 'and not only because the situation has changed. I am beginning to realize that I sometimes weary and irritate you. I must mend my ways. But I can only ask you to be patient – to wait a little. Can you do that?'

'I will try.'

'We are approaching a crisis. Till it's behind us – ' With an impatient gesture he walked away. 'Wait. I ask you to wait.'

'I must, if you say so.'

'And don't watch me!' he exclaimed – adding, as if to himself, 'But I suppose that's too much to ask. All the same – now what's happening? Who's that?'

I got up and looked out of the window. 'It's the Granger boys, they were to have tea with Francis.'

'Keep them out of my way, all of them,' he said hoarsely, strode into the library and banged the door. I saw him no more that day, nor for dinner. He left no message as to his whereabouts, or as to the time of his return.

That night was peaceful and tearless; waking late, I came down to a solitary breakfast, and was waylaid by Mrs Waring as I went up to the schoolroom. Stringham had seen Cripps in the orchard, and she was afraid that he might be 'after' Miriam or Grace. 'Those girls can't be trusted,' she went on, 'and though Alice has been walking out with Fred Bownall these two years, I'm worried for her as well, so I come to you, Miss, as Master's gone away.'

Accepting this news as though I already knew it, I agreed to meet Stringham, who was waiting for me in the library. 'I think it was the brother, Alfred,' he said, 'but he'd gone before I could get hold of him. And now' – producing a grubby envelope – 'he's left this for yourself, Miss.'

'For me? I've never set eyes on him,' I said, dropping the note on the nearest table.

Stringham's healthy colour darkened; he cleared his throat before replying, 'I doubt he's written on account of his licence for the races.'

'That's no affair of mine – ' I began, and paused as Stringham shifted his feet, avoiding my eye.

'No, Miss. It was Master got the Committee to take it away.'

216

'But what can I do?'

'I'm sure I couldn't say,' replied Stringham after another silence. 'Unless – well – he was to think you'd speak for him.'

'I should not dream of it.'

'No, Miss.'

'Next time you go into Belminster, please return this – unopened.'

'Very good, Miss.'

We stood looking at the note. Then I said, 'Mrs Waring is afraid for the girls. But she thought it was the other, the one who was groom here.'

'That's Jim, Miss. The one who brought this is Alfred.'

'Leave the note for the present. I think Mr Quarrendon should see it, then he can advise me. Is there anything else?'

'No, Miss, except for Miriam. She's afraid of Jim Cripps, you see.'

'I will speak to her. But now, Stringham – you have been here much longer than I. Cannot these two be got rid of, somehow or other?'

Stringham shook his head. 'Master would have to buy them out. And I don't see as how he'd care to throw good money away, after what he's spent already.'

'Already? What do you mean?'

'I thought you knew, Miss. Master gave Alfred Cripps the money for The Waggoners. But that was before you came here,' he went on, as I stared at him. 'And they say as he's done well enough to pay for the tenancy, interest and all. It doesn't seem right, does it?'

'That will be all, Stringham. Leave the note, please.'

I took up the letter, then let it fall. Presently I put it away. It would be better – safer – to read it with Mr Quarrendon, because of course he would be able to explain everything. Half an hour later, I began to go through Francis's English lesson, an essay on the prayer for the day. Its title – 'Keep us, O Lord, in all our doings' – struck me as so ludicrously apt that I burst out laughing.

Slowly, the morning went by till it was time for luncheon. After that, I decided to read the letter. It ran, 'Miss, this is a good plais, I ask you to speak for us for the lisen and oblige, yrs respecful A. Cripps.'

The opening seemed familiar. But that was all part of a blind, bewildering struggle against something unrecognizable which drove me out to walk in the orchard. Then I saw Stringham coming towards me. I went to meet him. He said, 'I did wrong, Miss, I'm afraid, telling you about that money. It was Jim Cripps let it out one evening when he was the worse. No one was to know, he said. But he's told others, so I thought you knew.'

As the sentences were uttered in jerks, my breathing became uneven. Gazing at Stringham's anxious face, I was silent, debating how to get away from him. At last I said, 'It doesn't matter. You are not to blame.' Realizing that I had not said the words aloud, I went on, 'No blame – ' so emphatically that he came nearer, then retreated. He said, 'Are you all right, Miss?'

I muttered something about the cold. He glanced up at the sky. Then I was able to walk past him, towards the house. He stood looking after me.

Later that afternoon Francis, meeting me in the hall, said, 'Aren't you going to get ready, Aunt Anne? We were having tea with Mr and Mrs Portman-Sinclair.'

Before I could reply, Sybilla, followed by Nurse, came in from the garden, exclaiming, 'Me too, I'm coming,' and was set aside by Francis with 'You're much too little, and you're not asked,' upon which she flung herself on the floor in an outburst of sobs. By the time she had been pacified with promises of tea in the garden and was being coaxed upstairs, the dog-cart had appeared and I hurried to my room. I came down to find Francis in the driving-seat and the cob increasingly restive. As I took the reins from him he said, 'If you'd remembered in time, we could have ridden there,' with a hint of reproach, adding, 'Blue Peter's nice and frisky today.'

'That is why I don't want you to ride him unless String-ham is with you.'

'Or Uncle Neville.'

'He can't – he will not always be able – you must have Stringham,' I said, uneasily aware that I was speaking too sharply.

'But Uncle Neville's a wonderful rider.' I said nothing, and he went on, 'Of course, he might not always want to come with me.'

After a short silence I began, 'You must not worry your uncle. Wait for Stringham, or me.'

'Well, but suppose he asks me – '

'Francis! Please don't make a piece of work about your riding, or we shall regret we ever let you begin,' I burst out, so violently that he stared at me in dismay. I pulled the cob into a walk, glanced at his downcast expression and leaned back, loosening the collar of my jacket. At last I said, 'What time is it? Are we late?' and was reassured. As we entered the drive I went on, 'Don't worry about your riding. I will see to it, but you must ask me – always – no one else. Do you understand?' and received a puzzled assent.

Much to my relief, we found Mr and Mrs Portman-Sinclair alone; Augusta and Major Briggs were visiting his relations. Claude Lang then arrived, without Susan, who had gone to London to see about her trousseau. Mrs Portman-Sinclair, thoughtful for others now that her daughter was, as she believed, happily disposed of, asked me if I was quite well, with real concern. It had not occurred to me that my looks might betray my state of mind; and I was further disturbed by the raging hunger that swept over me with the appearance of tea. But I was in the right company. If we had been visiting the Langs, their spare habits would have made for hesitation. The solid out-lines of the Portman-Sinclairs consorted with my craving; so I ate and drank avidly, was soon able to converse in an ordinary manner and even to show interest in Claude Lang's additions to his rock-garden, which he described at length.

'But this cannot amuse you, Francis,' said Mrs Portman-Sinclair. Turning to her husband, she went on, 'Why do you not take him to see the hound puppies you are walking?'

'I suppose', that gentleman put in, 'that you will be out next season, now that you have become a rider.'

'I don't think I shall be allowed to, sir,' Francis replied as they disappeared.

We were halfway round the garden when Claude Lang said abruptly, 'Your nephew is a very intelligent boy. Was his brother equally so?'

Mrs Portman-Sinclair, rather put out by this casual reference to a painful subject, waited for me to answer, and then began to outline her plans for a rockery. Claude persisted in his inquiries, which I answered briefly enough. Then he said, 'A riding accident, eh? It doesn't seem to have made Francis nervous. I caught sight of him on horseback on the downs the other day.' As I remained silent he went on, 'He'll come to no harm there,' in an omniscient tone.

'He is not allowed out alone – ' I began, intercepting Mrs Portman-Sinclair's warning look, which Claude disregarded, repeating, 'No harm out of doors – except for mole-hills.'

'His uncle and aunt must decide,' said Mrs Portman-Sinclair repressively, and Claude reverted to her gardening schemes. After what seemed a very long time, Francis and his host rejoined us, and we were able to leave.

I urged the cob forward, and managed to prevent myself refusing irritably when Francis asked if he might take the reins. As we came indoors he said, 'Are you really not well, Aunt Anne? We needn't read if you're tired.'

Bending to kiss him, I replied, 'Perhaps not tonight. Will you read to Sybilla for me?' and he nodded and ran upstairs.

Solitude was not achieved until after dinner; having sent away the tea-tray, I sat by the library window, trying to accept Mr Quarrendon's disappearance. The suspense was becoming unendurable. Then, remembering the children, a plan came to me, admirable in its simplicity.

I looked at the clock. It was not yet the servants' bed-time; they were probably still at supper. As soon as I had decided how best to put it, I would tell Waring to summon Nurse, and then announce our departure for Suffolk, there to stay until Mr Quarrendon came to fetch us back. The thought of his displeasure was at the same time a consolation and a stimulus. I rang the bell. Waring appeared. There was a short silence.

'Yes, Miss?'

'I rang – didn't I?'

'Yes, Miss.'

'Nurse – is she there?'

'She went upstairs, Miss. Should I fetch her?'

'Not yet. Soon.'

After a pause he said, 'Shall I bring in the tray, Miss? Would you be wanting the port – or some tea?'

'Wine. Bring the wine.'

'The white Burgundy?'

'Was that what I had just now – at dinner?'

'Yes, Miss.'

'Bring that, please.'

Reappearing, he said, 'And Nurse – should I fetch her to you now?'

'Yes. No. Later.'

'Very good, Miss.' He adjusted the tray and went out.

He had put a plate of biscuits beside the wine. I ate one; then I drank, slowly, thirstily, yet tasted nothing. Refilling my glass, I went over the orders for Nurse and the Warings, and resolved to give them out in the morning. For there was no need to hurry; we could leave in two or three days' time, after my own staff had been warned of our arrival. That entailed a letter to Ellen or Lucy; and as I tried to remember which was the elder, the wine-glass was emptied again.

It would be best to let the Pond House servants think that their master knew of the move – and also that I knew where he was; this required further thought. After deciding to say that he had left for London, it occurred to me that he might have told Stringham where he was going, on the way to the station: an unexpected complication. It seemed to throw up a barrier between me and the pale gold of the decanter.

It was not until I reached my room and was undressing that the picture of its being cleared away – empty – rose before me. Some hours later, I saw that my bedroom candle had sunk to the socket, and blew it out. Presently I began to dream.

I was packing a trunk – not mine, but a very large one I had never seen – with earth; and gradually I realized that I was stuffing into it the contents of a huge molehill. No sooner had I pressed down one handful than it was necessary to collect another; and all the while both trunk and molehill remained as before, one half-full, the other barely affected.

And then the molehill began to move, heaving and bubbling, as if it were alive – or as if some dreadful creature was trying to get out and spread itself over me. I was very cold: yet I could not move; and now the trunk was sliding away. Struggling, moaning, I called for help – and started up.

The bedclothes had fallen to the floor. The window was open, and the curtains were blowing inwards; the whole room seemed to be swaying back and forth in a light from below; and then I remembered that I had left the hall door ajar and forgotten to turn out the lamp; its rays were streaming over the lawn.

I dragged on a dressing-gown and went downstairs. As I turned out the lamp I saw that the library was still lit up. There, I sank down, staring at Mr Quarrendon's desk, which was as he had left it, piled with papers and ledgers. It would please him if he returned to find everything in order; and as I began to tidy it, I leaned forward. My hands, pressing down, released the spring of a secret drawer.

It was full of letters without envelopes – and the top one

was in Cecilia's writing. In her thick, sprawling hand – I used to tease her about it – I read, 'My own darling Neville – be kind to Anne. She will love you, as I do. She will understand why – '

That was all that could be seen. I took up the letter, unfolded it and read to the end.

8

'Isn't it kind of him?' Francis exclaimed. 'Now I can go there whenever I like. You won't mind?'

'Not at all, as long as you don't ride on the downs.'

'I'll walk, it's only a little way. Look at the key, Aunt Anne, isn't it enormous? But I don't understand why it's called a folly. It seems to me such a sensible thing to build. In Uncle Neville's book on them, it says the owners hardly ever went inside. What a waste.'

'There's one near me that I believe was never used: a temple. It's falling to pieces.'

'When are you going to take us to Little Glemham? You said you would before I went to school.'

The bowl of gloxinias I had been arranging looked incomplete, and I began to augment it with sprigs of honeysuckle; as if absorbed, I replied vaguely, 'I don't know, dear. Some time soon.'

'It would be rather a pity to go just when Uncle Neville comes back. If we went while he's away' – he glanced at me hopefully – 'he wouldn't be so much missed.'

'You miss him?'

'Don't you?'

'Now and then.'

'When is he coming?'

'Oh – before very long.'

'I suppose he's abroad.'

'There – that's done. Will you carry these vases for me into the library?'

As we left the alcove I used as a flower-room, Francis reverted to Colonel Hay's loan. 'You know,' he added confidentially, 'I could have broken in through the ground-floor window. I'm glad I didn't. Unless you want me, I thought I'd go there this afternoon – ' and consent given, he ran off.

I was on the point of calling him back. The rearrangement of all the flowers in the house had been an inadequate distraction, and his independence came at the wrong moment. Yet it must be endured, and the remembrance of what could only be described as Cecilia's subjugation faced.

Her letter, undated, had been written when she knew that she had not long to live; and the second will was not mentioned. Her circumstances seemed to have prevented an immoral relationship; for she was in the hands of nurses and doctors when she made that last request. Yet the fact that there were no other letters from her in the secret drawer did not entirely confirm her innocence; for he might have destroyed them; and her concealment of her state of health from me could not but add to my suspicions. Nevertheless, his connection with the second will was not, and probably never would be, proved. Herbert, Lucretia and Eliza Trevy would have seen this discovery as conclusive. Imagining their comments, I tried, vainly, not to do so.

Meanwhile, I could only wait, between hope and fear, for his return. I told myself that keeping a watch on Francis was unreasonable, and might result in the loss of his affection. My attempts to control this instinct were more successful than resistance to his uncle's power; for now I knew all its strength and all its dangers – and saw no escape. To leave Pond House, with or without the children, was out of the question.

One Sunday afternoon, Francis told me that he had met Jim Cripps walking on the downs with a girl. 'Which one?' I said sharply. When he replied that he had never seen her before, I went on, 'You are to keep out of his way, do you understand?'

'I don't want to bother with him. He's a bad lot, Stringham says.'

'You know I don't like those stable-hand expressions.'

226

'I'm sorry, Aunt Anne. But you see, riding so much with Stringham, one gets into the way of it.'

'I will give you that point,' I said, and we both laughed. So Francis and I rode out together; like much else that I had once enjoyed, these expeditions became an effort.

Because I dreaded the nights, the days went by with alarming rapidity; alternating between enforced wakefulness and haunted sleep (the laudanum left by Eliza soon gave out), self-control seemed to be slipping away, and increasingly irksome duties – the children's lessons, consultations with the staff – sometimes abandoned. When Mrs Waring said, 'I'm sure you should see Doctor, Miss, about those headaches,' I promised to do so, later, presently, guiltily aware how meaningless those too frequently used words had become. And then, after nine days, his telegraphic message arrived.

It was delivered during a visit from Arabella Lang who, having watched me while I read it, left the tea-table and went to the window, as if to show an access of tact. When I said, 'It is from your cousin, he returns tonight,' she replied, 'Good news indeed, how glad he will be to get home,' turning to stare at me.

Afterwards, alone once more, I felt hot and sick. When Waring came to clear away, I told him the news, adding, 'Send the brougham, it may rain,' in a harsh, uncertain voice. His quiet 'Very good, Miss,' sounded like a reproof, and I went on, 'Or the dog-cart, what do you think?' in a casual manner, and did not hear the answer.

As I sat wondering whether I had remembered to say that we must dine late, Francis came in, followed by Sybilla. We went into the garden; he suggested that we should play Grandmother's Steps. With a little help, Sybilla won the first round. She pretended to be frightened; I really was. A game embodying suspicion, stealth and terror had become symbolic.

Later, Francis and I settled down to the last chapter of *Kenilworth*. As I shut the book, he said, 'Well! Poor Amy. But she should have suspected Varney more, don't you think so? "Is the bird caught? Is the deed done?" I should like to act that. Jack and Tom and I could do it for our next entertainment.'

'And you would be Amy Robsart?'

'Oh, I expect so, we'd have to see. The staircase would be the difficulty.' I left him reading the passage, too absorbed to notice my escape.

The next few hours were got through somehow. Waiting, listening, I dared not look at the clock as I walked from the library to the hall and back again. Then Waring came in to say that the brougham had returned – empty. What orders had I for Stringham?

'There's another train, there must be!'

'No, Miss. That was the last.'

'I never heard the carriage.'

'He drove straight round to the stables, Miss. Should I serve dinner?'

'Yes – at once,' I said, and walked into the dining-room. There, I had to wait for the first course – and eat and drink – and so escape again.

Concealment – refuge from observation – drove me to my room. I locked the door, sat down and shut my eyes. Rage held me; he should be punished for this victimization. Then the thought of an accident, or of a sudden illness, rose in an icy glare; it yielded to furious resentment, and thus to self-disgust, self-accusation. For I alone was to blame; weakness and folly were leading into sin; and that quicksand was closing over me. Still, I listened – and heard the sound of horse-hoofs on the drive.

I ran to the window. He had dismounted and was looking round. Stringham came forward and led away the horse. As the front door opened I rushed downstairs. Then I was in his arms.

Afterwards – again and again since that moment – I tried to remember how long it was before we were sitting on the drawing-room sofa. He had held down my head and now, his arm round my waist, was helping me to lean back. As the giddiness diminished I heard his voice; the words were meaningless. I gasped out, 'What happened? Where have you been?' and made nothing of the answer.

After another interval he got up, returning with a cup of water. I said, 'That's from the tea-tray – ' and he replied, 'I know, it's still warm, but it must do for the moment – ' and taking out his handkerchief, wiped my forehead. Then he sat back, looking at me. As I tried to rise he held me down; his hand on mine, he added, 'You did not get my message, but that was not my fault.' I shook my head, and he went on, 'I arrived by an earlier train than the one Stringham met, went to the Arms and sent to him from there to fetch me. The Boots must have missed him. When I realized that he had gone home, I hired a mount and rode here.'

'I thought – an accident. Something dreadful.'

'I'm so very sorry. How do you feel now?'

'Better. But how – weren't we in the hall?'

'I carried you in here when you fainted. Now – let me get you some wine.'

'No.'

'A vinaigrette? There's one in the library.'

'No, thank you.'

'There must be something I could do for you.'

'You were away for a whole week – I didn't know where. Or how long it would be.'

He withdrew his hand and looked at the floor, frowning, as if to make up his mind. Then he said, 'I apologize. It was inconsiderate. But we did agree, I think, that I might sometimes leave you in charge – '

'Without a word! I never agreed to such a thing!'

'If I had stayed on, I should of course have written to you, as I did before. This time – I don't know. Thinking of you, I forgot to write. It didn't seem necessary.'

'What nonsense – do you expect me to believe you?'

'Perhaps not. It's true, all the same.'

A long silence fell. At last I muttered, 'It's no good – I shall never get the better of you.'

'Do you want to?'

'Yes – because I have been to blame. Everything – all I had, at least – is poisoned.'

'Poisoned?'

'You think I'm hysterical.'

'Not at all. But I don't understand.'

'Why did you set up Alfred Cripps at The Waggoners? As a bribe?'

He raised his head and looked across the room. 'I suppose you might call it that – yes,' he said smiling.

'You had employed him?'

'In a sense.'

'In Switzerland?'

'There, and elsewhere.'

'And his brother?'

'As he also was in my service, I had to provide for them both – for your sake.'

'Mine? What can you mean?'

He rose, and thrusting his hands in his pockets, paused by the fireplace; he looked at the clock, took out his cigarcase, and glancing at me, raised his eyebrows. As I made some sort of gesture, he lit the cheroot and drew on it. Then he said, 'As you have found out so much in my absence, it's best that you should hear the whole story. Because it concerns your sister, I wished to keep it from you. The Crippses were working in Vevey when I last stayed there. The elder, Alfred, was engaged to her maid, Marie-Louise. Cecilia told her, and she told Alfred, that we were going to run away together. When Cecilia died, Cripps threatened to tell you, and so blackmailed me. Naturally I did not want you to know of this – scheme – and for a reason which, even now, I would rather keep to myself. However – Cecilia was deluded. I had no intention of eloping with her; but in the circumstances I could not tell her so.'

'Because she was going to die?'

'Exactly. But as she had confided in the maid, and the maid in Cripps, and he then held this sword over me, I decided to pay up. Now, at least, I need no longer do so.'

In the pause that followed I realized that the coordination of this statement with what I already knew was beyond me. I then told him about Cecilia's letter, adding, 'I did not mean to spy on you. But this blackmailing – why should Alfred Cripps think that you would want to prevent my knowing that she hoped to run away with you? I might not have cared.'

'What she told me of you convinced me that, knowing it, you would almost certainly have blamed me, and refused to come here and help with the children. I could not risk that, I needed you. Till we met, I did not realize how much.'

'You wanted me here so that you could come and go as you pleased.'

'I don't deny that that was so. But now – do you really believe that I am simply making use of you?'

'Sometimes. This last week, I did.'

'And yet you stay on – for the children.'

'They need me.'

'Of course, you've seen to that. Their dependence on you is essential. That is' – he paused – 'buying love, rather than giving it.'

'That's not true!' I exclaimed. 'You don't understand. Cecilia was not always – she didn't know how to care for them as I did.'

'So you stepped in, and now they can't do without you. The fact remains that you had to make yourself – *yourself* – indispensable. I've watched you, I've seen it.'

'That's a cruel and mischievous thing to say! You know that I care for them.'

'Yes, as one cares for a possession – an achievement.'

As I stared at him, bewildered, aghast, I found nothing to say. He said, 'Why buy love, when you can have it free? Have you never thought that it's there, waiting? Listen' – as I began to protest – 'stop thinking of Francis and Sybilla as your raison d'être, your responsibility. The role of the perfect foster-mother will bore you in the end.'

'Even if you were right – and you're not,' I burst out, 'what's the alternative?'

There was a short silence. Then he said, 'Taking what you might value more – here, with me.'

'In the intervals of your disappearing when you happen to feel like it?'

'We might disappear together.'

'That's impossible.'

'I meant after Francis goes to school. Even you could trust Nurse and the Warings to look after Sybilla – unless you were afraid that she might learn to do without you.'

'You accuse me of hateful motives, and yet you expect me to do everything you want. I ought not to listen to you.'

'But you will – won't you?'

'Only because I can't leave this house unless you make me.'

'My dear child, why should I?'

'You threatened it.'

'Not seriously.'

'How am I to know when you're serious, and when you're – you're – '

'On my knees to you? It's you who call the tune.'

'Then why do you accuse me of what you call buying love? It's not only untrue, but a complication of something quite simple and ordinary. I've helped to care for those two ever since they were born.'

'And so they learned to depend on you.'

'What is wrong with that, pray?'

'Nothing – except that you have cut yourself off in the process.'

I stood up, shaking. 'From what? What have I missed?'

'I hardly like to tell you, when you look so angry,' he said, leaning back, his eyes on my face. 'It daunts me.'

'I don't believe you.'

'Ah – that's what I was afraid of. And when you describe love, of whatever kind, as something quite simple and ordinary, I don't know how to answer; because my experience – of marriage, for instance – has shown me that it's not so.'

'Neither of your marriages concerns me.'

'No – but another one might,' he said coolly, and getting up, stood facing me.

I tried to answer. No words came. I drew away, more frightened of myself than of him. Then, slowly, because my gown had suddenly become too tight and too long, I got to the door and went out.

I came down to breakfast to find him with Waring, who was saying, 'I think that is the case, sir – it's in the *Belminster Record* – ' glancing at the folded sheet as he began to wait on me.

'And I suppose', his master gloomily replied, 'that he won't leave until I have seen him. Give me five minutes, and then send him in.' As Waring went out he continued, 'It's Bownall, at his most tyrannical. Before he comes, I want to hear that you forgive me. I meant to leave London much sooner than I did. But I'll tell you about it later.'

'So that was where you were.'

'I am truly repentant. Are you still angry with me?'

'Of course not,' I said hurriedly. 'I was confused – and taken aback. Do you mean to see Bownall in here?'

'Yes – with your support.'

After an interchange of salutations the bailiff took up his stand with his back to the windows. His master, indicating the newspaper, said, 'You have come about the sale of the Priest's Way meadow, I suppose.'

'Yes, sir. If I might be so bold as to ask for your word now, I could get to the estate office before noon. There'll be others after it, as I think you know.'

'Of course I know. But on second thoughts, I don't want to bid for it, why should I?'

Bownall paused, gazing at the ceiling, as if in appeal to a higher power. 'It's not for me to go against your wishes, sir. But that meadow land – well – ' he shifted his feet, taking a firmer stance – 'you may have forgotten, for I'm aware as you've other things to think of, is the best bit of pasture in the county. Far and wide, as I may say, you'll not see another like it, no, not if you was to go over and over.'

233

'It's too dear. You've seen the reserve price?'

'Yes, sir. But I've reason to believe that that's as may be,' Bownall replied, lowering his voice to a conspiratorial tone.

'What do you mean?'

'There's reasons.'

'Whatever they may be, I don't want the land – unless of course it was to go for a peppercorn fee, and that's not in question.'

'Well, sir – if I might make so free – ' Bownall broke off, as one in awe of a stern master.

'Go on.'

'You might regret it, all your days, if you let it go to that Belminster Syndicate. Suppose they was to build there – what then?'

'Are they bidding?'

'That was the talk at The Waggoners.'

'You were there?'

'Not me, sir, no. It was our Fred heard it.'

'But really, Bownall, I don't think we need it,' Mr Quarrendon expostulated, visibly weakening.

'So I've not your leave to go to th' auction, even?'

'Go, by all means. Bid, if you insist – but not a halfpenny more than the figure you persuaded me to.'

Bownall sighed. 'We should have that pasture, sir, if you wish the place to make a fair return. But there – it's just what they call a hobby, I reckon.'

'You know as well as I do that I don't go in for hobbies of that kind, I can't afford it.'

'It's the return I think of,' said Bownall with melancholy resignation. 'But I'm ready to stand there, dumb, while others gets a bargain – *and* profits.'

'Dumb – at an auction? I can't imagine it.'

The bailiff, ignoring this attempt at humour, shook his head and glanced at me, with the result that I began to see myself as a subversive influence.

'Well – ' said his master in an exhausted voice, 'you can go up by another two hundred and fifty.'

I should say – but it's all according – that a good *round*

sum' – with encouraging emphasis – 'should come a bit higher. As it might be, well, three hundred.'

'Make it ten, why not?' exclaimed Mr Quarrendon irritably.

'No, sir, no, I know my duty. Adding on five, now, that's reasonable. But it'll go for less than your limit, mark my words. That Syndicate chap's timid. Afraid of his masters.'

'Won't there be other bidders?' I put in.

'Why yes, Miss, one or two no-account farmers. But there – I'd best not go, as Master don't wish it.'

'Go – and you can raise my price by four hundred. Take something in the kitchen before you leave – and ruin me – ' Mr Quarrendon added as the door closed. We looked at one another: and began to laugh.

9

' "And they will deceive every one his neighbour, and will not speak the truth; they have taught their tongue to speak lies, and weary themselves to commit iniquity. Thine habitation is in the midst of deceit ... " '

As I leaned back, my arm round Sybilla, I was listening to the sound rather than to the words. Francis, having found the chapter, had ceased to follow it, and was watching his uncle, whose head and shoulders, darkly sculptured above the lectern, had a formidable effect. His tone was resonant and slightly nasal. With 'Here endeth the First Lesson,' he paused to stare down the aisle.

As the service continued, so did my doubts about his being blackmailed by Alfred Cripps; yet although it was too far-fetched an explanation to be entirely credible, it could not be altogether dismissed. That Cecilia's love for him had conjured up the chimera of an elopement was in character; for as girls we had often indulged one another's tendency to romanticize; and she had never lost the habit.

Perhaps I had not either; and now, dwelling on his brusque mention of marriage, I might be similarly deluded. A younger, bolder woman would have asked him, *sans phrase*, what he meant, what he wanted. I could do neither; nor could I contemplate bringing up the matter of the second will. Moving in a phantasmagoria of disbelief and credulity, doubt and hope, I was lost, groping, helpless; his spells, whether consciously cast or not – and to know even that would have cleared the atmosphere – prevailed.

As we all settled down for the sermon, I glanced at him, and was afraid, then rejected the thought of danger as odious and absurd. With the blessing, came the resolve to tax him on one point, at least. I forgot to do so when, late in

237

the afternoon, we were walking through the woods to Limmerston Hall.

'As Craik had brought Ida, I stayed on,' he concluded. 'It was too good a chance to miss. He was in a surprisingly reasonable frame of mind.'

'Ida?'

'His daughter. He has placed her in a finishing school at Ascot. He stayed to see her settled, driving down there every day. We spent several evenings together. He has asked me to have an eye to her, as well as to the Hall.'

'And you agreed?'

'I might. The trouble with him is that he never makes a decision. He was on the point of leaving several times before he eventually went.'

'So nothing was decided about the Hall.'

'I am not sure,' he said after a pause. 'His circumstances have changed.'

We had passed the lodge gates and were walking up the drive. Sunlight drenched the façade in deepening gold; the figures on the roof stood out, darker and more solid. 'Wait,' I said, 'I like best to look at it from here,' and withdrew my arm from his.

Standing there in silence, we were united in tranquil pleasure; so bound, disagreement, perturbation, fear and shock lost their power, then ceased to exist. For the magic of the Hall was benignant, all-embracing. It held a promise; and that emboldened me to ask, 'Have Sir Charles's circumstances brought him to the point of considering a sale?'

'He has come into money, a fortune, in fact, so he's richer than ever.' What seemed to me a sentence of doom was pronounced with perfect composure; trying to speak as calmly, I asked what Sir Charles's plans were. 'I don't think he has any for this place. He said something about buying a larger villa, and refurbishing his house in Paris.'

'So he may never come back to England?'

'Who can tell? He's ruled by caprice,' was the answer, uttered in the same cool, detached tone, as we came into the atrium, to be greeted by Mrs Grant, who had just 'turned out' the principal bedrooms and desired Mr Quarrendon's approval.

She left us in the room of the Dowager's unmarried sister, which had been kept as if she were still alive. The four-poster, hung with amber brocade, was made up, the coverlet removed and the sheet turned down. Hand-mirror, brushes and combs were set out before the looking-glass. On the chimney-piece a blue vase containing paper roses was flanked by a pair of *potichomanie* ornaments and lustre figures of the four seasons. An enamel clock, a Bible and the miniature of a child were arranged on the bedside table. Miss Georgina's own watercolours and a needlework carpet completed the decoration of a room which was now a shrine.

I sat in the window-seat while my companion inspected its contents, pausing to take up the Bible, from which he removed a velvet marker. 'That's strange,' he said. 'She has underlined two verses. If you and I were superstitious, we should take them as a portent.' Then his smile became fixed; his hands shook a little, as he read out, ' "And thorns shall come up in her palaces, nettles and brambles in the fortresses thereof; and it shall be an habitation of dragons, and a court for owls. The wild beasts of the desert shall also meet with the wild beasts of the island, and the satyr shall cry to his fellow; and the screech-owl also shall rest there." Odd,' he continued, replacing book and marker. 'Did she foresee the desertion of her home? Or was she thinking of Lady Henrietta's ghost? According to the Grants, she haunts this room, weeping for her dead children. Perhaps she sounds rather like an owl, what do you think?'

'It's such a pretty, cheerful room. I can't imagine that.'

'A rooted sorrow,' he said, coming to sit beside me and staring at the floor.

'You never cease to surprise me,' I began. 'While Sir Charles's access of fortune leaves you unmoved, you're put out by those verses.'

'I know. Isaiah has an unpleasant gift for the *mot juste*. But it's something to have surprised you.'

'There are other problems.'

'Can I solve them?'

'You may not care to. However – I have thought that it might be Cripps and not Henry Craik who made that attempt on Sybilla by mistake for Francis.'

'Have you, indeed? And his motive?'

'I don't know. I felt, and I still do, that he is dangerous.'

'It seems to me', he said slowly, 'that your intelligence does not inform your feelings. I can't defend those two, as far as what you already know of them is concerned. But they are perfectly sane.'

'I don't deny that.'

'Well, then – why in the world should one of them attack either of the children? There was every reason, if one can call it that, for Henry Craik to do so.'

'You don't think Cripps let him escape?'

'He might have. But that cannot be connected with your suspicions.'

'Did you ever ask him about it?'

'Of course, and he denied everything.'

'I wish – I do wish – that you could get them out of the neighbourhood.'

'I am trying to,' he said gently. 'Give me time. Now – shall we look at the other rooms? The great bedchamber is rather fine.'

Here, the huge plumed and curtained bed stood on a dais; its hangings were of gold tissue, studded with semi-precious stones: cat's-eyes, tourmalines, topaz and turquoise. 'It is a German seventeenth-century piece,' said Mr Quarrendon. 'I believe Wyatt and his employer had quite a set-to about its being put here. But I find in it a sort of splendid vulgarity, such as Louis Quatorze might have appreciated.'

'Did Sir Charles's ancestor really sleep in it?'

'Oh yes, the goose-feather mattress is still there. But

come, let us go, I'm sure you've seen enough,' he added, and we went downstairs.

As we walked towards the fountain he asked me which of the bedrooms I liked best. 'The maiden lady's, it's so gay and pleasant. She must have loved all those things – even the *potichomanie* vases.'

'You can't imagine yourself in any of the others, the – ' he paused – 'the larger ones?' As I shook my head he went on, 'Married life there might also have been pleasant and gay.'

'We never looked at the nursery wing,' I said hastily.

'The children were relegated to the third floor, with their nurses.'

'So that if they were ill-treated, their parents didn't know?'

He laughed. 'The thought obsesses you – even in the case of dead and buried children. Is that why – but I won't go on. We have been happy here this afternoon, haven't we? Somehow, I don't believe it will become an habitation of dragons or a court for owls, with the satyr, whoever he may have been – perhaps he was rather like Cripps – crying to his fellow.'

'No – it's too beautiful to become evil or sinister.' My arm and hand were in his; he pressed them to his side as we sat beneath the nereids and the sea-horses. 'There's the new moon,' I said. 'We must wish, and turn our money. But I haven't any with me.'

'I have – a five-shilling piece. Will you have that, or a half-sovereign?' I took the gold, stood up, curtsied and gave it back. 'Keep it, for luck,' he said. 'But you should not have turned it in a glove – ' and he began to take both mine off, smoothing them out as he did so. The process was prolonged, and I wondered how often he had practised it.

'I shall not ask you to let me keep one,' he went on, 'but to lend it to me, so that next time I am in London I may make a better gesture. And I shall not ask your leave to do what should have been done long before this. So unless you can answer prettily, you had best not speak at all.'

I laughed and handed him the glove. We sat on in silence till the light began to fade. Then we walked slowly home.

Mr Courtenay dined with us that night, and as soon as we were alone spoke of his host's purchase of the Priest's Way meadow. 'Of course,' he said, 'although you gave a fancy price, it was well spent, at least I suppose so.'

'It is watered by a stream that has never dried up,' said Mr Quarrendon coldly; his glance at me indicated that the moment had come for my withdrawal. As I rose he went on, 'If I were to let it for building –' and was interrupted by a horrified protest. They were still discussing the point when they joined me; his curt replies to Mr Courtenay's objections made it clear that he did not wish me to know how much he had spent.

Next day he described Mr Courtenay as a tactless gossip who knew nothing of business, and added, 'Whatever Bownall's feelings, I intend to let a portion of the land to Burrows and Harding.'

'Not for building?'

'If you are taking his side, *I* shall have feelings – very disagreeable ones – so be warned.'

'I should not dare.'

'I don't trust you, I never have,' he said, taking my hand, 'but I am helpless, as you very well know.' His approach was more than usually disconcerting; it made another barrier between us and enhanced his mastery.

For the next few days he seemed to take pleasure in drawing attention to what he called my dangerous powers. I replied amiably enough until he remarked, 'And then, too, you are elusive.'

'So are you!' I exclaimed. 'It's all very well – but there must be a limit.'

'To what, pray?'

'To being charming – and secretive.'

'What do you want to know?'

Having got to the point of asking him about the second will, I was speechless. I muttered, 'It doesn't matter,' and walked towards the orchard, where Francis was making a tree-house. Mr Quarrendon let me go; I did not turn to look at him.

Francis, descending, then announced, 'I've had a great talk with Uncle Neville. He said I might tell you about it,' and described his uncle's plans for Sybilla's settlement from the sale of the villa. 'And of course,' he concluded, 'I shall see to that, it's only fair, she might get a richer husband if she had some money of her own, don't you agree, Aunt Anne? Aren't you pleased?'

'Indeed I am, my dearest boy. It's such a – such a – ' As he stared at me I managed to say, 'A relief.'

'Relief?'

'I did not mean that, exactly. I want it for her, just as you do.'

'Well, it's all arranged now, you see,' said Francis in a soothing tone. 'I must say, he thinks of everything.'

As soon as I had time to consider it, I realized the uselessness of passing on Francis's account of his uncle's actions to Herbert and Lucretia. I could imagine Herbert saying, 'Of course he thinks of everything,' with satirical emphasis. Triumph over their suspicions could only be effected by the climax of my relationship with the friend he had dared to vilify; and that must come soon; everything pointed to it. Yet self-discipline was now more necessary than ever before.

Repentance, thankfulness and the search for guidance entailed set times for communication, and for rereading what had lately been neglected. Turning from the Old to the New Testament, I found St Paul's admonitions too severe, and substituted the Acts for the Epistles as being a surer antidote to suspense, anxiety and the sudden attacks of horror I could neither define nor withstand. The course of such studies is generally arduous; mine did not always blot out the beckoning visions that drew me on against my will.

These obscured any contemplation of Francis's immediate future, which entailed his uncle's selection of a school; he had settled on a small establishment near London, returning from it with a report for my approval. 'He is too intelligent for an institution where they think more of games than of scholarship,' he said. 'I had thought of sending him to Belminster as a day-boy, but the standard is not high enough,' and he handed me a leaflet and some photographs.

'I will look at them as soon as I come back.'

'Where are you going?'

'To afternoon service, at St Saviour's.'

'On a weekday?'

'I have been doing so lately,' I said, uneasily aware of his cool scrutiny.

'Have you ordered the brougham?'

'I am driving myself in the dog-cart, and leaving it at the inn.'

'I will do that for you.'

'But during the service – '

'Do you object to my coming to that too?'

'Of course not. But Mr Clare's sermons are apt to be rather discursive.'

'I have heard him on the lost tribes, and on the journeys of St Paul. Before you came here, I was more enterprising,' and he took his gloves and hat from the hall table. As he did so, something rattled to the floor, and he picked up the Roman dagger. 'Who moved this?'

'I think Francis was using it for one of his dressing-up games; he should have asked leave.'

'He should indeed.'

'I will tell him – ' I began, and stopped to watch him test the blade; then he put it on top of a chest.

Driving back from St Saviour's, he described the school, breaking off to ask where Francis was. 'He went on one of his mysterious expeditions to the Belminster folly. I told him to be back for tea, as the Grangers are coming.' He said nothing; as he whipped up the cob, I added, 'We are in good time, they won't be there yet,' and he looked at me sideways, still without speaking.

Rather to my surprise, he drove straight to the stables, at the same speed, and jumped out as Stringham appeared. I thought he had forgotten to hand me down until he turned back to do so. As we walked towards the front of the house he said, 'I shall be late, I have letters, don't wait for me,' and preceded me indoors.

As I stood in the hall, trying to decide whether the bowl of sweet peas on the tea-table should be renewed, I was drawn back to St Saviour's. There, he and I had been isolated. Those rhythms of supplication and praise, the music, the patches of coloured light had created a microcosm in which the world of every day was forgotten, by me at least. That setting had been wonderfully serene. With the Grangers' arrival I returned to the struggle.

Mrs Granger's explanation of her sons' absence went on until we were seated. 'It is just as well', she continued, 'that dear Francis is not here, he would have been counting on them, but really, their father and I positively cannot let pass some kinds of naughtiness, so they have been sent upstairs to copy out the Lesson for the day. The hens, poor things, will probably not lay again for weeks, after being chased all over the yard and out into the garden. When it comes to Red Indians – '

'I hope we are to see your nephew,' the Rector put in, 'I have the book he wanted to borrow – '

' – their catapults have been confiscated – '

' – and a print on which I should like his uncle's opinion.'

'They will both be here quite soon. I'm sorry about the boys – and the hens.'

'I wished to consult our friend about this matter of a curate, now that Blow is retiring,' Mr Granger continued. 'I understand that the young man who used to tutor Francis – Lambton, is it? – has taken Orders. In that case, would Quarrendon recommend him?'

'Does he want to return to the neighbourhood?'

'He does indeed. Ah now, here you are, my dear fellow, just as we were saying – ' and after an exchange of greetings the inquiry was resumed.

Mr Quarrendon seemed not to hear it; he said, 'Is Francis back?' and I shook my head. He then began to cut the cake

245

– and went on cutting it till the slices covered the plate. Mr Granger said, 'Poor Blow, his health enforced this step. But as to young Lambton – '

'I can't imagine anyone less suited to the Church. Will you have some cake, Mrs Granger?'

'Thank you. Is he not serious, then?'

Mr Quarrendon, the plate of cake still in his hand, began to laugh. The Grangers stared at him. Then the Rector said, 'You don't think I should ask the Bishop to appoint him?'

'By all means, if you want someone subservient. Do take some of this, won't you?'

Mr Granger, who had just helped himself to bread and butter, looked rather puzzled. 'Presently, if I may. But has Lambton no qualifications? Or has he Puseyite tendencies?'

'None – no tendencies, Puseyite or other,' replied his host, helping himself to cake and then staring down at his plate as if he saw it for the first time.

'Dear me. His letter was most sincere.'

'That is his tendency, now I think of it – over-sincerity,' said Mr Quarrendon, leaning back, his eyes half-closed.

'I don't quite see – '

'What I mean is that he tends to ecstasize. It taxed my nerves, as I am sure it would yours. He may have a vocation – but – ' Drawing out his watch, he added, 'That boy is much too late,' glancing at me.

'Shall I send out to look for him?'

'No, no. Well, as to Lambton – but you are not eating – ' and again the cake was offered and refused.

As the conversation passed from the curacy to bulbs, then to bird-watching and so to lawn-mowers, unexplained dread, rising to fear, came over me. It would have been possible to send for Francis unobtrusively; I did not do so. Meanwhile, Mr Quarrendon's talk, now rapid, now disjointed, whirled about us. His high spirits should have reassured me; as I tried to think that they did, I glanced out of the window, and saw only the gardener and his boy, one with a box of plants, the other with a wheelbarrow; they stopped, blocking my view of the drive.

Cups were refilled; the conversation, now of book-collecting, became more animated. Mr Granger produced his print; his wife asked after Sybilla, adding, 'I am sure she will be very pretty one day. I remember Susan at that age –' and was no longer heard. Forcing myself to look at the clock, I realized how very late Francis was; and as he had been expecting his friends, that was odd. He might be waiting for them at the entrance to the drive; but this seemed unlikely. My hands shook; I had to use both to manipulate the urn.

Then I heard Mr Granger say to his wife, 'My dear – you are absurd –' in a tone of tender amusement that struck away my distraction. The picture of a happy married life, shared over more than twenty years, rose, shone, and slowly faded, unobtainable, on the far side of a gulf.

Resignation to single life had not always precluded a corrosive envy; such attacks were rare; this one ceased as Mr Quarrendon, glancing at me, said, 'This afternoon we deserted your parish for St Saviour's. But Clare can hardly be described as a rival, I should imagine?' turning to the Rector with a smile; his tone was that of someone expecting a malicious response.

'He is very hardworking,' Mr Granger replied. 'That his ritualism doesn't suit village people has never discouraged him. One can't but admire a man who –' He stopped as the door was flung open. Francis stood before us.

His appearance was received in silence; we sat gazing at him as if he had made a dramatic entry; and yet, apart from the fact that he was dirty, dishevelled and out of breath, he seemed much as usual. Looking from one to another of us, he began, 'I'm very sorry – how do you do, sir, I'd better not shake hands, it's not really my fault, I'll go and wash –' and was halfway across the room when Mr Quarrendon said, 'What have you been doing? Stay where you are,' in an exhausted, barely audible voice.

Realizing that he had been very anxious, and might now

be enraged, I tried to catch his eye in the hope of sparing Francis a scolding in front of the Grangers. His look, fixed on his nephew, was incredulous and horrified.

'I am most truly sorry, Uncle Neville,' Francis repeated. 'I did run all the way back. But you see, something rather extraordinary – ' His voice died away as he paused, held by that icy stare.

'Perhaps he had better go and wash, then he can tell us,' I suggested, and, silenced by a gesture, began to wonder to what extent my fears had been shared.

'No,' said Mr Quarrendon, 'you can do that when you have told us what has happened.' As Francis, rather intimidated, began, 'Well – ' and hesitated, he added, 'Go on – speak!' his voice rising.

'I went to the folly, you said I might.'

'You were alone there?'

'Oh yes, I've got the key,' Francis replied, as if rather surprised.

'Well?'

'Someone has broken in since I was there, through the window. I'm afraid Colonel Hay will be angry, but of course it can be mended – and – '

'Kindly tell us – briefly – what has happened.'

'Nothing very special, except that when I got to the top – ' Francis turned to me – 'It was rather funny, I mean odd, because I was thinking about Amy Robsart, my play, you know, and I had some matches, luckily, otherwise – well!' Suddenly radiant, he exclaimed, 'It was just the same, Aunt Anne! I went up the stairs, and then – there was nothing. That handrail on the top landing had been wrenched away, I looked down and saw it, right at the bottom. That's why I'm so dirty, you can't think what the dust was like.'

'Do you mean', the Rector put in, 'that if you had not struck a match, you would have gone on – and fallen?'

'Yes, sir, all the way down. You remember, in *Kenilworth* – '

'That's enough! Go and wash yourself,' said Mr Quarrendon.

Pausing in the doorway, Francis said, 'I climbed down lowly, and then I looked to see if I could find out who – I mean – ' Again he broke off, gazing round the table. He then left the room.

'Oh dear, what an escape, who could have done such a thing?' Mrs Granger exclaimed. 'If he had not had matches – '

'He always carries them,' I put in. 'Most boys do, I fancy.'

'Mine don't. If they had been there – but all is well.'

'Yes! Very well,' said Mr Quarrendon loudly. 'Saved – by a box of matches,' and silence fell.

'Boys of that age have nine lives, I have always said so,' Mr Granger began.

'Oh – nine – that's the minimum,' his host replied, and held out his cup to be refilled. As I reached for it, it slid from the saucer on to the tea-tray and broke in half. 'Leave it,' he said. Rising, he went on, 'We have all finished, I think? Be so good as to tell them that Francis will have tea upstairs – ' and opening the hall door, he waved the Grangers forward, with 'The garden now – as usual – ' and all three walked out into the sunshine.

I sat on, facing the wreck of the tray; for his cup had been almost full; tea was flowing over the edge into my lap.

As if wound up to move, I went to my room, changed my dress – and began to rearrange the gloves and handkerchiefs, already neatly piled, in the dressing-table drawer. This must have taken some time, for I set about it very deliberately. Returning to the hall, I found that the Grangers had left.

Then I knew what I had to do. Walking into the dining-room, I looked for the decanter. It had been moved from the sideboard to the table – and was empty. A tumbler, also empty, stood beside it in a pool of wine. The mess must be cleared up before Waring came in to lay for dinner. I stood there, staring in front of me.

10

'Mrs Waring wishes to know, please, Miss, what you'd
fancy for dinner. There's a nice drop of soup, she says, and
she's made some chicken patties.'

'Thank her, Alice, and say that I shall be down for
dinner at the usual time.'

'Then you mean to get up, Miss?'

'Certainly. It was nothing, just a little faintness.'

'When should I come to help you dress, if you please?'

'I will do that for myself. But you may put out the
lavender brocade.'

Looking round the room, which was filled with flowers –
not all from the garden, vases of bee-orchids and marsh
marigolds stood in the window – I took out Mr Quarrendon's note, but decided not to read it again. For his
concern about my collapse had brought me to the point of
wanting to protect him from my own hideous, and, as it
then seemed, evil suspicions. Those few lines had convinced
me that he had been as horrified as I was by the trap laid in
the folly.

Now, fearful conjecture and renewed trust must both
give way to a cool and unbiassed assessment. I felt sure of
being able to judge him without prejudice or emotion. His
power over me had ceased to operate, first with the advent,
and finally with the disappearance, of shock and terror.
Forty-eight hours of rest, isolation and prayer had brought
back the independence of mind I had unwittingly lost. All I
had to do was to announce my plan of taking the children
to Suffolk, and carry it out regardless of his authority. If he
forbade our departure, I should defy him. Nothing he
could say or do would alter my decision.

Standing by the library window, I saw my surroundings
much as when I first came to Pond House. The Roman

emperors, their eyes fixed on nothing, appeared slightly more forbidding, the marquetry bureau less suited to its setting, than before. Only the ranks of books seemed familiar and, somehow, welcoming. From the nearest shelf I took out a volume of poetry, opened it at random and began to read. 'I said – "Then, Dearest, since 'tis so" ' – and that former sense of intimacy was recalled: the echo of a spell, no more. Then the door opened. He came towards me, holding out his hands.

I took them without a tremor. He said, 'Should you really have come down? I can't regret it – but I am still anxious.'

'You need not be. I am quite recovered, as you see.'

'You look pale – ' he began, breaking off as dinner was announced.

He was rather silent during the first part of the meal; and it then occurred to me that he was still suffering from shock. His eyes were unusually brilliant and his pallor accentuated; idly, I noticed that he had had his hair cut and so brushed back as to add to his height, thus enhancing – did he know it? – the outlines of his profile. He described Francis's first lessons in Greek, Mrs Lang's calling with a doll for Sybilla, and his interview with the Bownalls about the cottages he intended to build, adding that he had nearly won them over to his plans.

As we ate, drank and talked, my resolve hardened, and with that came a renewal of strength and calm. Yet the impact of his appearance – as always, he looked his best in evening dress – although undiminished, was no longer disturbing; nor did the sound of his voice distract me from what I intended to say as soon as we were alone.

With dessert, the moment came. Then, reflecting that we should not be sitting on for more than half an hour or so, I began to watch his hands as he peeled a peach for me. He said, 'I have news about the attack on the folly. It was made by some gipsies, who have now been arrested. They camped there, and so were traced.'

'But Francis saw no signs of them?'

'No; I imagine he was too anxious to get home.'

'Have they admitted to breaking in?'

'Such people never admit to anything. The signs are unmistakable. A kettle – the ashes of a fire – they must have left in a hurry. But I have told Francis that he must not go there alone.'

'Are you certain – about the gipsies?'

He did not answer till he had placed the fruit before me. Then he said, 'You are not, it seems. Why?'

'I didn't know that gipsies camped on those downs.'

'Well, they have,' he said, smiling. 'Or are you going to tell me that they have been wrongly imprisoned, and that your chosen villain was the culprit?'

'I don't know what you mean.'

'Were you not thinking of Cripps?' I said nothing, and he went on, 'I can only tell you what the police have discovered. Ask Colonel Hay, if you like. I saw him this morning. In any case, the matter of the Cripps' departure is in hand. In a week or so, they will be gone.'

'I don't doubt what you say – but – '

'I think you do – sometimes,' he said, leaning forward to snuff the candles. 'I must put up with that, I suppose. Now – tell me how you feel. Have you been able to enjoy your dinner?'

'Yes, thank you.'

'The children have missed you. And so have I.'

'You speak as if I had been ill for weeks,' I said, rather disconcerted.

'Without you, this house – but that brings me to the next step in our lives.'

The last phrase shook me a little. At last I said, 'Please tell me what that is.'

'I have to go to London. Craik wants me to meet him there. But let us move to the library, and then I will explain. I hope you won't be displeased.'

My resolve to leave Pond House had now to be put forward. By the time the tea-tray had been placed between us, I was ready, waiting for him to speak first.

He stood by the fireplace, his cigar in one hand, the other

253

on the chimney-piece. 'The time has come', he began, 'for you to take Francis and Sybilla on that long-promised visit to Suffolk, where, I am sure, they have missed you almost as much as I shall, in London.'

Within a few seconds rage overcame astonishment. The power, the resolution that had enabled me to behave in a normal, friendly manner, were now destroyed. That independence of action was no longer possible – that the words had been taken out of my mouth – struck me into a furious silence. It seemed a long time before I managed to say, 'So you are getting rid of us,' in a thick, uncertain voice.

I was looking at the ground, my hands clasped in the folds of my gown; then I became aware that he was sitting opposite me. He said, 'But is not that what you wanted?' I did not answer, and he went on, 'Of course, if you would rather stay here, you are more than welcome to do so. The decision rests with you. But as I have to leave – '

'Yes!' I interrupted, 'and that's all you care for! He has only to raise a finger for you to be at his beck and call, in the hope of getting possession of that place. Nothing else matters – ' and I got up and walked away.

After a short silence he said gently, 'Why are you angry? Tell me.'

I knew the answer to that question. But to say, 'Because you care more for Limmerston Hall than for me,' would have been shameful and disgusting. Already, I felt myself ridiculous. At last I said, 'It doesn't matter. I was going to tell you that I intended to leave, with the children.'

'And I forestalled you. Is that an offence?'

'It's your disposal of me – and of them – that I object to.'

'But my dear – I have just told you, begged you, to do whatever you like.'

'It's very good of you. We will leave as soon as possible.'

'In anger?'

'I am well aware', I said, turning to face him, 'that I have neither right nor cause to be angry.'

'You have the right to be anything you like. I wish to please you.'

'You please too many people.'

'What an accusation,' he said as he got up, threw his cigar into the fireplace and took my hand. 'And it's not even true. I should explain that Craik has sent for me because he is coming over to see a doctor, a specialist. He has quarrelled with his man in Monte Carlo, and wants me to advise him. I said I would – do you blame me? I know a physician who might help him, that is, if anyone can.'

'Do you mean that he is seriously ill?'

He laughed. 'No, indeed, he is a hypochondriac of the first water. Now he thinks he's in a decline. It takes him that way sometimes. But if you object to my going, I'll stay here.'

'Of course you must go,' I said, withdrawing my hand.

'And I am forgiven?'

'There's nothing to forgive.'

'That's what people say when they are still angry. You have not forgiven me.'

We said no more for some minutes. Then I began, 'It was you who sent up those flowers – the bee-orchids and the marigolds?'

'Yes. I was trying to paint them; but I am out of practice.'

'Please show me the painting.'

He went to the bureau and drew out a small portfolio. 'I would like to give it you, if you care to accept it.'

I took the watercolour over to the lamp. 'I like it very much. It's – I can't quite think – serene.'

'And are you?'

'Yes.'

'That's a pity. Anger becomes you.'

'Please – '

'What?'

'I don't want compliments. Being cross makes me unhappy.'

'But being admired – needed?'

Taking up the sketch, I held it between us. 'You said that I bought the children's need of me, and their love, do you remember?'

'I did, and you do. But there are some kinds of love that can only be given. And I don't know, even now – ' he took the sketch and laid it on the bureau – 'whether you are a giver.'

'Are you?'

'I could be. But now we must have some wine.' He said no more till our glasses had been filled. 'I expect you remember', he went on, 'the Italian toast – "I drink to what I see in your eyes, and you to what you see in mine." '

'I see nothing,' I said, putting down the empty glass.

'No? Then we must try again.'

As we sat there, the decanter in front of us, I began to feel dizzy. I put my hand to my head – and drank again; and again the glass was refilled. Presently I got up; his hand was under my elbow. So we reached the door; I waited while he lit my candle. Then I said, 'I'm sorry I was angry. I wanted us to have a happy evening – because I suppose you will be away for some time?'

'I will let you know. That's a promise.' In the pause that followed I felt the tears rising. He said, 'I don't think I shall be away very long. And you will be glad to see your home again.' As I shook my head he went on, 'You need a change of scene. You are not quite recovered.'

'It's not that. I don't know – what I need.'

'A rest. Give Francis a holiday.'

'Very well.'

'Don't cry – please.'

'It's nothing – I mean, there's nothing to cry about, not really,' I said, turning away.

'So it's good-night?'

I nodded and stumbled upstairs. In my room I cried for a long time. When I came down next morning, he was gone.

Three days later, I had a letter from him, and after that, another. When we arrived, Nurse and the children and I, at

Little Glemham, a third was waiting for me. They were not long, but lively and amusing; one contained a drawing of himself and Sir Charles Craik which made me laugh. I used to reread them before I went to bed.

Meanwhile, it was reassuring to be surrounded by the treasures of the past; my father's portrait in the hall, that of my mother in the dining-room: their collections of Limoges enamels, Chelsea groups and Jacques Petit statuettes: the *ébéniste* furniture I had hitherto merely tolerated and now saw in the light of visits to Limmerston Hall: the feather and shell bouquets left me by an aunt whose work they were. But the rooms of Manor Farm ('Why do you call it that when it isn't one?' Francis asked) seemed small compared to those of Pond House, its Jacobean panelling rather sombre, and the garden too exposed to the wind from the heath.

Fortunately, the stream running below the house was so shallow that the children could play by and in it without supervision; and as the barn, combining stables and lodging for my gardener-coachman, was being re-thatched, they hung about it in the belief that they shared in the work. When Miriam joined the household as between-maid, there was no risk of my faithful Ellen and Lucy being overtaxed: and their welcome to her was tolerantly kind.

All the rooms had been filled with flowers, not very well arranged, in bowls and vases I decided to give to the next charity bazaar. The neighbours I liked best, a childless couple who wrote travel books, collected Palissy ware – and were not ornithologists – called very soon, and others followed; but as it was not the custom in that part of the county to entertain in the evenings, I dined in solitude, wondering whether I might not sink to meals on a tray when the weather called for a fire in the drawing-room.

Faced with the beaker of barley-water that had always been freshly made for this meal, I began to consider an innovation. The wine and port laid down by my father had been brought out only when Lucretia and her husband and, on one occasion, Herbert, came to stay. I hesitated to

I

send for them now; but when both Ellen and her sister commented on my altered looks ('You're that thin and pale, Miss Anne, we've been quite worried'), I had both decanted as being prescribed by the doctor. One glass at a meal was, in their view, the accepted quantity, and I thus confined myself for the first few evenings, increasing consumption by slow degrees and drinking coffee instead of tea. So a sleeping draught became necessary: and I renewed the supply of laudanum usually kept for Eliza Trevy.

Presently I realized that Mr Quarrendon and I had together drunk a great deal more wine during and after dinner than that now produced, and that I had been agreeably, if unwittingly, affected by it. Of course, he had not intended this; he must have forgotten, or did not even know, how abstemious most middle-aged women were. I had never drunk spirits and felt sure I should dislike them; but when an inspection of the cellar revealed the existence of some cherry brandy, I tried that, and found it palatable.

So the first week passed contentedly enough. Then Francis, who had rejoiced in having no lessons, became *désœuvré* and rather tiresome; he teased Sybilla, left books out of doors all night and tore up his Amy Robsart play. When questioned, he admitted missing the Granger boys; brought into contact with the son and daughter of the local doctor, he dismissed them as dull, silly and only interested in cricket, adding, 'I used to like playing, but with Mary and John Lawson it's hopeless, and they seem unable to do anything else. But of course,' he went on, 'I'll help you with them whenever you want, I suppose their parents have to get them out of the way sometimes.'

Then Sybilla, having insisted on coming to church, burst into tears during the sermon and had to be removed. Later, she described our elderly and bearded incumbent as a nasty giant. (He was immensely tall and cadaverous, and his flowing surplice gave him the aspect of the ghost in *Hamlet*.) She also proceeded to go through a destructive phase, beating her dolls and tearing up her picture-books, while Nurse reported her as 'faddy with her food'. Gradually both children settled down; but I knew that they looked forward to returning to Pond House, and unwillingly shared this feeling. Within a fortnight, mild uneasiness turned into irritable boredom.

As this aimless routine became increasingly oppressive, almost any diversion would have been desirable. It came in the form I most dreaded, that of a letter from Herbert Graham, imploring me to see him. Arriving at Pond House two days after my departure, he had returned to London, and now proposed to visit Suffolk; he added that what he had to say could not be put in writing and was of the utmost urgency. 'Do not think', he concluded, 'that I shall offend you by abusing or even criticizing Neville Quarrendon. Although he is in London, I have not seen him, nor do I propose to do so. I humbly beg you, my dear Anne, for the sake of our old affection, to grant me an interview.' Curiosity and alarm resulted in consent.

He arrived in time for dinner, which we ate hurriedly, in strained conversation. He then proposed that we should go into the garden. I said it was too cold, sent away both tea and coffee, and took up my work. Herbert, standing over me, cleared his throat, began to speak, moved over to the window and stood looking out. At last he said, 'Just over a week ago, I met Charles Craik in the Reform Club, to which we both belong. When I used to stay with – that is, we saw a certain amount of each other before he left England. Some ten years have passed since then. But he is not much changed.'

Something in his tone made me put aside my work and look at him. He had become very pale; with a shaking hand, he pushed back his hair – it was thinner since our last meeting – and began to walk about. I said, 'Pray sit down, and tell me everything. You know that I am ready to listen – though I can't imagine how your meeting Sir Charles Craik concerns me.'

He seemed to feel that this remark was an interruption: for he shook his head, and continued, in a slightly louder tone, 'He told me that he has removed his daughter Ida from her finishing school, and has made other arrangements for her future. These include marriage.' He paused, and came to stand opposite me. As he appeared unable to go on, I made an interrogative sound. This had no immediate effect. Then he said, in an almost inaudible voice, 'He has settled everything – all his possessions – on her. Her dowry is enormous.'

In the ensuing silence, I saw the axe descend on Limmerston Hall – and on the hopes I had not been able to prevent myself sharing. Sooner or later, it would become part of this girl's inheritance. It was useless to try to conceal what I felt. Dropping my work, I got up.

Then a thought came to me – that I might, somehow, make up for this loss and soften the blow by devoting my life to the victim of it. I had no plan, of course; but surely one would develop when we were together again. I might even ask Herbert's advice; though it was odd that he should be so concerned about this news. As soon as I could command my voice, I said, 'At sixteen! Her father will have to protect her from fortune-hunters.'

Herbert took my hands in his; he was trembling. He said, 'She was married yesterday.'

I stared at him; then I edged away. His agitation made him look slightly ludicrous. I decided to tell him that Ida Craik's future was of no interest to me, and so end our conversation. Yet I could neither move nor speak.

Herbert said, 'She is married – to Neville Quarrendon.'

11

Herbert and I had been married for nearly three months before we were able to talk about the reopening and occupation of Limmerston Hall. This delay was due to the illness from which I was still recuperating when we settled into the furnished house he took in London as soon as I was allowed to leave Little Glemham. The attack was diagnosed as a nervous collapse, necessitating several weeks in bed and the 'absolute quiet' so glibly prescribed and so difficult to achieve.

If Herbert had not sent for Lucretia to take charge of the household – if she had not been able to settle her own boys, Francis, Sybilla and Nurse with a sister – I should probably have remained as she found me for many months. As it was, she brought me back to something approaching normality, and thus to the point of agreeing to marry her brother.

Recollection of the weeks preceding this step became increasingly vague. Very much later, I realized that almost total inertia, speechlessness and difficulty in swallowing had been the prevailing symptoms. For a short time, brain fever was anticipated; when this did not materialize, extreme weakness and insomnia reduced such strength as was left. Then, suddenly, I heard myself thanking Lucretia, asking about the children and failing to take in the answers.

Once, I became aware that Herbert was talking to her at the other end of the room. As he saw me look towards him, he came to the foot of the bed, and seemed to be waiting for me to speak. I said, 'The flowers – those downstairs – they're dead, aren't they?' Lucretia, joining him, replied, 'All the vases have been replenished with fresh ones.'

I whispered, 'Give them away.' As she bent over me, I

saw that she had not understood and went on, 'The vases – for the bazaar. See to it,' and she nodded. Then I fell asleep, waking up on the way to recovery. I had been lying with my eyes fixed and open for so long that to shut them and breathe deeply was exquisite happiness. I desired nothing else; but the struggle towards convalescence had to be gone through; and it was not till then that I was able to cry, helplessly, and in fear of losing my reason.

As I had never before stayed in bed for anything worse than a feverish cold, this whole strange experience was transforming. I became utterly dependent on Herbert and Lucretia; and so marriage with him was a foregone conclusion; I should have made the offer if he had not. He proposed against his sister's advice; she thought him too precipitate, and was afraid that I might change my mind when I regained strength. In fact, there was no question of reversing a decision I knew to be irrevocable. I could never again live alone; and that Herbert would nearly always be kind and considerate was almost a certainty.

Within a few weeks of our marriage, I perceived that it was possible to ignore certain aspects of his character, either by agreeing with everything he said, or by ceasing to listen. He was neither stupid nor gross; and his pride in his tact did not detract from its effect when he chose, rather obviously, to exercise it. His self-confidence was only exacerbating when he spoke of his determination to 'win' me. The odious modern colloquialism of 'being caught on the rebound' was not in his vocabulary.

Lucretia's warmth of heart had extended to a complete and tender care for Francis and Sybilla. She relieved her brother of any communication with their guardian about their future, with the result that an agreement was reached within a fortnight of his marriage to Ida Craik. Both children were handed over to Herbert and me on the understanding that accounts of their progress would be submitted to their uncle at regular intervals. Lucretia then prepared Francis for school, visited him there and reported him as well thought of and contented; his letters showed him to be absorbed in, if sometimes critical of, his new life. She could not help indulging Sybilla, whom she came to love as her own child. On this point she and Nurse were sometimes at odds, but only at intervals.

With my return to health, despairing rage and a passionate desire for revenge took a stronger hold, enforced by the need to know what was happening in Limmerston. I therefore entered into a secret correspondence with Arabella Lang, stealing downstairs to collect her letters while Herbert was in his dressing-room. There was a hideous satisfaction in reading her account of the effect made by the girl bride ('Not pretty exactly, but elegant, unusual looking and rather shy'), of the rehabilitation of the Hall ('They expect to move in before Christmas') and of the gossip about her parentage.

'Some people say', wrote Mrs Lang, 'that she is Sir Charles's daughter by another woman, not his wife – and one PERSON, *whom I will not name*, actually declares that her mother was *Neville's wife*, and that her birth took place after Leila ran away with Sir C.! ! ! And this in the face of Neville's telling me (as his nearest relation, I was of course *the first to hear*) that Sir Charles adopted her when her parents, old friends of his, were drowned in a yachting accident – but *jealousy* is the cause of this *detestable slandering* of an innocent *girl*.'

Meanwhile, daily life with and gratitude to Herbert were made possible by my determination ultimately to confront the man he now thought of as his defeated rival. But first, I must know the whole truth: whether he had deceived me about his guilt (I still did not always believe in it), if so, how, and to what extent. I therefore suggested to Herbert that the time had come for an analysis and explanation of all that had happened after Cecilia's death.

When he demurred I pointed out that uncertainty was more distressing than any revelation he could make, 'Although', I added, 'I am not yet convinced that your suspicions are justified. And still I don't see how they can be proved.'

'I wish', he said despondently, 'that we could have postponed this discussion.'

Perhaps a wet Sunday afternoon in a tastelessly furnished drawing-room was not the best setting for a talk of this kind. I was about to suggest putting it off, when Herbert, glancing about him, went on, 'We are not likely to be disturbed, it's true. And the change in your attitude' – he looked away – 'makes it possible for me to speak frankly.'

'As an old married couple,' I said, taking his hand, 'surely we can say anything to each other?'

He smiled; then, sitting opposite me, he began, 'I should not consent to embark on this very painful subject if you were still involved with a person whose behaviour has destroyed any feeling you might have had for him.'

Herbert's habit of describing me to myself – his omniscient assumptions – created a barrier that was rather protective than otherwise. It provided privacy, while enabling me to withdraw from him.

'I suppose', I said casually, 'that if it had not been so, you wouldn't have asked me to marry you.'

'My dearest Anne, you underrate me. I have always been devoted to you,' he replied, in the tone he used when announcing that he would be home early.

At this point, it would have been helpful to take up my work; feeling that he might look on such a gesture as unnatural, I sat idle.

After apologizing for any strain entailed, he asked me to give him as detailed an account as possible of my stay at Pond House, from the moment of my arrival – 'when he was away – but his absences are equally relevant.'

'To what? His condemnation?'

'My dear – '

'I'm sorry, Herbert. Give me a moment – then I will begin.'

I did so without much difficulty; as I continued and his deductions became sharper, I was roused to a form of defence. If he did find me hostile, he was not perturbed;

and I began to realize that he might have been a successful barrister.

It was impossible wholly to refute his final summing-up, which came very near to proving his case. I had to admit that the dismissal of tutor and governess and the departure of Eliza Trevy had been followed by an attempt to remove me to the Dower House; that, this having failed, I had been approached with a view to seduction, together with misleading hints of marriage; that references to being 'on the edge of a very deep sea' and 'a crisis' were significant; that the protection of Jim and Alfred Cripps might show them to be employees, just as speeches about future plans for the children were meant to deceive; that the supposed intervention of Henry Craik and the gipsies was part of a plot.

Overriding this evidence, which I still claimed to be suppositious, was that of Cecilia's subjugation and her second will – and finally, most damning of all, the determination to acquire Limmerston Hall. Some other aspects of the case were rejected by Herbert. He had no use, he said, for Claude Lang's 'vision', which he described as hallucinatory; he thought nothing of the, to me, alarming pictures of flowers and wild animals ('a taste for the macabre is not unusual'), he saw no connection between criminal intent and the possession of the Roman dagger ('I have seen such antique weapons in half a dozen households') and, while deprecating the relationship with Mademoiselle Hébert, found it irrelevant, adding that Francis being allowed to ride was equally so. He concluded by saying that, two attempts on the boy having failed, marriage with an heiress had been substituted for his elimination. 'He risked nothing when he persuaded Craik, who thinks himself seriously ill, that he would be a suitable husband for the girl. Now, at least, it is clear that Francis is perfectly safe, quite apart from the fact that his uncle has virtually abandoned the guardianship of both children.'

A long silence fell. As Herbert got up and looked down at me, I returned his glance steadily enough, forcing into my mind that this interrogator, this judge – this destroyer –

and I were husband and wife: that he was neither a stranger nor an enemy; that he must be treated as became a rescuer; that my life was bound up with his; that I was responsible for his well-being. The picture was fantastic; and I burst out laughing.

'It has all been too much for you!' he exclaimed. 'Let me get you something – or should you lie down?'

'No – no. I am laughing at myself,' I said, wiping my eyes. 'When one has been made a fool of – ' I stopped, breathing rather fast.

'You have been monstrously used.'

'Oh, that, yes. I dropped into the middle of a melodrama. The trouble was that I didn't know my part.'

'Dearest Anne – '

'It's over, don't worry.'

'How can I help it? But you insisted on this – these explanations.'

'I did indeed.'

'We should have waited.'

'Certainly not.'

'I hope – so much – to make it up to you,' he said, bending over me, his hand on my shoulder.

'You have. We're married,' I said, and moved away.

'You don't regret – '

'Why should I? Oh – I did forget one thing. Those notes – and the spelling on the photograph.' As he stared at me I went on, 'I'm talking of what I found in a book, a photograph of Edwin, with "good plais" ' – I spelt it out – 'and then again, the same word, the same spelling, in a note from Alfred Cripps. Is that what you would call significant?'

'I don't know,' he said doubtfully. 'It might be. But now – we must try to put this whole matter behind us.'

'Naturally – at once.'

We stood looking at one another. Then I said, 'It's time for tea,' and rang the bell.

'You do believe', he began, 'that Lucretia and I were justified in warning you?'

'Of course. And we must not forget Eliza. She also meant well.'

'In the circumstances, it was natural that you should have stood up for him.'

'Yes! He's so insinuating, isn't he?'

The tea-tray appeared. As I sat down to pour out, my hand fell on the urn, which was scalding. I snatched it back, overturning a cup, and Herbert bent forward to replace it. I cried out, 'Leave that alone! I'm still capable of giving you a cup of tea – although I was taken in by Neville Quarrendon.'

It was the first time that his name had been uttered by either of us; and an unseen presence seemed to dominate the room. In silence, we began to eat and drink hastily, as if we had just been summoned away.

12

Herbert's return to England and his purchase of a country home had been combined with the establishment of a branch of his Canadian office in London. He now suggested that this little seventeenth-century manor should be chiefly furnished by my possessions, because such an arrangement would 'distract' me. I had determined to fall in with all his plans; his choice suited me well enough, for it was within easy reach of the City, which entailed his being away at regular intervals.

The alterations and improvements of Long Welston necessitated our remaining in London till after Francis returned to school. 'And this', Herbert pointed out, 'will enable you to keep in touch, should the occasion arise, with the most highly qualified physicians.' I submitted, secretly resolving to have nothing more to do with the faculty; the cure for my sickness – if it was one – lay with me, and in recourse to supplication for self-command. The resultant struggle was at first rather destructive than otherwise; one face, one voice, in settings lost for ever, recurred to break me down. Then, as the establishment of Nurse and Sybilla in the household became a major issue – for Nurse had made up her mind that London was unhealthy – I began to feel myself more successful as an aunt than as a wife.

In the latter role I failed to achieve peace of mind, while apparently pleasing Herbert. We did not discuss that other marriage, or its consequences, until he told me that Lucretia had received a letter from Neville Quarrendon inquiring after my health and adding that he had held back his to me when informed of my collapse. 'He seems to think', Herbert continued, 'that you expect to hear from him, and he apologizes for what he has the insolence to call his apparent remissness. Silence is of course the only answer to such an approach.'

'Of course. Dignified silence – as dignified as possible.'

Herbert, who had been about to leave the room, paused and said anxiously, 'Perhaps I should have spared you this communication?'

'I don't think so. Are you going up to dress?'

'We are dining with the Griersons. But if you do not feel up to it – '

'Is that the paralysed judge?'

Herbert frowned. 'He had a slight stroke some six months ago, from which he has almost recovered. As old friends of mine, they are naturally anxious to meet you.'

'What shall I wear?'

'Everything becomes you, my dear Anne. I should add that Mrs Grierson has published three historical novels, set in ancient Rome.'

'Gladiators and Early Christians?'

'I seldom read fiction. I believe her tales are extremely popular.'

'Did she write *Hilarion or Below the Cross*?'

'It is possible.'

'Then I have read that one. I can tell you about it as we drive there.'

'My dear, take care. It may be the work of another writer.'

'I'll find out when we go upstairs, and then if it is hers, I'll nod at you, and you can pretend you've read it.'

'You are incorrigible,' he said, and left the room.

With what promised to be a strenuous evening ahead of me, I allowed myself to fall back on Arabella Lang's last letter, of which the postscript ran, 'Neville and Ida are in Paris and won't be back until the New Year. I do hope she will not turn out to be one of these *gadding* young wives, but we must not judge *too soon*.'

So the postponement of the meeting, on which I was more than ever determined, had to be faced, and that took a little time. I then dressed for the Griersons' dinner in the only gown of which Herbert disapproved; its cut, he said, was inappropriate for a party of elderly persons. When I offered to change it, he pointed out that unpunctuality would have a worse effect than an unsuitable *décolletage*, and I sent for a shawl.

So the weeks went by, agreeably divided, according to Herbert, between duties and pleasures. I got through them in dazed acceptance, rather surprised by his approval of my efforts – which he did not recognize as such. When I refused to consult his doctor about a stimulant, he said, 'It therefore falls upon me to prescribe. I plan to lay down a modest but interesting cellar at Long Welston. I have heard of some white Burgundy which might suit you.'

'I cannot imagine anything I should dislike more.'

'You won't try it?'

I turned away – and burst into tears.

Such scenes were rare; they were forgotten when Francis joined us for the Christmas holidays.

He returned with a prize for English, a mild interest in football and plans to meet two friends from school. Schemes for entertainment – pantomimes, children's parties and the usual lionizing – were arranged for him by Herbert, into which he entered with his customary zest. But something was wrong; and when I told him that next holidays he would find us established at Long Welston, he asked, 'Will my things from Pond House be there? The books and the games, and everything?' Reassured, he was silent for some time; then he said, 'I wrote to Uncle Neville, but he didn't answer –' and began to poke the fire, averting his face.

'When people are newly married, they do forget things.'

'I know,' said Francis slowly. 'But I did think – after all, he chose Bramley Hall, which I quite like, though some of it's boring – he would be interested.'

'I expect he is, even though he doesn't write,' I said rather desperately.

'You haven't heard from him?'

I shook my head, and after another silence, began,

'I'm sure you will like Long Welston. We are arranging for a pony – and we could ask Tom and Jack Granger to stay.'

Francis seemed not to hear; then he said in a strangled voice, 'Uncle Neville always liked Syb best. But I can't help missing him. He's such a – well, he's cleverer than anybody. I used to think that if Mamma hadn't died, he might have married her.'

'Men – and women too – seldom marry as one expects,' I said, forcing out the words.

'Oh, I know, and he's, well, rather different anyway. But I couldn't help wondering. He is, I mean he was, our guardian. Is he not going to be, any more?'

'I think – I'm not sure – that he thinks you will be better placed with us. His wife may not be used to children.'

Francis got up, and thrusting his hands in his pockets, walked away. 'Mamma left us to him,' he said gruffly.

'Yes, dear. But these arrangements don't always work out as they were meant to. She wanted me to help, and now I – we – can do more than ever before. You'll have a real home, and we'll always be there.'

'I thought that Pond House – ' He stopped and scrubbed at his eyes.

Not daring to put my arms round him, I sat still as his pride fell between us. At last I began, 'It turned out to be temporary. But Long Welston won't be, I promise faithfully. You do believe that?'

'Yes – thank you – ' with a muffled sob.

'I'm so very sorry, dearest Francis. But there's nothing I can do, except to make this new home as good as, and better, I hope, than the other. And there will be no more changes – none.'

Francis blew his nose and straightened his shoulders. 'I don't understand, quite. I never thought he just simply wouldn't write – or anything. I suppose – do you think – he doesn't want to see any of us, ever again?'

'Truly, Francis, I don't know. When you are grown up – '

'He might be dead by then,' Francis interrupted. 'He's pretty old now. And just look how people die! Edwin, Papa, Mamma – you can't count on anything.'

'Oh, I think he'll live till you are old enough to decide for yourself whether you want to see him,' I said rather sharply. 'He's not the sort that dies easily.'

'But it's now. I did like it there – and Little Glemham. I suppose there's no stream at Long Welston?'

'No; but we could perhaps make a pond or a lake in the garden, it's quite large. I'll ask Uncle Herbert. I can't promise. We might all go down there for the day, and see about it.'

'Uncle Herbert's very kind,' said Francis in a subdued voice.

'He's extremely fond of you both.'

Again silence fell. Francis turned and came back to the fire. Looking down at it, he said, 'You know, it's funny, I really didn't mind being an orphan, once I got used to it. Now it's as if I had to start all over again.'

Controlling my own tears, I muttered something about ill-luck and plans for the future. Francis said, 'Well – there's the pantomime next week – and the Tower. Do they let you go on the scaffold?'

'I'm afraid not. But the block is shown, and the axe – and Little Ease. They let you stand inside it, I seem to remember.'

'How long for?'

'We'll tip the guide, and then you can stay in it as long as you like.'

'That'll be nice,' said Francis gravely, and sat down. After a pause, I began to talk of other visits, and the party Lucretia was giving for her boys, to which he was invited. No more was said, either then or later, about our common loss. His consolation should have absorbed me entirely; but my efforts were those of a cripple.

Meanwhile, Sybilla, hearing of our move to Berkshire, produced what Nurse described as a tantrum, in the form of a passion for London life. 'It's the Park, Madam, she's

273

taken notice of there,' she said in disapproving tones. I decided not to enter into that particular struggle.

Yet I could not help being equally concerned for both children. Although the attack made in the summer seemed not to have affected Sybilla for long, she had changed since then. She was now aware of her own charms and set on exploiting them; any man, young or old, who glanced at or spoke to her, was greeted in a manner described by Nurse as forward, yet with an anxious desire to please, in which there was a hint of fear, as if she were placating a possible enemy. As she preferred Herbert's company to mine, and he was inclined to spoil her, I tried to even the balance by taking her for walks and telling her stories. Sometimes these diversions were combined; we had returned from an expedition to the Baker Street bazaar and were still on the doorstep, when I heard my name called, and turned to see an almost forgotten figure: Cecilia's personal maid, Marie-Louise. She looked distraught and shabby; clearly, she had fallen on evil days.

Having disposed of Sybilla, I asked her in and offered to help her. After some hesitation and many assurances of loyalty to me and to my dead sister, she told me that, having run away with Alfred Cripps, she had found herself penniless. She then threatened to 'betray' him if he did not support her and their child. This narrative, poured out in a mixture of French and German, took some time. When I asked her what hold she had over him, she shook her head and muttered something about having no proof. I said, 'I cannot help you unless you tell me more' – and she began to cry.

I waited, trying to remember if she was truthful, and could only recall Cecilia saying that, although honest and hardworking, she tended to dramatize trivialities and quarrel with the other servants. At last, drying her eyes, she said, 'And Monsieur Francis? Is he not here?'

'He lives with us. He is spending the afternoon with some friends.'

'Thank God, Madame! I was afraid for him – ' and she

entered into a long, confused explanation about her search for me, which had begun in Belminster and been achieved through the Langs.

'Belminster? Then you kept up with those men?'

'It was necessary. I had no money. He gave me some, because he was fond of the child. Now that it is dead, I need never see him again. I am *blanchisseuse de fin* in a good house. But I had to know – after Monsieur Edwin – you understand me?'

'No, I do not. What do you mean?'

'Madame, this is hard for me. But I was not sure – I mean, that his death was indeed an accident.'

'If that was the case – ' I stopped, partly because I had begun to feel sick. Then I said, 'You must give me your reasons.'

'I cannot! I was not to blame – ' and another burst of tears.

A long, disjointed conversation followed, during which she became hysterical, refused to enlarge on or verify her suspicions, gasped out abuse of the Cripps brothers, and finally rushed from the house.

I sat on, shaking and cold, till Herbert appeared. I then told him that I was ill – but not ill enough to see a doctor – went up to bed, swallowed an opiate and slept till late the next morning. I came down resolved to keep secret my interview with Marie-Louise.

I knew that this was the decision of a coward – and that I should probably regret it for the rest of my life. But it was part of that other scheme, which had now become an obsession. No matter how long the waiting, I was going to seek out Neville Quarrendon, and force him to tell me the truth.

It had occurred to me that Sybilla might be his child; but I did not intend to tax him on a matter which could never be cleared up, and had ceased to be of any importance.

13

I soon realized that to force an admission was impossible, and that adjuring, if necessary, begging, him to tell me the truth was the only hope. My knowledge of his character led me to believe that he seldom told a superfluous lie, and that he would trust me with any secret, however dreadful. Also, his position was impregnable; if he had been guilty of destroying one brother and planning the elimination (I remembered his use of that word) of the other, it could never be proved. That Edwin had been killed and that Francis had twice escaped a similar fate could not, legally, be connected with the uncle who would have profited by both deaths; so Herbert said, and I believed him. And the acquisition of Limmerston Hall had made its owner harmless; having got what he wanted, he was no longer dangerous – if, indeed, he ever had been.

I could not threaten him, even if I had wished to do so; but I thought that an appeal might produce, if only through caprice, a confession which would help me to lead a normal life; for this corrosive and agonizing uncertainty was rapidly becoming a disease, which must eventually destroy any chance of repaying Herbert, in whose debt I was and on whom I had become morally dependent. I desired above all things to make him happy; and that could only be achieved by complete knowledge. However horrible the revelation – and I was prepared for it – I should then be able to accept the present instead of dwelling on the past; or so I believed.

Out of the past, memories of Limmerston Hall predominated, often to the exclusion of its occupants. A re-creation of its impact was thrust upon me when we returned the call of a retired law lord shortly after our establishment at Long Welston. His mansion was of the same date as the Hall, although not so well placed and oddly uninspiring. As we got out of the carriage and came indoors, I said, 'In spite of its elegance, that house is disappointing, I wonder why.'

'I think I know the answer – and the remedy,' Herbert replied, taking up his stand by the fireplace. 'Additions – tactfully applied. Good old Mereworth, a clever man in many ways beyond his profession, has no notion of such matters. If he were to ask my advice – but as he has not done so – '

'What do you mean by additions?'

The tone rather than the interruption itself brought Herbert up short. He glanced at me as if disconcerted, and went on, 'You know my tastes, indeed you share them. A bow-window here and there – ' he made an illustrative gesture – 'a tinted glass porch over that severely pillared portico – what is the matter, my dear? Are you unwell?'

'Perfectly well, thank you.'

'Perhaps this room is too warm for you?'

In the pause that followed I was able to suppress the outburst which would have led to inquiries, solicitousness and too familiar recommendations to rest. At last I said, 'I think it is. In any case, I must go and dress,' and moved away. As he followed me to the door I added, 'Why do you say warm when you mean hot? But it doesn't matter – ' and left the room.

When we met for dinner I apologized. Herbert kissed my forehead, patted my hand and said that he must really keep a guard on his tongue, adding that in his own way he was as great a stickler for accuracy as myself.

Such passages – they could hardly be called scenes – were still infrequent. I knew that they would soon cease to be so unless I took action.

Yet I could not bring myself to write and ask him to meet me, although I tried, again and again, with tears, enraged, and in torments of self-disgust. I would begin a letter – and then remember his saying that he found most people negligible. Sometimes I was sure that he had not found me so; sometimes I felt myself condemned, *in absentia*, from the judgment-seat of his disregard. And then, suddenly, the solution, unimagined, grotesquely fortuitous, slipped into my hands.

Lucretia Mary, who was virtually separated from her husband – she did not even know where he was – wrote begging Herbert to accompany her to Oxford, to interview her elder son's tutor; for the boy, now in his first term, had got into trouble and was in danger of being sent down. His uncle's famous light touch with young persons was therefore invoked, and he prepared, not without complacency, to leave at once. On the morning of his departure he received a catalogue from a firm of London auctioneers which he had not time to go through and which he asked me to mark for him with a view to acquiring such furniture as might fall within our means and would be suitable for Long Welston.

I now dreaded Herbert's absences; solitude brought on recourse to sedatives, alternating with stimulants I had hoped to forgo and could generally do without when he was at home. Then, listlessly applying myself to the catalogue, I came upon the words, 'Two suites of historic interest, formerly the property of the Craik family of Limmerston Hall, Gloucestershire.' It appeared that these and other items would be available for viewing some days before the auction took place.

His discrimination in such matters would, I was almost certain, entail his inspection of these pieces before deciding to bid for them. As women were not in the habit of frequenting auctioneers' premises, he would be alone. I therefore had a valise packed, took the first train and a room in an hotel looking over St James's Park, some five minutes' walk from the sale rooms.

I had not long to wait. He came down the steps of the building in the late afternoon of the second day as I approached them. I stopped and gazed up at him. Then I raised my veil.

Looking taller than usual in his dark London clothes, he

stood there, unsmiling, his eyes fixed on me in a long, piercing, penetrating stare. He seemed to be on the watch, as if I had come to make a scene. Then he said, 'If you wish to see the exhibits, I shall be very glad to escort you,' and offered me his arm.

That he spoke as if to a stranger or a chance acquaintance helped to steady me; for I had begun to shake; now, the phrase I had ready came back, and after a few seconds' pause I was able to say, 'No, thank you. I came here because I wanted to talk to you.'

Still contemplating me with that immovable preparedness, he said, 'Where? In the rooms?'

'No – out of doors.'

'In the park, then. Or will that be too cold?'

I shook my head. We walked down the steps into the street in silence. As we reached the gates he paused to look round.

It was a gentle, clear spring day, much like that on which I had first seen Pond House. A bed of daffodils, still in bud, lay between us and the lake; froths of green swayed from the tops of the trees; above, a few clouds patched the uncertain blue; sunlight struck, wavered and sank away, as if blown out by the breeze. Here and there, groups or couples or solitary walkers were strolling, some towards the water. Three small children with their nurse passed, carrying baskets of bread and chattering about the ducks. As they ran towards the bridge we faced an iron bench under a weeping birch.

We walked over to it and sat down. He took off his hat, placed it beside him, slowly removed his gloves and dropped them inside. His deliberation, his expectant composure were oddly reassuring. I began to feel almost calm. Then I turned to look at him.

He was gazing ahead, his eyes half-closed. So I had often seen him when trying to guess at his mood. If he had prepared for a battle, he was certainly above it.

Yet I could not speak as I had planned – nor at all, unless he did. He had once been kind; surely he would be so again, f only because he must know by now that I was not going to upbraid or reproach or cross-examine him. I had a right to one question, one demand: but that seemed unutterable. As he leant back and glanced at me, I saw the change.

His serenity, no longer formidable, was that of one at peace with himself; though he was still grave, he appeared neither hostile nor on guard. This tranquillity was infectious. We were together again. I no longer cared about what I had come to ask. I said, 'Are you going to bid for the Craik items?'

He seemed to consider. 'For one, perhaps – an escritoire. There is a Sèvres dinner service of some elegance, but it is incomplete. I shall have to see how it all goes.'

'A Sèvres dinner service – could one use such a thing?'

'I think so – on certain occasions.'

In the silence that followed, despair struck and held me. I would have got up and walked away, if I had been able to move. On certain occasions – yes! The faceless figure who would share that feast, move about those rooms, stand, triumphant, by the spray-washed nereids and river-gods and the streaming water, rose before me. All was lost. Death – of any purpose in life – has many forms: and this was mine.

Yet we must go on talking. If we did not, he would ask me why I had sought him out, I should find no answer, and he would leave me sitting there, as if turned to stone. As I searched desperately for an opening, he said, 'Are you quite well now?'

'Oh, yes. We're living' – I spoke hurriedly, running the words together – 'near London, it's more convenient, Berkshire, the train service is very good except on Sundays and of course one doesn't need it then, and on weekdays there are only two stops and sometimes none at all.'

'I suppose', he went on, after another pause, 'that any further personal inquiries would be – discordant. But I should like you to believe that I have been concerned. No excuse is acceptable: so I shall make none.'

'Excuse – that's a strange word,' I said, rather pleased to

be achieving something like an ordinary tone. 'Why should there be any – I mean – one lives as one can.'

'As one must. But that was not what you wanted to talk about.'

'No, I – there is something. It won't take long.'

'There's plenty of time.'

'You are staying up for the auction?'

'My agent will do that.'

Those five words sufficed to create, not only his new life, but the gulfs and chasms that now lay between us. Beyond them was the desert. I pushed back my veil. Glancing away, he said abruptly, as if to test me, 'The Cripps brothers are on their way to Australia. They seemed glad to go.'

'The Bownalls must be thankful.'

'Yes. Those two were a nuisance, from first to last, even in Rome.'

'You employed – you knew them so long ago?'

'One had English grooms there in those days. When I left – under a cloud, as it's called – they followed me.'

'A cloud?'

'Oh, quite a slight one.' He smiled. 'There was a scene. I hadn't thought of it till just now. Odd, how these things come back. My first wife, poor girl, left that rather gloomy barrack we were living in, in the small hours. And so – talk, gossip, commiserations, conjectures – you can imagine it. I stayed on. Ostracism didn't worry me then. Now, I have learnt to avoid it.'

The incongruity of this conversation, its complete disassociation from our respective circumstances, appalled me. Yet because we were talking as if nothing of any moment had happened to either of us – as if we were sitting in the library of Pond House at the end of a quiet day – I was hypnotized, subjugated into response, even into mild curiosity, about events with which I had no concern. No doubt this was what he intended; for he went on, in the same, casual, reminiscent tone, 'I was more to blame than she. But I did not at first realize that fright, terror in fact, had driven her out. Nevertheless' – his face darkened – 'she

282

should have warned me that she did not like cats. When the ill-treated one I had rescued from a gang of children, I retaliated. The cat died. In the general view, that was of no consequence compared to my bringing home to her that she had been – unwise.'

After another silence, I managed to say, 'Why do you tell me this?'

'I can't imagine,' he said with a laugh. 'I must be getting old, maundering on about the past. Forgive me.'

'Was that story a warning?'

'What a notion. Of course not. In any case, why should you be warned?'

'I'm not sure.'

'I seem to remember that you were inclined to imagine things.'

'That's true. But after imagining, you sometimes guess. Then, you begin to suspect.'

'And that may result in delusion.'

'Not always.'

'How does it work out in your case?' he said, smiling.

'Differently. It varies.'

'That must be confusing.'

'It can be misery.'

'Do you know,' he began, in an expansive, friendly tone, 'I don't really understand what we are talking about. You are getting quite Delphic. And I'm in the dark. Will you enlighten me?'

'I came to appeal to you.'

'Well – why don't you?'

'It is difficult; because you are without compassion.'

'You have always found me so?'

'No. But then I was deceived.'

'By me?'

As I looked at him without speaking, he said gently, 'I see. In other words, I'm in the dock, not for the first time, on a charge of – what? Conspiracy? Knavery? Or just general caddishness?'

'You turn everything into ridicule.'

'And that too is a crime?'

'It can be a form of cruelty.'

'Cruel – pitiless,' he said, suddenly grave. 'And withou[t] evidence. Is not that rather harsh?'

'I don't mean it to be. I came to those rooms, I waited fo[r] you, to ask a favour.'

'It's granted. Go on.'

'My peace of mind depends on your answer.'

'Then I must be very careful what I say.'

'Whatever that is, I shall never speak of it to anyone.'

'Except, of course, your husband.'

'To him, least of all.'

His eyes, fixed on mine, narrowed a little. 'You don'[t] trust him?'

'It's not a question of that. What I must know has nothing to do with him.'

'With what, then?'

'With my future happiness – if I'm ever to have any.'

'That's serious,' he said after a pause. 'Is it fair to make me responsible?'

'I think it is, because you have everything you once wanted. You wanted it desperately, hopelessly: and now it's fallen into your hands.'

'If you mean Limmerston, I was not quite hopeless. I thought Craik might come round.'

'You were not sure, though.'

'No: I couldn't tell. One can't, in a case of that kind.'

'So you had to think of how else to succeed.'

'As to that, I thought of all sorts of ways, but – well' – he shrugged his shoulders – 'I did not at once hit on the obvious one. Meanwhile, you have condemned me as a fortune-hunter.'

'I don't care whether you are or not!' I exclaimed. 'What I have to know is – ' I pressed my handkerchief to my forehead and leaned forward, so as not to look at him – 'what you planned, and what you did, before coming upon that obvious solution.'

'Why? Does it matter?'

284

'Yes.'

'It concerns you so deeply?'

I waited, gathering strength. It seemed to me that we had been sitting in that aqueous shade for many hours. The moment had come. I was about to make what amounted to a hideous accusation. Then he would leave me; and we might never meet again.

At last I began, 'I should have asked you about Cecilia's second will as soon as I knew of it.'

'There was no secret,' he said calmly. 'What do you want to know?'

'It was made during your last visit to her. Was that through your influence?'

'She consulted me about it. She had already made up her mind.'

'Without telling me.'

'She thought you might object. You saw her letter. But we have been through this before.'

'She trusted you – entirely.'

'You make it sound slightly sinister,' he said, and drawing out his case, lit a cigar. He had never done so before without leave; and the omission of that trivial formality seemed to indicate that he was on the alert.

'She did not know', I went on, 'anything of your feelings for what you now possess.'

'She didn't know much about anybody. She was a romantic.'

'And in love.'

'She thought so. As I once told you, she was deluded.'

'By you – as I was.'

'You assume too much,' he said, leaning forward to knock the ash off his cigar. 'I had no designs on her.'

'But on her sons?'

'I don't follow you.'

'You stood to inherit – enough – if they died.'

'Enough?'

'To buy the Hall.'

He turned and looked at me curiously; then he smiled. 'I

understand! Of course – the wicked uncle. Why did you not say so before?'

'Because I could not believe – ' I paused for breath.

'But others did?' I bent my head. 'Well,' he said reflectively, 'perhaps I should have thought of that. How long have you had this notion in your mind? I can guess who put it there.'

'What does that matter? If you would only tell me – if I knew for certain, one way or the other – I could – I could bear it.'

'Bear what?'

'My life.'

There was a long silence. The smoke of his cigar rose between us. Then he said, 'Is this the favour you were going to ask? Are you serious?'

'I was never more so. You can trust me, you know that.'

He leant back, gazing in front of him. 'You must forgive me if I refuse to descend to this rather absurd level. I can't do it, really.'

'Don't – don't make it more horrible! Can't you see – can't you understand that if I knew – what I mean is, nothing matters but this. You had to get me on your side, because you couldn't turn me out, as you did the others. I don't reproach you for that, or for – for anything. I was happy there, with you. Now, it's all gone.'

'All but the memory. It sounds like a drawing-room ballad.'

'For God's sake – I implore – '

'Ah! yes – I thought we should come to that.'

'Have you no pity? Nothing?'

'You said just now that I was without compassion. In fact, I am generally sorry for hysterical women.'

After a short struggle, the effort to appear composed succeeded. In a flat, subdued voice, I said, 'I wonder whether you were as cruel to that girl in Rome as you are now.'

'She was more frightened than hurt. But I may have been too severe.'

Forcing myself to look at him, I began to hope that

286

somehow, even now, the barrier between us might be raised. His repose was that of one whose patience had not yet reached its limits; he seemed to be waiting for me to return to sanity. He had never looked more nobly serene, more tranquilly self-assured. And so it was that the progress of suspicion halted; for it might be that his rejection of my demand was justified – and that because we had once been allies and friends, he was ready to tolerate the outbursts and appeals of a misguided victim. I prepared to accept his denial and ask forgiveness.

This change of attitude crept over me by degrees; and in that frame of mind which illumines the irrelevant, I watched a blackbird hop towards us; we were so still that it took us for part of our surroundings, and did not retreat as the hand holding the cigar moved back and forth. Meanwhile, the sun had gone in and the breeze had sunk. The park was almost deserted.

He had been cruelly scornful; but I had brought that response on myself. Now there could be no escape. I was in a straitjacket of my own making : and so must continue to play the part of a crazed captive, the pitiable prisoner of a self-induced obsession. All that remained was to speak quietly, deliberately, as if making an ordinary, everyday inquiry.

'Did you do it?'

After a short silence, he rose and looked down at me. I braced myself for further mockery. It did not come. In a tone of withering contempt, he said, 'You are impertinent–' and turned away.

As he walked towards the water he took out his gloves and put on his hat. He paused on the bridge, looking down. I heard a rush of water as a bevy of ducks gathered below. He gazed at them, drawing on his gloves.

Slowly, he crossed to the other side. There, he waited for a group of people to pass. Once more, he paused, as if making up his mind. Then he walked on, a black shape, gradually diminishing, till, reaching the trees, he was engulfed – and I saw him no more.

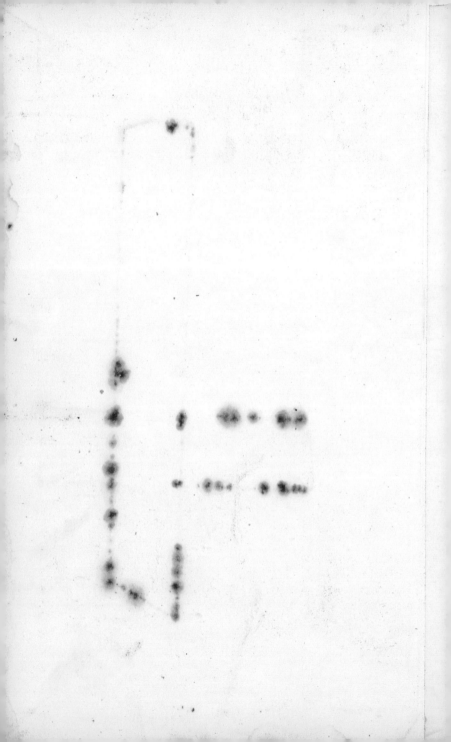